Robin

Rose Harvey

To Mum,
for being my first reader and constant support.

Content Warning

This book deals with some challenging themes, including sexual assault.

Reader discretion is advised.

Also by Rose Harvey

The Ice Flame Trilogy
Heir to the Ice Flame
Heart of Ice
Fire on the Ice

The Order Series
Robin

Prologue

The stranger looked through her sunglasses at the small cottage in front of her. It had been hard trying to find the family inside. When she had last seen them, it'd been six years earlier and they'd owned a completely different house. This new one was made of red brick and there wasn't a fabric shade cloth in sight. The stranger sighed, momentarily saddened by how much an act of stupid recklessness had changed this family's life forever.

Taking a deep breath to steady herself, she reached out and pressed the doorbell.

The door was opened by a woman in her early fifties.

'Well, hello,' she said, confused. 'Can I help you?'

The stranger smiled, and prepared herself for the painful memories to return.

'Hello, I'm Jane Rallen. I would like to ask you a few questions on the neighbourhood and the issue of house fires. I'm a reporter for *The Robin*.'

'*The Robin*, eh?' the woman asked, as a shadow filled her eyes, 'I've not heard of that newspaper. But never mind. Come in, come in.'

'Thank you,' Jane said, relieved that the first part of the ordeal was over and that the woman had believed her story. However the next part of her tale would be even more difficult to lie about.

'Tom!' The woman called as they entered a tidy lounge room. 'We have company.'

'Coming, love,' a man's voice called.

'Cup of tea?' the woman asked Jane.

'Yes, please.' Jane took out a notebook, to give the effect of being a reporter. 'Would you mind if I wrote down your names?'

'Of course, Miss Rallen. I'm Gretel Jefferies, that's spelt J-E-F-F-E-R-I-E-S,' she said, as she watched Jane write the name into her notebook, 'and this is my husband, Tom.'

As if on cue, a man strolled into the room and sat down next to his wife. Jane caught herself just before she began to stare at Tom Jefferies, who was not at all how she had pictured him during the past six years. He was balding and portly, and the wrinkles on his face were tight and strained despite the smile he now wore. It looked like he hadn't laughed properly for a very long time. Jane felt another pang of guilt at the thought of the bad memories which she would awaken in this couple.

'Pleased to meet you,' Tom said, interrupting Jane's thoughts.

'Now, Miss Rallen, you wanted to ask us some questions?' Gretel prompted, having noticed that her guest had fallen silent.

'Yes,' Jane said, jerking back to reality. 'I'm investigating the impact that house fires have on a community, and I understand from police records that you and your family relocated to this address after an arson incident.'

Gretel and Tom had both frozen in place, and for a moment their expressions were unguarded, revealing their shock and pain. Before they had a chance to react, Jane took a deep breath and gathered the last remnants of her strength. She had come so far, she couldn't turn back now.

'I understand that this might be a confronting topic for you both, but my publisher was adamant that he wanted to hear about your experience. But before I begin I'd like to tell you a story. I'm afraid that I cannot ask my questions until you have heard the whole story in its entirety. Would you mind if I use up some more of your time?' Even to Jane's ears, she sounded absurd. But it had taken so long to find them and she couldn't bear it if they threw her out after what she had sacrificed to be here.

'I could listen to a story any day.' Tom said with forced joviality, his voice breaking through her thoughts. Jane noticed how his hand was shaking slightly as it held Gretel closer.

'I suppose,' Gretel added slowly, but she couldn't help noticing how Jane's gloved hands kept clasping and unclasping. She did the same thing when she was nervous. For a moment she wondered why Miss Rallen had reason to be worried at all. Then she smiled: surely it must be the first interview for the poor girl. But why did she have to interview them about house fires? That would just dig up old memories. The past continued to haunt her daily. No number of questions could ease it, and she sighed in resignation, privately wishing that Tom hadn't accepted Miss Rallen's request.

Her eyes took the reporter in, noticing the crisp, neatly cut grey suit and the shiny black high heels. She looked like she could be a lawyer instead of a reporter. Gretel had always imagined reporters to have pencils behind their ears, ragged jeans and a laptop bag slung across one shoulder. Jane Rallen was anything but that stereotype. She was wearing white satin gloves, which were tightly folded in her lap. Her face was slightly angular but with the large black sunglasses Gretel couldn't distinguish what colour her eyes were. Jane flicked her hair out of the way. As she moved, her hair shone like glazed copper. A memory came to Gretel's mind from many years before, and her heart flipped. *Her hair…*

She blinked in shock when Jane turned to Tom and asked, 'Do you have anything stronger, Mr Jefferies?' as she placed down her teacup.

'I've got some sherry, Miss Rallen,' Tom said slowly, 'I can pour you some if you'd like.'

'Thank you,' the reporter replied, a vague image of Christmas Eves long since passed coming to her mind's eye, before draining the glass in one gulp. 'The story I'm going to tell you began a long time ago, and sadly I don't know the ending. But please hear me out, because it contains things that are completely out of the ordinary.'

Gretel and Tom looked at each other in surprise. Each was wondering the same thing: what had they gotten themselves into?

Part One

Six Years Earlier

Chapter One

'Shit!' the teenager hissed, 'they're coming!' His two friends turned around, disorientated. One was slightly green in the face and clutched his stomach nauseously.

'What the fuck have we done?' he asked, horrified, when his glazed eyes took in the flames. The ecstasy he had felt before was rapidly draining, replaced by fear and horror. 'What have *I* done?'

'Come on!' their leader cried and dragged his stunned friends over the neighbour's fence and into the back alley, where they ran as fast as their stumbling legs could carry them. It hadn't been an accident in his mind. Fred Jefferies would deserve what he got– a hot wake-up call to the Australian summer and a realisation that it was useless to try to steal Billy Tyler's girl. He had enjoyed pouring the alcohol on the windowsill, before lighting it and watching the flames spread across the overhanging shade cloth and wooden joists. The invigorating rush brought on by lighting the fire and his need for revenge was wonderful, ecstatic. Yes, this would teach Fred Jefferies and his family a lesson. He would learn not to interfere from now on in other people's business. He smiled to himself and dragged his friends along roughly, slipping into the shadowy alley.

The cheerful Christmas Night party for the next-door neighbours had been ruined; everyone was screaming and running in all directions, panic-stricken. The hosts ran to the fence shouting desperately, trying to rouse the family inside the burning house, but to no avail. Over the sound of the roaring flames their voices could not be heard at all.

No one had noticed the arsonists leaving except for two darkly clothed figures, who were standing next to two creatures resembling horses in the alleyway, watching silently as the trio ran further and further away.

'Master, can I follow them and make them pay for what they've done?' the shorter figure asked, eyes burning.

'The Door here will close soon,' the other replied, 'but do not concern yourself; they shall spend the rest of their lives filled with guilt for what has happened tonight.'

From the house there came a loud crash, and both figures turned to see part of the roof collapse.

'I think we should make sure that the family is alright before we leave,' the taller one said, placing a fatherly hand on the other's shoulder.

Inside the bungalow, the family awoke when the fire alarm started to ring and part of the roof crashed to the floor. The daughter opened her eyes with a start and leapt out of her bed. She pushed open her door, getting hit by the sign that read '*Laura's room*' as the door swung closed behind her. She muttered something indiscernible and froze, as she took in the broken remnants of the roof in front of her.

A wall of fire barred her path, separating her from her family who had gathered on the other side of the flames. At that moment Laura regretted not having a bedroom in the front of the house, like her brother and parents.

'Mum! Dad! What am I going to do?' she screamed over the ringing alarm and roar of the flames. Tears of fright and sweat mingled together, rolling down her face.

Her mother shouted something, but she was unable to

discern a word. Suddenly an idea formed in Laura's mind: if she could push open her bedside window, then she'd be able to escape and meet her family around the front of the house.

Laura turned and ran back into her bedroom, as more pieces of the ceiling collapsed behind her. The high pitch of the fire alarm filled her head and she stumbled, coughing in the smoke. Laura shut the door, hoping that the barrier would give her some time to open the window. She grabbed a silver necklace which her family had given her for Christmas, and hurriedly put it in her pocket as she ran to the other side of the room, tripping slightly over the piles of schoolbooks and shoes which were scattered around her floor.

'Shit!' she cried as she stubbed her toe on her bed, hopping closer to the window.

Fingers scrambling, she tried to open the window, but when it was only a few centimetres open, the mechanism jammed.

'Come on. *Come on!*' she yelled at the window, 'open!' She tugged harder, but the window didn't budge.

'Damn!' Laura hissed, glancing back at the door, which was beginning to smoulder in the heat. There wouldn't be much time left before it fell.

In a frenzy, she picked up a stool from the corner of the room and smashed at the window, again and again.

The glass shattered and Laura wriggled out, ignoring the pain as the glass pierced her flesh. But she came to an abrupt halt when her nightdress snagged on one of the protruding pieces of glass. Behind her, she heard the door of her bedroom crash to the ground.

As she tried to dislodge herself, the nightdress got soaked in blood from a wound in her leg, making it harder to distinguish where the dress stopped and the window began. She became even more frantic and, disregarding the pain, her fingers slipped on the glass, trying and failing to dislodge herself. Her hands were stained red and soon Laura couldn't grasp onto anything.

'Help me!' she yelled, as the heat of the fire licked at her feet.

Yet again she tried to crawl out of the window, wriggling like a fly caught in a web, but she only got herself more stuck than before. Another shard of glass slashed down her thigh and she screamed, kicking out, trying and failing to avoid the hungry flames.

Suddenly, Laura felt hands clasp her own as another pair of hands dislodged her nightdress from the piece of glass.

On being lifted into someone's arms, she clung on, whimpering quietly as the world began to spin.

'We have to get her away from here,' one of her rescuers murmured in a deep baritone voice. 'They won't arrive in time to help her.'

'Where are our mounts?' the person holding her asked, glancing down at Laura, eyes dark and worried. 'She needs a doctor.'

'Geranium and Iris are around the corner.' The other man said. Why were the creatures named after flowers? What were they? Who were these people taking her away from Mum, Dad and Fred? Laura struggled weakly, and tried to call out. What would her parents think? She couldn't let them believe she had burned to death.

'Mum! Dad! I'm here! *I'm alright!*

'Be quiet, child,' one of the men said, 'it won't be safe for you to stay here.'

'*Why?*'

He didn't answer. Mouth set in a hard line, the man

moved onwards.

One of the first things Laura noticed about the two men, was how fast they walked. Who *were* they? They sounded strange, their accents indistinguishable. They didn't sound Australian. Why had they saved her? And, perhaps most importantly, *where* were they taking her? What did the man mean by it not being safe for her here? It didn't make any sense. Her head swam and she moaned.

They rounded a corner and she realised that they were in the backstreet behind her house.

In front of them were two creatures which resembled Pegasi, yet their bones were barely contained within their skin. They appeared to have dark fur but when she looked closer, Laura realised that it was rough and leathery.

'How can they carry us?' Laura asked faintly. Her rescuers jolted, obviously having thought that she had fainted.

'They're stronger than they look, little one.' The taller man replied, smiling at her. She was too weak to shrink away. Her nightdress clung to her body, soaked in blood, and she felt more trickle down her skin. A tortured moan escaped her and the man's grip around her tightened.

'I'm... not... *little*.' She protested faintly. Her captors chuckled.

On mounting the strange creatures, they leapt into the air, circling the burning house below them. Her head swooning from the sudden movement, Laura flopped against her captor's chest. As the air flew past, she was reminded of some of the rides she had been on in one of the annual travelling fairs. Had she been feeling remotely comfortable, she would have shrieked with exhilaration. A rush of heat blew past her cheek and she looked downwards, towards her home, her head spinning.

'No!' Laura whispered, wriggling in the man's arms, 'that's my family down there. I need to get to them; they'll think something's happened to me.'

'I'm afraid we can't let you go, child,' one of the men said grimly, 'now that you're with us, we must take responsibility for you.'

'Why?' Laura sobbed; how could this be happening? Her family meant everything to her, how could these people expect for her to just move on and forget her parents and brother?

Looking down, she felt tears well up in her eyes as she saw her family.

Her mother was crying on her father's shoulder, then she raised her face to the heavens above, eyes tightly shut. Had they been open, mother and daughter would have seen each other. A wordless scream of denial escaped her lips, mingling with the shouts from the fire-fighters who were struggling to put out the flames. Defeated, she sank down onto the ground and bent over, heartbroken sobs wrenching her frame.

'Mum, Dad, look up. I'm here. I'm here,' Laura cried faintly, her voice breaking into a whisper. She tried frantically to wave her arms, but they were starting to go numb and were not responding to her wishes. They hung by her sides, lifeless.

'It's no use,' the man closest to her said curtly. 'They can't hear you.'

'Let me go home!' Laura wept, 'Don't you understand? I don't know what to do without them. Let me go back. They'll think I'm... they'll think I'm...' Choking sobs rose up her throat, forcing her to stop for a minute. When she was able to speak again, the creatures that they were riding on had already left her burning house far behind. 'They'll think I'm dead,' Laura croaked, eyes full of tears and stinging as the wind rushed past. It must be impossible for her to cry anymore, she thought.

'We can't go back.' The man said. Laura turned on the back of the creature and weakly punched her fists into his chest, yet more tears streaming down her cheeks.

'Let me go *home!*' she repeated, ignoring the bursts of pain from her wounds and the blood which made her head feel woozy. All that mattered was that these people– even though they'd saved her from the fire– were taking her away from the only home she knew. Laura couldn't bear it, and found the stranger's silence infuriating.

His eyes, which gleamed in the glow of the full moon, were hard, decided.

'We can't go back now,' he answered eventually, 'it would be too late if we took you back, child. I'm sorry.'

Laura turned back, if only that he wouldn't see the new tears in her eyes. Her shoulders slumped in resignation and exhaustion. Maybe, when she woke up, this crazy fantasy would turn out to be a nightmare and her mother would bring in breakfast on a tray with a glass of freshly squeezed orange juice, like she did every Boxing Day morning.

That was right, *had* to be right. On waking she'd discover it was just a bad dream. Sighing, Laura shut her eyes. Her right hand grasped the heart-shaped necklace inside her pocket. Tomorrow it would be back on her bedside table.

'It's just a dream,' she murmured, leaning back against one of her rescuer's chests and fainting, just as one of the strangers began to sing in a mellow, rich voice to the full moon.

Chapter Two

Laura awoke after dawn had broken, and she stretched, moaning as the movement wrenched on the multiple injuries on her body.

'Are you okay?' One of her abductors leaned over her. He looked only fourteen, not that much older than Laura herself.

'I don't know,' she answered truthfully, glancing at her hands, which had been bandaged overnight.

The boy laughed, 'I'm Crow. Timothy Crow. You can call me Tim if you like.'

'I'm Laura Jefferies,' she replied, automatically politely extending her bandaged hand. The way he'd said his name reminded her of some old James Bond movies she'd once seen. She might've laughed if she'd not been so worried.

Tim shook it gently, so as not to cause any more bleeding.

'I'd better get the fire started,' he said suddenly, glancing at the sky, 'Kylan will be back soon.' Laura shrank backwards with a muffled whimper of fear, the vivid memory of flames scalding her feet sharp in her memory.

'Don't talk about fire,' she whispered, white-faced, 'please, I can't bear it.'

'Ah.' Tim said, but Laura could hear the lack of sympathy in his tone. All the same, he moved away from her and began piling up sticks, continually glancing conspiratorially at her.

'Is this distance from you alright?' he asked finally, and she nodded.

'You mentioned someone before: Kylan. Who is he?'

'My master,' Tim smiled, 'he's teaching me to be one of the Robins.'

'How can you be a bird?' Laura asked, curious despite herself. 'It's impossible.'

Tim looked at Laura again and laughed, 'you mean you don't know? Are you joking? You honestly don't know what a Robin is?'

Laura shook her head, 'Should I?'

Tim now looked amazed. 'You're serious?'

'Of course I am,' Laura thumped the ground in frustration, regretting it instantly as her wounds gave a painful throb. 'Just get to the point.'

'Okay, calm down. A Robin is someone who can travel from this world into another without coming to any harm.'

'What?! Stop lying.' She said, 'there's only *one* world— my world. Earth. And robins are small birds with red breasts which sing pretty tunes.' She paused, breathless, 'now you can't tell me that there are any other worlds. That's just fantasy, fiction— like in books. But it's not *real!* In any case,' she paused again and looked around, taking in her surroundings for the first time. She appeared to be in some sort of clearing, enclosed by tall trees which resembled pines, minus the needles. The horse-like creatures were on the other side, munching comfortably on the lower hanging branches. A shiver ran involuntarily down her spine. Now, in daylight, she could clearly discern the leathery skin which barely contained their bones. Their wings didn't seem to have feathers, but hung low on the creatures' backs, made of the same leathery skin. How was that possible? Perhaps they were crazy people who thought they lived in a fantasy world. She had to find out where the nearest phone or road was– she had to get home. Laura pulled her eyes away from the bizarre creature and took a steadying breath. 'Where are we? I've never seen anywhere like this in Adelaide.'

'I told you,' Tim said impatiently, 'we aren't on Earth anymore. We're in…'

'That's not *true!* Laura interrupted angrily. Did he think she was stupid? What game was he playing? 'Not one word of it.'

'I'm afraid it is, my dear.'

Laura jumped and turned slowly around to see a tall man approaching, a pair of rabbits in his arms.

'Kylan, you need to help me persuade Lily…'

'*Laura!*'

'Laura, I mean, that there are worlds other than *hers.*'

Kylan stared at them both for a second, and his gaze made both of their eyes drop to the ground, humbled.

'I'm sorry to be the one to tell you this, Laura,' Kylan said, 'but my apprentice, Tim, is right. There are other worlds, and we are in one of them now. This is where Tim was born, and it's called Venetica. I'm from this world also, but have travelled to many others. For now, though, you must stay here. You can't go back.'

'What?! *Why?* Laura asked, a million thoughts racing through her head. How could she get to a hospital? What would happen to her family? Her friends? They would think she was dead by now. She had to get back, so her last memory of her mother would not be one of the inconsolable loss she now felt. 'Why can't you take me home?'

'Once you've seen us, it is unsafe for you to go back to the life you knew unless you become a Robin also. If you travel between worlds without singing the correct incantation, you shall be incinerated.' His voice was harsh and final, but it wasn't a good enough explanation for Laura.

'Then how did I survive when I came here?' Laura demanded, adding, 'if your story's true.' Of course, she thought to herself, it's insane. There's no way that what they say could be true. It's impossible. She glanced around, searching for an escape route but the trees were clumped thickly together, and she didn't think that she would get far even if she could make a run for it.

'Every being has the ability to pass between worlds just once. That in itself drains the soul, so after that one time we must protect ourselves. So, we sing an incantation of protection.'

Laura felt the sense of unreality which had been with her since she awoke overtake her and she struggled to make sense of the situation. 'If it is supposed to drain the soul, how come I'm feeling alright?' Laura objected, 'shouldn't I be tired or something?'

Kylan smiled. 'You were sleeping for three days. Your body had to recover from the experience.' Laura froze in place, too shocked to speak.

Kylan continued, 'I tended to your wounds as best I could, however I didn't learn a lot of healing incantations when I was studying. We shall have to take you to Yorket; we can find a healer for you there.'

'What'll happen once I'm better?' Laura asked cautiously. Kylan's brows came together in thought.

'We'll cross that stile when we come to it,' he answered coolly.

'What about my studies?' Tim demanded.

'We can continue them, and Laura can partake in them as well, if she wishes.'

'Maybe.' Laura said, feeling a spurt of curiosity which she immediately stamped down. 'They *will* be able to teach me how to go home again, won't they?'

Kylan paused, 'Perhaps in time.'

She sighed but was beginning to understand that on *that* subject, she should keep silent. She eyed her two companions warily, still not quite sure if what they spoke was true or some delusion. They both were adamant in believing their story.

'Here,' Tim handed Laura an apple, 'you must be hungry.'

She was. After taking a large bite, it suddenly struck her that she wasn't hungry, but ravenous. In moments she had eaten the entire apple, core and all, ignoring Tim's look of distaste.

'Geranium! Iris!' Kylan called into the air, and almost immediately, the two creatures from the night before landed in front of them. Laura gasped; during the conversation with Kylan she hadn't noticed them leaving the clearing.

'What are they?' Laura asked curiously, amazed at the sheer impossibility of the creatures. Had they really been telling the truth about alternate worlds?

'Willowings.' Tim responded smugly, 'Let me guess, you've never seen them before either?'

'Tim…' Kylan began, but Laura cut the older man off.

'No, I haven't,' she flashed back at Tim, 'how about you tell me about them?'

Tim was caught off guard, 'Well, Willowings are strong and are used to transport heavy goods. Despite their appearances,' he smirked at Laura, 'they are capable of anything.'

'Indeed, then I take it that they can fly to the centre of the earth?' Laura's tone was laced with sarcasm and perversely she enjoyed watching him react.

Tim sighed in exasperation, 'well, no, of course not.'

'And you just said they were capable of *anything!* Really, Tim, you must get used to using the correct words for the right things. Only then you won't embarrass yourself.'

Kylan laughed, 'Well, she's got a sharp tongue hasn't she, Tim? We're going to have to control this one.'

Tim glowered at Laura, who smiled brightly back.

'I hope we don't have a problem,' she said with false sweetness, trying to hide the sudden rush of anxiety that Kylan's words had caused.

'No,' Tim growled, before mounting the Willowing called Iris. 'You can ride with Kylan. You're just plain annoying.'

'I don't think so,' Kylan interjected, 'a man like me needs a lot of space. I'll crush you otherwise.' This statement made Laura giggle despite herself and provoked an, 'I don't care if she does,' from Tim.

'You two can ride together and try to become friends,' Kylan continued, suddenly serious, 'I don't want to have two children who hate each other constantly jibing.'

He mounted Geranium and leapt into the air, pretending not to hear Tim's yell of 'I'm not a child!' aimed at his back.

Tim turned around to face Laura and said resignedly, 'come on.'

Laura attempted to rise to her feet but could hardly move. Tim rolled his eyes, dismounted and strode over to her, lifting her with strange gentleness, over to Iris' side.

'How can I get on?' Laura eyed the creature nervously, unsteady on her feet.

Tim sighed impatiently, 'here, I'll put you up in front of me.' He did so and they lifted into the air. The sensation of a Ferris wheel came sharply to mind and Laura smiled from the thrill. For a long time neither spoke. Tim kept his eyes fixed straight ahead and Laura gazed down at the trees and fields which rushed past beneath them. Twisting blue rivers flashed in the morning sunlight, and at one point they were joined in the sky by bright orange and yellow birds which looked vaguely like storks. So far, she conceded, it looked nothing like Australia. Perhaps more like a European country, although she was sure that even they didn't have trees which walked through fields or fish which flew over the rivers, tiny scaly wings flashing with water droplets. Was it still possible that she was just dreaming this?

'How long have you been with Kylan?' Laura asked after the storks had flown down to a far-off lake.

'Three years,' Tim responded abruptly, 'anyone who wants to be one of the Robins must leave home at eleven.'

'Don't you miss your family?'

'Yes, of course. But when I signed the contract to be Kylan's apprentice, I was forbidden to see them again. That's why there aren't many Robins. It's not too bad...'

'No, that's *terrible*,' Laura interrupted, and Tim looked at her in surprise.

'It's the way things are though,' he said slowly, 'by the decree of The Robin, himself. Most apprentices have to make the choice themselves or be orphaned.'

'Hang on, aren't you trying to become the Robin?' Laura asked, confused.

'No, only *a* Robin. Not *The* Robin– there's a large difference. *The* Robin is the leader of the Order.'

'Order?'

'The Order of Song.'

'And he's in charge of everything in the Order?'

'Yes,' Tim replied simply.

'So The Robin makes the rules, and only he can re-write them?'

'Yes, but I wouldn't advise trying to let him change *that* rule.'

'Why?'

'The Robin is well known for having a heart of stone, Laura. No one dares approach him.'

'He's that bad?'

'I'm not sure, but rumours about him aren't complimentary.'

'But they're just rumours, stories, nothing more. Surely there's no truth to them,' Laura scoffed, turning around to see his reaction. His face remained like a slab of marble, hard, unmoving. But his eyes were full of suppressed fears as he replied,

'You're wrong.'

The town of Yorket was like nothing Laura had ever seen before, but then, nothing that she'd seen since she awoke was remotely familiar. Yorket was in the middle of a large forest which, from the sky, seemed to stretch for miles and miles. The town was in the treetops, with large swaying bridges in between any gap. They looked almost exactly like the rickety bridges in the old adventure films her father had enjoyed. She was sure that if she placed even a toe on one, the bridge would break. As her eyes travelled downwards, towards the forest floor she realised that there was no ladder or contraption to ferry people down to the shadowy ground.

'I know what you meant about the Willowings now.' Laura murmured. Tim laughed,

'It's really something, isn't it? They live up here so as not to get eaten by the Dragutash.'

'The *what?*

'Dragutash are monstrous creatures,' Tim shuddered, 'it was one of them that did this.' He pulled up his sleeve roughly and she saw a jagged scar running down the length of his left arm. It was ugly and horrific, and Laura flinched instinctively.

'I was six when it happened,' he said. 'One day, I'll find the beast that did this and I'll kill it with my bare hands.' Suddenly he seemed to be acutely aware of her staring at his arm and hurriedly pulled the sleeve back down, turning away, ashamed. 'I mean… I'll have my revenge one day.'

'I think you're really brave,' Laura whispered.

'Uh thanks,' Tim said awkwardly, hoping that Laura wouldn't see his cheeks redden.

'Tim,' Kylan called from ahead of them, 'Let's land near the inn on this side of town. Aim for the stables.'

'Alright,' Tim yelled, his hands tightening on Iris' reins, gently manoeuvring them downwards towards the town.

With a slight jolt, they landed on one of the wooden platforms. Kylan, who had already dismounted, walked over to Laura and lifted her down. Behind them, Tim led the two Willowings over to the stable door and paid a ragged boy whilst handing him the reins. When he re-joined them, they set off towards a lopsided building which Laura thought would most definitely fall to the ground far below when the next storm came.

'We're staying there?' she asked, eyebrows raised.

'Yes, is there a problem?' Kylan asked brightly, glancing down at her.

'Won't it fall down?' she said, looking meaningfully towards the ground.

'No, it's been here for many years,' Kylan replied. 'I know that it doesn't look like it could support a person, but this inn is like the Willowings: it's stronger than it looks.'

On entering the inn, Laura sighed, it was almost as if they were on the ground. Inside you couldn't tell that you were hundreds of feet in the air above the forest floor until the wind blew and the inn began to wobble and sway. This gave the effect that they were in a large boat, which made her feel sick. She grasped Kylan's arm so tightly that her knuckles turned white.

Tim patted her shoulder, with surprising thoughtfulness. 'It's okay Laura, you'll get used to it eventually.'

'Yeah, easy for you to say,' she grumbled.

Tim laughed, wandering over to where some girls were standing at the bar. Wrapping a carefree arm around one of them, he drank from a cup which had miraculously sprouted out of nowhere. The girls clustered around him, giggling incoherent words.

'Come on, Laura,' Kylan spoke over the raucous noise of the inn, 'there are some people I want you to meet.' Seeing as she couldn't support her own weight, Laura had little else to do but nod her agreement. She was taken over to a group of men, who were laughing companionably together around a large table in the corner of the room. Kylan placed her into a nearby chair to rest her throbbing legs and she looked at them all in turn.

One looked like a tree stump; his hands, which rested in his lap, were gnarled and rough. Her eyes widened as she realised that he had no hair, only twigs and leaves. His eyebrows were clumps of moss and two beady eyes watched her, gauging her reaction to his bizarre appearance. A memory of her mother telling her off for staring came to mind, and she quickly averted her gaze to the man on the Tree's right. Luckily, he looked more human. He was tall and had a long curly beard, with glasses perched on his nose. In his hands, the man clasped a book which, on peering closer, Laura could make out to be called *Interaction with Inhabitants of the Eyja Peninsula*. She wondered vaguely in which world the Eyja Peninsula was and was relieved that the title had been in English. The next man had flaming red hair and seemed to have a large grin permanently etched on his face. He kept fiddling with a pebble, passing it between the fingers of each hand.

'Do you want to see something special, little chick?' he asked, a mischievous glint in his eyes. Laura nodded, completely bewildered. In a second, he flicked the pebble upwards, and she watched it flip once, twice, three times before it was caught by a paw. She blinked, then looked at the man, before crying out and recoiling in horror. In front of her was a creature which had the head of an eagle and the body of a lion. Its tail flicked impatiently and the wings fluttered, brushing against the wooden seat. The beak clicked before the man's voice said, 'I believe the words you're looking for are spectacular, astonishing or simply bombidextrious!'

'Bombidextrious?' Laura repeated faintly, her heart beating at a million miles an hour. How was it possible that the man had disappeared, yet his voice remained? Did the creature swallow him alive? Frantically, she looked at the other men who all wore smiles of bemusement yet seemed unfazed by the sudden change of drinking companion.

'What… how… where…?' she began, unable to piece together her thoughts to make a coherent sentence. 'He was right there and then…' Luckily Kylan came to her rescue.

'Don't worry, Laura. Lukas is just being, well…'

'Himself,' the fourth man completed, 'he shouldn't even be allowed to use magic. Disgrace to all of us.'

'I heard that,' the Griffin said, 'I still have ears.' The pebble flew into the air again and flipped thrice. By the time it had finished, it was caught in his, once more human, palm. Laura looked back into his eyes and felt a weird sensation in her fingertips as they instinctively reached towards the pebble. In a second, the pebble disappeared into the folds of Lukas' robe and he regarded her sternly.

'Don't you know not to touch dezmians?' he asked sharply, and Laura pulled her hand back quickly, surprised at his sudden change of tone.

'Of course she doesn't,' Kylan replied, 'in her world there is no such thing as magic. I'm sure that she believes it all to be quite overwhelming and strange.' Lukas looked slightly abashed but didn't bring the pebble back out again.

'That ought to teach you not to judge newcomers before you know what world they come from,' the man on his left said, 'you always did jump to conclusions, now you've frightened the poor girl.'

'I'm sorry little chick,' Lukas said, 'I just assumed…'

'Of course, you *assume*,' the Tree said, 'you never pause to *consider.*'

'It's okay,' Laura said quietly, 'but what is it? The pebble? And why are you calling me "little chick"?'

'What's a pebble?' Kylan asked, eyes alight with curiosity.

Laura stared at them for a moment as the realisation of what he had just said struck her.

'You know,' she began, although they obviously didn't, 'it's that rock you were throwing before.' She pointed at Lukas' sleeve where the pebble had disappeared. Lukas withdrew it, the dawning light of understanding on his face.

'You mean the dezmian?' he asked, and received a nod in reply. A collective sigh of 'ahh' was released from the other men.

'Pebble,' the man with glasses said, as if tasting how the word felt on his tongue, 'that's simply bombidextrious!'

'What does "bombidextrious" mean?' Laura asked, remembering the word from before.

'It's like saying that something is really, really good,' Kylan said.

'Or something's absolutely-fabulously amazing,' Lukas added.

'Or fascinating,' the Tree said.

'Okay,' Laura said. 'But why did you call me "little chick"?'

'Because you're training to be a Robin, aren't you?' Lukas asked, 'and all birds have to be chicks before they become fully fledged.'

'She isn't training to be a Robin,' Kylan interrupted quickly, before turning back to her, 'Laura, I'm afraid I didn't introduce you to my friends. These are fellow members of the Order of Song: Lukas, Paul, Neal and Jadjet.'

'Pleased to meet you,' she said smiling, shaking each of the men's hands.

'Nice to see that you can still remember formality, Kylan,' Paul said as he placed *Interaction with Inhabitants of the Eyja Peninsula* on the table.

'We saved her in one of the worlds,' Kylan said, ignoring Paul's comment, 'Tim and I pulled her from a burning house. She was badly hurt, in fact,' his eyes roved around the room, 'that's why we're here. Is Healer Lionel still around? Laura needs medical attention as soon as possible. Tim and I just used some basic healing spells, but we never followed the path of Healers.'

'Yes, he is,' Paul said. 'I wonder, Laura, would you be willing to share some stories of your world with us? I'm sure that they must be fascinating.'

Laura paused, unsure whether she really wanted to tell strangers about her home. As overwhelming as this world was, she still hadn't come to terms with the fact that she wasn't able to leave it anytime soon.

As if sensing her feelings, Kylan said, 'If you don't want to talk now, Laura, you don't have…'

'But it would brighten up my day if you would tell us just one story of that world.' Lukas interrupted, as he drained a tankard of mead. 'You don't know how boring it is, listening to the same tales every time we see each other.' The other men chuckled as a waitress replenished their tankards.

'I'm not sure,' Laura replied unsteadily, fingering the coarse linen tunic she had been dressed in. 'There aren't a lot of interesting stories for me to tell. Not any that happened to me, anyway.'

'Poppycock,' Lukas said, 'I'm sure that you can remember folk tales or mythology.'

'Oh, please do tell some,' Jadjet added, his leaves and twigs fluttering in excitement.

Perhaps it was due to the strangeness of being begged to do something by a tree, but Laura relented, and for the rest of the evening she told her audience about Snow White and the Seven Dwarves, the Sleeping Beauty and the Frog Prince. Only Kylan noticed the way her eyes kept darting back to gaze at Tim with his female entourage.

Secretly, Kylan smiled.

Chapter Three

Kylan decided that they should stay in Yorket for a couple of weeks, using the time to get some supplies for their journey and to wait for Laura's wounds to heal.

The day after their arrival, Kylan carried Laura to a small hut near the tip of one of the treetops. As they climbed up a rickety staircase, Laura glanced down and felt a wave of vertigo overcome her. Clinging onto Kylan's neck, she looked back upward, hoping the dizziness would soon pass. Thankfully they soon left the staircase, which had swayed unsteadily through the course of their climb, and Laura felt her nausea subside. They approached the hut and Laura noticed a small plaque on the door which read 'Healer Lionel – Apothecary'. She wondered what an *apothecary* was but decided against asking, whenever she asked those sorts of questions Kylan just smiled and Tim guffawed.

Kylan opened the arched door and they entered a small circular room scattered with chairs. Tim closed the door behind them.

'Lionel! Come on out, you lazy idiot!' Kylan shouted, which, Laura thought, was a very unceremonious way of addressing anyone.

A man dressed in a brown robe came out of another room, his expression mingled between exasperation and amusement. Her eyes were drawn to the wooden amulet he was wearing, it seemed to glow with a pale green energy and she felt a tingle like the one she'd had when she saw the dezmian. It must be magical.

'When will you treat me with respect, Kylan?' the healer asked as he approached them.

'No idea.' Kylan replied good naturedly.

'Who's this?' Lionel asked, smiling encouragingly down at Laura.

'I'm Laura,' she replied.

'Nice to meet you.' He said, 'and what can I do for you today?'

Kylan told the apothecary shortly and precisely about Laura's injuries from the night of the fire. As he spoke, Lionel's face clouded in worry, and he insisted on attending to Laura at once. Taking her from Kylan's arms, he took her into another room, where he lay her on a bed. Within moments, he had removed the bandages which Kylan and Tim had wrapped around her. Using a poultice from a small tin, he carefully applied it to the burns and deep slashes in her arms and legs.

'Thank goodness there is no glass in the wounds,' he murmured, as Laura scrunched up her nose. The poultice he was applying smelt of seaweed mixed with cinnamon. It was pungent.

The healer leaned over her legs, long fingers holding the amulet which brushed her wounds, and he murmured something incoherent under his breath. When Laura listened more carefully, she realised that he wasn't speaking words at all, more like different intonations of notes, rising and falling up and down an unknown musical scale.

'How long will it take to heal?' she asked Lionel when he had finished and was briskly packing his equipment back onto shelves.

'Hopefully in a few days you'll be better. It all depends on how quickly the poultice heals your injuries. I'm afraid that they will leave scars; you didn't arrive soon enough for me to remove traces of those. But rest that leg for as long as possible, Laura. I'll come around to check on you tomorrow.'

'Thanks, Lionel,' Kylan smiled as he and the healer shook hands.

'My pleasure, old friend. Now, tell me about your latest adventure to Earth. Did you find some medical supplies which I can study?'

To Laura's amusement, Kylan nodded and brought out a packet of Band-Aids, a packet of antihistamines and some pills of paracetamol. Lionel took them with the reverence of a scholar handling an ancient manuscript. His eyes lit up with amazement and joy, marvelling over the pills and Band-Aids.

'Wonderful,' he smiled, 'truly wonderful.'

'Laura,' Tim said suddenly, interrupting her thoughts. She jumped, not having realised that he had entered the shop.

'What?'

'How old are you?' he asked shrewdly, and was met with wide eyes.

'I'm thirteen in May.'

With a strange expression on his face, Tim persisted by saying, 'which date?'

'The fourteenth. Why?'

'I was born on the twelfth.' He replied. 'Do you have any brothers or sisters?'

'I have… *had* a brother. He was seventeen, his name was Fred.'

'Really?' Tim paused for a moment before adding, 'why did you say "had"?'

Laura shrugged, a heavy weight constricting around her chest as she spoke, 'As everyone has made it obvious that I won't be able to go home, I'm as well off as apprentices in the Order of Song. My family thinks I'm dead. I'm as *good* as dead.'

'No,' Tim said quickly and gripped her shoulders, glancing at the men who had stopped and were looking at him with bewildered expressions.

'I mean,' he continued, removing his hands slowly, 'that it's too early for you to give up hope. Trust me, we'll find a way to get you home. Even if it may not be for a while yet. I promise we'll figure it out.'

Due to Lionel's orders, Laura was confined to her bed for several days, and at first she didn't take it well, complaining under her breath.

'You're saying that I have to lie down for days? Why isn't there electricity and normal things like that here? If I could watch T.V. it'd make time go faster, but *no*, all you people have in this world is magical pebbles and flying horses and tree houses.'

'The only excuse for you to exit your bed is when you need to go to the privy and eat your meals.' Kylan said smoothly, but this did little to console Laura, especially as she didn't understand what a privy was. 'You have to get used to this new way of life, Laura. You can't go back.' His words stung, as did the way his eyes tightened with suppressed anger.

'I'll be stuck here, bored out of my mind, while *he* can hang around with all of those girls. Look at him; he's having the time of his life.' She grumpily pointed towards Tim, who had an arm around one of the scantily dressed bar girls. 'I just want to go back home.'

Kylan let out a deep, throaty laugh, the anger fading as quickly as it had come. They were sitting in the main dining area of the inn, having just finished a meal of roasted meat and boiled vegetables. Laura's eyes didn't stray from the bar, and Kylan patted her hands which were folded one over the other on the tabletop.

'Tim,' he chuckled, 'he's a ladies' man, Laura. Don't worry, he can look after himself, although he'll be touched that you were thinking of him.' Kylan winked conspiratorially at her, which infuriated her even more.

'I don't care about his *safety*,' she snapped back, 'It's just so unfair that *he* can do whatever he wants and *I* can't. If I had it my way, I would be back home.'

Suddenly all of the laughter disappeared from Kylan's face and he regarded Laura sternly. She'd gone too far. His hand withdrew, and when he spoke, his voice was chilly and severe.

'Amazing though it may seem, Laura,' he began, tone clipped, 'Tim is as badly off as you are. Even though he's not confined to his bed for a few days, he is denied the one wish of his heart. Like you. And being ungrateful will get you nowhere. As I said before: you need to get used to this world now. You cannot– you *will not*– go back.'

Laura sat there for a few moments, absorbing what he had said, so when she glanced at Tim and the girl, she felt stirrings of shame. She couldn't look into Kylan's eyes. Was she really ungrateful? Why was Kylan so adamant that she would not go back home? If he wasn't prepared to take her home then who was?

'Laura,' Tim said, interrupting Laura's confusion, 'this is Amelia.' He pointed to the girl beside him before he turned to her, 'Amelia, I saved Laura from the heart of a fire single-handedly.' Puffing out his chest proudly, he clasped Amelia to him and kissed her. Laura stared at Amelia, who, back home, would've been a model. She was slim, with long golden hair and bright, cornflower blue eyes. She looked like a fairy-tale princess, all grace and poise. She made Laura feel quite small and insignificant in comparison. It did nothing to add to her already low spirits.

'Really,' Amelia drawled, once the kiss had finished. 'She doesn't look worth all that effort, Tim darling. In fact, this *Laura* looks like she has the same amount of worth as the dust under your feet. She's not even attractive. Why can't you take me with you instead of her, dearest?' she crooned, stroking Tim's cheek. 'I'm sure I could make a much more… *desirable* companion. I know you'd prefer that, darling.'

A brief frown crossed Tim's face at her words, and he pulled slightly away. Laura flinched, shocked by the sudden bitchiness. She wasn't used to other girls treating her like that.

'Timothy,' Kylan said angrily as he rose to his feet, 'A chat. Outside. *Immediately.*'

'Sorry,' Tim muttered to Amelia, 'maybe next time.' Amelia pouted and strutted back to the bar, hips swaying provocatively. He followed Kylan outside the inn, his head held high.

Laura rose and, with difficulty, climbed the stairs as quickly as her injuries would allow. Was she really that ugly? Really *that* worthless? On reaching and closing the bedroom door behind her, Laura gazed into the mirror.

A young, almost innocent-looking girl stared back. She was neither too tall, nor too short, with a pale, heart-shaped face. Long coppery hair fell past her shoulders and wide hazel eyes blinked back tears of humiliation. The necklace her parents had given her hung around her pale neck, the silver pendant resting just in the hollow of her throat.

No, she wasn't exceptionally pretty, but she wasn't ugly either. But she could never be as beautiful as Amelia. Not even if she wanted to be.

Her mother had always said she was odd, but that once she got to high school she would find a wider group of friends who would accept her eccentricities. She had been a bit of an outsider in the last few years, always feeling slightly out of place in the classroom. If Kylan knew that, he would probably ask her why exactly she wanted to go back. Tim would laugh and Amelia would sneer, whilst her eyes would encourage Laura to do the world a favour and leave sooner rather than later.

Laura tried to force a smile, which did little to help her rising sobs and she moved towards the bed, lying down on it as her tears started to fall. She just wanted to go home, to have her mother and father there to tell her it would be alright. Her heart was aching, mourning the space that they had once filled.

From her bedroom window, Laura was able to hear the argument taking place below, outside the door of the inn.

'What were you thinking?' Kylan asked furiously.

'I didn't know that Amelia would be such a bitch to her. Honestly, I didn't.' Tim replied defensively.

'Did you even see the poor girl's face, Tim? Those words cut deep, and don't you think that Laura's going through enough already?' his teacher snapped. Why was he suddenly taking her side? He had been so cold mere moments before.

'She's too sensitive. If Laura wants to live the hard life with us, then she needs to toughen up.' At this Laura flinched, hurt.

'Oddly enough, Tim, Laura's been through a lot recently. Her house burnt down. Her family thinks she's dead. We took Laura away from her world against her will! Can't you try to show some *sympathy*?'

Even from her bed she could hear Tim grinding his teeth in annoyance.

'Why don't you talk to *Amelia* about it? She's the one who caused all this trouble.'

'And who stood there with his arm around her waist, allowing a *bar girl* to offend our friend?' Kylan's voice lashed out like a whip into the near silence, leaving a long, angry pause behind.

'All right, if *that's* what you want. I'll go and apologise to Laura.' Tim's voice was tight and strained, and Laura already knew that his apology would not mean anything.

'Thank you, Tim.' Kylan sighed, and Tim left, his feet beating out a sharp rhythm on the wooden floor.

Chapter Four

A week passed.

For Laura each day dragged; it was as though this new world had already turned against her by not letting the clocks tick faster. Tim tried to make her time bedbound more enjoyable by bringing books of local tales for Laura to read, but none of them grabbed her attention long enough to really be a distraction. It didn't help that none of them were written in English, and so he had begun to teach her Venetican to help her translate them. The extended lessons aggravated Tim more than it did her, and he would eventually give up and go back to Amelia. His apology had been, as she had expected, lacklustre at best, but she was still grateful that he made the effort to keep her company. She found that when she was alone, her homesickness began to creep up on her, and she would often stare up at the ceiling, unable to fight back her tears.

Kylan's friends Lukas, Neal, Jadjet and Paul came to visit her as well, each with his own set of questions and were all too willing to continue her language lessons in exchange for her knowledge. Lukas was interested in the politics and governments on Earth, whereas Neal and Paul came to hear the stories of Thumbelina and Jack and the Beanstalk. Jadjet was interested in biology, and often ended up asking Laura questions which she did not know the answer to. However, he would smile at her replies as if they meant more than a whole scientific essay on the subject.

'The only thing I know about plants and animals is what we learnt about when we were studying mangrove swamps and ecosystems at school,' she told him one day. 'There were issues with pollution killing and hurting the animals, and the animals had a food chain.' Jadjet had been taking notes on some parchment and then stood up and thanked her before he left.

Healer Lionel came every day, and sang several healing incantations so that within four days there were just scars where her injuries had been. On his last visit, Laura's mouth hung open, staring at her legs, amazed. The scars themselves were still a shiny pink and were unpleasant to behold, but nevertheless Laura was awestruck. It seemed unreal, and she still couldn't get her head around the fact that *magic* had lent a helping hand to her recovery. It seemed ludicrous, and yet the results were before her eyes. Even whilst Lionel had chanted his incantations, she had been unsure that it would do any good in the long run. But the results were undisputable. Magic was *real*.

Earlier in the week Kylan had brought in a tall, hook-nosed woman to measure Laura. She didn't speak and didn't smile, which had made Laura feel quite awkward and nervous. Finally, the woman left with a nod from Kylan and within two days had returned bearing a large box. Kylan paid her some large silver coins and the woman left without a word. Laura opened up the box and found, to her astonishment, that inside were three plain dresses, two petticoats, several pairs of thick stockings, one green shawl and a pair of sturdy leather shoes. On beholding them, Laura felt immense relief, up until that moment she had had to borrow some of the Kylan's clothes, which were altogether too large and uncomfortable. She missed her shorts and t-shirts, but she would take the dresses over hand-me-down tunics any day. She was even more grateful when the hook-nosed woman helped her into the clothes, demonstrating how to tighten the fastenings so that she could wear the dresses properly. Laura was sure that she noted a brief spasm across the woman's face, which could have been interpreted as an attempted smile.

Despite his original thoughts that Laura could be included in Tim's lessons, Kylan had not let her attend one yet. His only explanation was that he didn't want her to over excite herself, or so he said. Laura wasn't sure if he was telling her the truth, although he would give no other explanation.

This didn't bother her that much, especially since Lukas came to visit her more frequently than all the others. She always liked his visits the most. Within a few days her grasp of written and spoken Venetican had increased in leaps and bounds which made her feel more confident. Furthermore, once Lukas realised that she knew absolutely nothing about politics or governments, he told her more about dezmians. Each day he would spend time showing her the art of throwing the dezmian thrice and being able to catch it with closed eyes. Laura practised with a small stone and could never resist laughing at his frequent tricks.

'Why do I need to know how to catch it with my eyes closed?' she asked one day after failing continuously to catch the stone.

'You'll be in our world for a long time,' Lukas said, 'and during that time it is inevitable that you learn the basics of magic. When you get a dezmian, it will conduit the magical energies of the earth around you and focus it so your will can be achieved. Sometimes you'll be doing several things at once, maybe even performing magic surreptitiously, and then you'll be glad that you can catch it as easily as breathing.'

'How can you change into other things?' she asked, 'like on that first night when you became a griffin?'

'You will learn that later, little chick,' he said, and then leaned closer and whispered, 'can you keep a secret?'

She nodded.

'I think that you will learn how to conduit magic sooner than you know. I'm sure that you'll find that it comes more naturally to you than many others who have spent long years training under mentors.'

'How can you know that?'

He laughed, 'That is a good question, little chick. Unfortunately, it's not one I can answer. But just looking into your eyes can show me some of your potential. When you see me change shape, they brighten and glow, they grow hungry with the idea of future possibilities. I may not be the one to instruct you in this field of study, little chick, but I know a man who will. Kylan will not appreciate my meddling, but I will write to him for you, and hopefully he will answer. Now look at that, you've been catching and throwing that stone without even being aware of it. Well done.'

'That's bombidextrious,' Laura murmured as she looked at the stone in her hand. Lukas' words had filled her with confusion, and she wondered if she would really be able to learn how to use magic. A previously impossible concept was now starting to strike her as a possibility.

On the seventh day of their stay, Kylan received a letter. After the messenger placed it in his hand, Kylan had retreated to his chamber to read it in private, and had not returned downstairs until suppertime, when he placed a letter in the courier's bag without a word. Despite multiple questions posed by Tim and Laura, neither discovered what the mysterious letter had contained until the night before they were to depart the town of Yorket.

Kylan called them to his room and, with a serious face, asked them to sit down.

'Tim, Laura,' he said gravely, eyes lingering on Laura's face as he spoke. 'As you probably both know, I received a letter on Friday. It contains important information.'

'What information?' Tim asked instantly. His impatience was contagious, and Laura perched on the edge of her own seat, leaning towards Kylan.

'Read it, and tell me what your opinions are.' Kylan's eyes met Laura's inquisitive gaze as he passed the letter to Tim.

It was more of a note, really, Laura thought to herself as she peered over Tim's shoulder and saw a faded piece of parchment. It was written with purple ink, but the cursive handwriting, for her, was very difficult to read.

Kylan, it read, *I request that you and your apprentice, Timothy Crow, along with your recent ward, come to The Temple of the Nest. I'm sure that Timothy Crow shall enjoy delving into the library. There are several of your old companions who are staying here as well. As for the girl, I shall decide her fate once I meet her in person.*

The Robin.

Beneath the letter was a seal and, pressed into the wax, was the image of a four-pointed star. Embedded within the star was the tiny silhouette of a bird.

'What does it mean?' Laura asked, her finger tracing the imprinted star. Something shifted in her memory, but it was gone before she even registered that it was there.

'So, we've been summoned to the Temple?' Tim asked in an awed whisper.

'Indeed, we have,' Kylan replied grimly. 'But I'm not sure about what The Robin's intentions are towards Laura.'

'I could protect her,' Tim said instantly, meeting Laura's surprised eyes and looking down, embarrassed.

'I'm sure you could, Tim,' Kylan said, 'but I'm still worried about her safety. We don't know what the Temple holds for us. I haven't been there since I was initiated as a Master of the Voice, and that was almost ten years ago, before The Robin took over from his predecessor. Since then, there have been far too many rumours spread about him for my liking. I don't know if we should…'

'I don't want to be the reason that you don't go to the Temple,' Laura suddenly interrupted. 'Kylan, you'll probably be able to meet old friends and colleagues. Tim can enjoy the library. So, I'll go too, and whatever happens, I'll hold myself responsible.' She remembered what Lukas had said a few days before, about her potential to learn magic. Could he have written to someone at the Temple of the Nest about her? He had seemed so secretive, but she had felt a stronger connection with him than she had to date with Kylan. If she had to choose between following Lukas' advice or Kylan's, she knew who she would prefer to listen to.

'Well spoken,' Kylan acknowledged, 'but I'm still not so sure…'

'Don't worry, Kylan,' Tim said impatiently, 'we can protect her and will leave if, somehow, Laura is in danger.'

'Why are you so worried about my safety, anyway?' Laura asked, 'you're acting like The Robin is a really bad person and the Temple holds nothing that can interest me.' Besides, she added silently, it was you who decided to bring me here. You may have saved me from the fire, but you also chose to take me away from my home.

'It's hard to explain,' Kylan began awkwardly, and made to change the subject. But Laura was one step ahead.

'Stop.' She said, raising a hand. 'If we're going there, then I think I have a right to know some of these rumours.'

Kylan paused for a long moment and considered her, before nodding in acquiescence.

'Well,' he began, 'no one actually knows how he became The Robin, Laura. He joined the Temple as a young man, many years ago, and stopped at nothing to reach the top. His magical affinity was noticed by the former leader of the Temple, and he took him on as his apprentice. Nine years ago during his initiation, he and many of the Robins went into one of the worlds, accompanied by his Master. One of those who joined him was my previous mentor, and several of my friends. No one knows what happened but only The Robin returned from that world, and he became our leader. True he was badly injured– could barely walk– but tales were spread that he had somehow planned for the other Robins to be… disposed of. We have barely seen him during the past years, so people are starting to worry that his ascension to leadership was forged through innocent men's blood.'

'That's it?' Laura asked. They had no proof, only speculation, that he had supposedly murdered his mentors in that other world. In her mind, this wasn't a good enough reason to blacken his name. Especially if he was the one Lukas had written to about her. If anything, this unknown history only made him more interesting.

'He doesn't like women,' Tim said, interrupting her thoughts. 'He doesn't treat them well. I've heard he gets very sullen and brooding when he sees them. That's why he stays in the tallest tower in the Temple, so he doesn't have to see anyone. No one knows what his real name is or whether he actually is human. He acts differently, so it's not hard to believe that he came from another world.'

'Tim,' Kylan said, aghast. 'He's not…'

'You've heard the stories too, Kylan.' Tim retorted, 'surely Laura should hear everything we do.'

'But they're only rumours,' Kylan snapped. 'We've never met him to find any truth to them.' Laura found herself agreeing with him, although she found it ironic that, only seconds before, Kylan had been as certain about other rumours to do with The Robin as Tim now was.

'Why defend him?' Tim cried, blood rising to his face.

His mentor was silent, but the look in his eyes made Laura shrink back. Kylan turned to Laura, and when he spoke his voice was frigid. 'The Robin has never had a lot of close contact with Robins, only with Romulus, his advisor. Romulus runs the school and reports to him. The Robin is rarely seen, except on important occasions, like the graduation of the apprentices. He isn't married and almost never leaves his tower unless on important business.'

Laura wondered why The Robin would be that way. Perhaps it was to do with what had happened in the other world all those years ago. *Or,* he could just be antisocial or working on something private that he wanted no one else to know about. As someone who had spent a lot of time alone for the past few years, she thought she could understand wanting to keep to one's own company, especially if he was aware of the rumours being spread about him.

'So, he likes solitude?' she asked Kylan absently, he and Tim were glaring at each other, but he glanced up and nodded,

'So we all have assumed.'

'Well, I guess that we must meet him,' Laura said finally, 'since he seems to want to decide what happens with me.' As she spoke the words, Laura felt the heaviness she'd felt when Kylan and Tim had told her she never could go back home, descend once again. It seemed that her destiny wasn't allowed to be in her own hands once again, but had eluded her, passing into The Robin's control.

'You're certain you want to accompany us?' Kylan asked worriedly, interrupting her thoughts.

'Where else would I go, if I didn't?' Laura replied, a bit sharper than she'd intended. She ducked her head, wishing to avoid their stares.

'True,' Kylan said pensively, 'I have already informed him that we shall set off at some point this week.'

'Then why ask us all these questions?' Tim demanded, the colour rising in his face. 'You could have just said…'

'I wanted to make sure that you both agreed on us leaving, and I was having second thoughts. I don't want to leave Laura alone here, but I'm not sure if I want her to go to the Temple either.'

'We'll be there,' Tim said forcefully, 'Laura won't be alone.'

Kylan smiled at his apprentice, before saying, 'in that case we shall leave for the Temple of the Nest tomorrow.'

'Come on,' Tim called from the other side of the swaying bridge.

Laura sighed and rolled her eyes; *he* didn't have to worry about pulling apart the scar on her thigh. Healer Lionel had been adamant that she shouldn't run until next week.

'Hurry up, Laura!' Tim yelled again.

She stepped onto the bridge and, almost immediately, began to feel sick as it rocked precariously. She stepped forward a few steps and it swayed more violently as the wind blew harder, pushing it to and fro. Laura screamed and clutched onto the handrails made of rope.

Instantly, Tim was running towards her, looking concerned. This only made the bridge rock harder and Laura moaned as she tried to keep down her breakfast.

'Are you okay?' he called.

Well, of course I am, Laura thought, apart from the fact that I'm not good with heights and swaying bridges, I'm perfectly…

'Fine,' she replied as he reached her. 'Oh, stop it, you're making it worse.'

Tim looked at her carefully for a moment before chuckling. 'You're scared!' he cried, and he began to shift his weight from one side to the other, on purpose this time, forcing the bridge to rock in the same direction.

'Stop it!'

'Aw, not comfortable with that, Laura?' Tim asked as she tried to push past him, clutching onto the handrails for dear life.

Suddenly he slung her over his shoulder and said, 'Come on, I can get you there much quicker.'

Then he began to run, and she squealed at him to let her down, hitting his back as the bridge swung again.

'You won't be allowed to do that at the Temple.' Kylan said, as they reached the stable and mounted the Willowings.

'Why?' Laura asked curiously.

'Because it's a place for the learning and study of the arcane arts. The teachers will be very annoyed if you run around and make a lot of noise. It's not acceptable.'

Kylan clicked his tongue and they leapt into the air. As Laura glanced back at Yorket, she saw Lukas waving good-bye, and felt a tight lump enter her throat. She was already missing his teasing smile and the way he would call her 'little chick'. In a few short days she had warmed to him more quickly than Kylan, and she could only hope that he would follow them to the Temple. Maybe then he would help to teach her more. Or, even better, he could explain some of the things he had hinted at in their last conversation.

Chapter Five

It wasn't until five long, cold days later that they finally caught sight of the Temple. Laura was relieved, she had had enough of sleeping on the ground and her bones ached from the hours spent in flight. The Willowings may have been gentle creatures, but they weren't like the comfortably padded seats one might find on an aeroplane or a car. Not to mention the fact that they had to ride through any weather. Laura often found herself daydreaming about having a roof and heating readily available.

Night was starting to fall as they approached the Temple. It was on the peak of an exceptionally high mountain, and the tallest tower rose up to touch the evening sky. A forest spanned the sides of the mountain and Laura felt a rush as she stared downwards, the shivering dark green mass seemed to breathe like a living creature. The Temple itself looked like a reclusive lord's sprawling castle from a fairy-tale. The walls loomed high and forbidding, almost like they had been scorched by the darkening sky. There was no light to be seen, save a small glimmer from the top of the tower. Laura shivered, partly from the cold twilit air and partly from foreboding.

'It's not exactly welcoming, is it?' she said timidly.

Tim and Kylan laughed, and she felt herself blush awkwardly. 'It wasn't meant to be funny.' She muttered, glancing downwards again, catching sight of thin waterfalls plummeting downwards to a dark lake below. She gulped, suddenly nauseous. If she were to fall…

As if in accordance with her thoughts, Iris bucked in the air, and Laura clutched onto Tim, all too aware of the hundred metre drop between herself and the ground. Kylan reached out and steadied the creature with the touch of his hand.

'Sorry Laura,' Kylan replied, but a smile still tweaked his mouth. 'The Robin enchants the forest so that any outsider approaching shall turn around. Robins spread rumours so that The Temple remains safe. That's why Iris is a little nervous; this is her first time to the Temple as well.'

'But what about traders?' Laura asked, 'surely *they* must come occasionally.'

'No,' Kylan said, 'Robins go to the nearby city, Boowlra, to get food and wine and all their necessities.'

'If it weren't for Willowings, no one could get here anyway.' Tim said as they began to approach the sprawling building. Laura returned her gaze to the Temple.

The Temple had a large courtyard in its centre and four covered walkways branched off to domed buildings. Another corridor intersected the courtyard, leading towards the tower Laura had noticed before. Now that they were closer, she could see that it had a long silver spire like a weather dial on its roof.

'See those buildings?' Tim said loudly over his shoulder. 'That is where the men's and women's quarters are, the dining hall is over there, and the library is on the other side of the cloister. You see?'

As he spoke, Tim pointed to each separate building. His eagerness was shown in every fibre of his being; his eyes were alight with passion, his muscles slightly tensed and his grin stretched from ear to ear. Laura silently wished that she could feel as enthusiastic as he did, but she couldn't help the words *'I shall decide the fate of the girl when I meet her in person'* from running through her mind. Fear gnawed at her insides, and she felt a strange tugging feeling in her stomach. She hoped she wouldn't throw up on Iris' back.

'There doesn't seem to be much room for study, apart from the library,' Laura commented to distract herself from the fear. 'Or anything else for that matter, most of the buildings are only one storey. How can they house a lot of people?'

'The buildings are much larger on the inside. They don't look like it from up here, but they have levels which go underground, almost to the bottom of the cliff.' Kylan replied. 'We'd better land; there seems to be a welcoming party for us.'

As they descended, Laura noticed that Kylan was right. A small group of about twenty people were waiting in the courtyard to welcome the newcomers. Laura's hand clasped her stomach, the odd feeling that she was being pulled was getting stronger. It felt different to the nausea from before, and her brow creased in confusion. The ground was coming closer and closer until they landed with the now familiar juddering shock as the Willowings' hooves hit the cobbles. On beholding the faces of strange people, the sensation disappeared as quickly as it had come.

'Hello, old friend,' an elderly man smiled as he moved to shake hands with Kylan as they dismounted.

'Romulus, it's good to see you.' Kylan answered with a small bow over the man's hand.

'Is this your apprentice?' Romulus inquired, turning appraising eyes to Tim.

'Yes, this is Timothy Crow,' Kylan replied.

'Hm.' Romulus scrutinized Tim carefully, finally nodding in approval and reaching out a hand to the boy. Tim bowed in a similar manner to Kylan.

'And this must be the mysterious ward, Kylan.' Romulus now turned to Laura. 'Even we have heard of her, and how The Robin himself has requested an audience.'

Kylan forced a smile, but his eyes reflected all his fears.

'I didn't know I was that famous,' Laura muttered to herself.

'Why indeed you are, my dear.' Romulus smiled, catching her off guard, 'you came between worlds, having not joined the Order first. Also, I think that… yes, I think I see why now.' His strange, disjointed words left the travellers at a loss as to what to say. 'Here we have a humble community,' Romulus continued, 'twenty women and twenty-five men. We only allow a selected few to reside in the Temple.'

'We're honoured to be here,' Kylan said with another bow.

'Now, I believe that we can see to your belongings and place them into your dormitories. The Robin is expecting you immediately; I'll probably get into trouble for keeping you all for just this conversation.' With a laugh, Romulus pointed to the tower, 'He's on the top floor. You know the way, Kylan.'

Kylan nodded, lips tight, and led Laura and Tim away.

Inside the tower they began climbing the winding staircase and soon felt as if they'd keep going up and up forever.

'Well at least the view shall be beautiful.' Laura said, trying to lighten the mood of worry and anxiety. Her heart felt heavier than ever, almost as if she were going to her doom.

'Except that it's dark.' Tim muttered. Laura stuck her tongue out at his back, annoyed. They continued in silence until finally reaching a small door. Kylan stopped, took a deep breath and knocked.

'Come in,' a deep voice called from the other side.

As the travellers entered the room, they were met by the warmth of a merry fire, along with the smell of hot food. Laura felt confused– hadn't Kylan and Tim made The Robin out to be a cruel, heartless man? Where were the chains, cold stone floor and black tapestries?

'Sit down, please,' a tall man said. His face was submerged in shadow and his accent sounded vaguely Italian. Laura began to feel uncomfortable as she felt The Robin's eyes scan over her, taking in everything from the pendant around her neck, to the leather shoes on her feet. She started to become embarrassed and looked down at a deep green carpet. There were some red stains on it at the opposite end of the room, which looked vaguely like blood. Laura shivered and turned away. Perhaps there didn't have to be chains and mildewed walls for it to be scary after all.

She faced the fireplace where three upright chairs sat. They were finely carved, with intricate designs resembling dragons, fairies and water nymphs decorating their backs. The fire started to rise, flames waving up into the air, and she could feel the heat radiating from them. Laura broke out into a cold sweat and froze, eyes watching it in silent terror. Suddenly everything came back; the flames licking the soles of her feet, smoke filling her lungs and screams filling her ears.

'Laura?' Tim asked, reaching out to touch her arm, but his voice seemed distant. She turned to him and stared blankly into his eyes, still caught up in memories. Family life before the fire: Christmas Day, her sixth birthday with all of her friends dressed up as fairies, her parents and brother laughing as they strolled through the botanic gardens while she ate an ice-cream…

'Laura, are you alright?' Kylan inquired, eyebrows drawn together in worry. Emotion welled up within Laura's breast and she stepped hastily away from the fire, tripping over the carpet and falling against The Robin's chest. She gave a little shriek as her balance shifted but was silenced when he caught her in his arms and righted her.

'Thanks,' she muttered, embarrassed. Something about The Robin reminded her of something, maybe a dream or long distant thought, but however hard she tried, she could not remember it.

'Not keen on hearths then?' The Robin interrupted her thoughts; his voice seemed to have a thread of remorse laced through it. Looking at Kylan and Tim, Laura realised they hadn't heard it and gazed up at the man behind her.

'Not really,' she replied, as evenly as she could. 'Not after recent experiences with fire.' The last word was a whisper, but the look in The Robin's dark eyes kept her from glancing away. His eyes were gentle, something she hadn't anticipated, and they seemed to smile at her from the shadowy darkness.

'Then we shall sit by the window,' he said graciously, and to Kylan and Tim's surprise, he lifted two chairs effortlessly and carried them across to a wide panel of glass which seemed to cover at least half of the wall. Had the sun been shining, Laura was certain the window would provide a panoramic view of the surrounding mountains for as far as the eye could see. She glanced at Tim and Kylan and grinned at their dumbfounded expressions; seemingly the meeting with The Robin was not going exactly as they'd expected either.

The Robin by now had moved the final chair next to the glass and gestured for the three travellers to take a seat. Once they sat down, they received bowls of chicken soup. Laura felt another grin spread across her face, but it disappeared almost instantly. It was one of the few dishes which reminded her of home, when her mother would make chicken soup during the winter. A jab of pain ran through her heart, and she slumped in the chair.

The Robin stood opposite them and stared intently at Laura, who gradually began to eat with the fervour of someone who'd been starved. Somehow, he managed to remain in darkness, which seemed to follow him like a cloud.

'So, this is your ward, Kylan.' His cool, clipped voice made Laura feel shy and embarrassed at her bad table manners.

'Indeed she is, sir,' Kylan replied, a hint of terseness in his tone.

'I understand from my sources that you took her from her world against her will.' The Robin continued, his voice becoming emotionless. 'What gave you the *right* to do such a thing?'

Kylan sat up straighter in his chair. When he replied, his voice only had a slight tremor in it. 'I saw it as my duty, sir.' He said, 'she was stuck in her window, the glass had caught her and if we had not intervened, she would have been burnt alive. Her own people would not have come in time to save her. We were lucky enough to get her through into our world alive.'

'If her state was so fragile in the first place, why didn't you just deposit her with her own family?' The Robin demanded. 'Surely she would have been better off...'

'I thought it was the right decision at the time,' Kylan interrupted, 'I wasn't sure if her parents were alive and when I realised they were, it was too late. The Doorway would have closed and Tim and I would not have gotten out of that world alive. My decision may have been harsh, but it was for the best. For all of us.'

Laura stared at Kylan, speechless, and felt anger well up in her chest. She rose shakily to her feet and moved away from him. His eyes were full of demons as he turned to Laura.

'Laura, I'm sorry,' he said, 'but you must understand, I did it for the best, you were hurt and we needed to get to safety. There was no time to take you back. It was the only way.'

'You kidnapped me,' she hissed. The words seemed foreign in her mouth. And yet, it wasn't until this very moment that the truth of what had happened to her struck her for the first time since her abduction. True, there may have been no bad feelings intended towards her, but she'd been taken away from her world all the same. The injustice of it rose up within her as she took another step backwards, shaking. 'You *kidnapped* me!' she repeated hoarsely as tears filled her eyes, 'this– all of *this*– is your fault!'

'Laura!' Tim cried, surprised, 'there was no other option. Kylan made the best decision at the time, he told you so. You called for help and we answered. We saved your life, surely that is worth the fact that... well, for the moment you can't...' He trailed off; Laura's large accusing eyes stared into his own. He held her gaze firmly, his own eyes reflecting only honesty and truth.

'Had there been time we would have returned you to your family.' He repeated, 'I swear.'

She didn't reply, but continued to stare at him, unsure about what to believe. The two older men watched on, Kylan's eyes a troubled hurricane of emotions. The Robin's, on the other hand, gave nothing away about his own private thoughts. Finally, Laura looked away and returned to her seat. She still couldn't entirely face Kylan's relieved expression and turned her head in the opposite direction. She didn't realise she was facing The Robin until he tilted her chin upwards, examining her profile in the light.

'What is your full name, child?' he asked Laura.

'Laura Helen Jefferies, sir.' She answered, and in the shadow she thought she saw a strange expression flash across The Robin's face. In a blink it was gone and she assumed it had been a trick of the light.

'How old are you, Miss Jefferies?'

'I'm twelve, sir.'

'Really?' he muttered, his brow creased in thought. It was almost like he'd forgotten the presence of the visitors.

'My apprentice, Tim Crow, is looking forward to the advantages of the library, sir.' Kylan said awkwardly, breaking the silence.

'And I hope that it can provide them,' The Robin responded. 'Let's call for the next course.' He threw his dezmian and their bowls disappeared, reappearing covered in rice and a dark meaty sauce. Laura took a hesitant bite, and an eruption of spice filled her mouth making her splutter and cough, eyes watering. The men watched in horror as she turned bright red.

'Chillies,' she said, 'I can't handle them.'

After a moment, the men continued to eat without saying a word. Breathing a silent sigh of relief, Laura glanced around as her curiosity got the better of her. Apart from the green carpet and darkened windows there was a painting, depicting a battle with a rearing horse and a rider wearing silver armour and brandishing a sword above his head. Bodies sprawled at the horse's feet, sightless eyes staring up at the knight, who looked determined, but Laura could see a hint of something else in his tight expression. Was it exhaustion?

Her gaze moved to a large bookshelf which rose from floor to ceiling, leather bindings evenly aligned along the shelves. Peering closer she could make out some of the faded writing on the spines.

Histories of Venetica: A Warlock's Perspective.

Faerie Protection in Ghernin's Woodlands.

The Complete Guide to Dragutash.

Provinces of Kinet.

The Basis of Barriers and How They are Formed. Laura was just wondering what a 'Barrier' was, when The Robin's voice broke the silence.

'Miss Jefferies, it is never polite to stare, especially when not given leave to do so.'

Her head jerked around, and she felt her neck crack. A flash of pain shot down her spine as she gazed at The Robin's feet.

'I'm sorry,' Laura said, although racking her memory, she could not remember her mother telling her it was rude to stare at another person's house. Especially the bookshelves, weren't books meant to be admired?

Kylan was watching her carefully out of the corner of his eye, and she felt embarrassed again. She hadn't meant to stare, it was just from what Kylan and Tim had implied when they'd spoken about The Robin, she'd thought this place would be different. But there was something about this room which made her feel safe. It was strange, but the sense of safety made Laura's curiosity overrule all other feelings, demanding to be satisfied. Why should she feel this way when this was a completely different world? Planet, even. It made Laura's head spin when she tried to imagine that she was no longer standing in the same solar system.

Wouldn't scientists love to discover Venetica? she thought wryly. This place would be a dream come true.

'Well,' Kylan said, voice cracking with tension. 'I think it is about time for us to leave.'

The Robin seemed surprised, although it was hard to tell through the shadows.

'But we haven't had dessert yet!' Tim said irritably, 'you can't expect me to sleep with an empty stomach!'

'It won't be empty,' Kylan replied coolly.

Caught off-guard and red-faced, Tim clamped his mouth shut and said not another word. Laura was looking from Kylan to The Robin and back again.

'Very well,' The Robin said smoothly, turning to her. His eyes were burning; if it was with anger, she wasn't sure. 'I'm sure that Romulus will be kind enough to show you to your rooms. I bid you goodnight.'

Kylan nodded sharply and turned, hands on Laura and Tim's backs, he pushed them towards the door. Laura tried to avoid his touch and Kylan's hand moved to fasten firmly on her shoulder. She shrank away, her anger still simmering beneath the surface.

'Miss Jefferies,' The Robin said, 'tomorrow I would like you to return here at ten. Please be prompt, I don't approve of time wasters.' Even though his voice was relatively quiet,

Laura could feel it reverberate with authority in the silence. She hesitated, uneasily aware of Kylan's hand– which by now was shaking slightly– but she also could not avoid The Robin's strong, demanding gaze.

Looking once around the room, Laura replied, 'I doubt that I really have a choice, sir. But, if you wish to talk to me about how I can go back home, then I will come.'

'Indeed, that is what I wish to speak of, Miss Jefferies, along with a proposal. But I won't delay you any longer, as you must find your dormitory. And Miss Jefferies,' Laura, who'd been already propelled closer to the door by Kylan, dug her heels into the carpet.

'Yes?'

'Tomorrow, come alone. I don't appreciate,' his eyes flicked to Kylan's back, 'interferences.' With that, he turned away, and in an instant seemed to have blended like a chameleon back into the shadows.

Laura glanced at Kylan surreptitiously to see what his reaction would be. Surprisingly, he didn't show any signs of having heard what The Robin had said. Confused, she looked at Tim, yet he too seemed oblivious to what had happened. Deep down she was sure that, for some inexplicable reason, Kylan and Tim hadn't been able to hear what The Robin had said at all. It had been only her.

'I'm so pleased that you are staying, Kylan,' Romulus smiled as he led the three of them towards the dormitory blocks. Kylan made a noise of agreement in reply. Romulus turned to Laura, 'could you wait here for a minute please, Miss Jefferies, while I show your friends to their dormitories?'

She nodded and saw Tim smile encouragingly. Kylan turned towards her as well, but she ignored him.

'Night,' she said, her lips slightly numb with cold. This would be one of the first times she was separated from Kylan and Tim, even in Yorket one had almost always remained with her. Now, as Laura watched the men disappearing through the doors to the male dormitory block, she felt utterly and completely alone.

The stars twinkled far above, and she craned her neck backwards, breathing in the air and wishing that she knew the constellations. It seemed like an age passed until Romulus came back, grinning from ear to ear. Together they started heading back towards the female dormitories, their footsteps echoing around the courtyard.

'Are you going to study here?' Romulus asked, a hint of curiosity in his voice.

'I have no idea,' Laura replied truthfully, wishing that he'd stop watching her so closely. 'It all depends on whether or not *He* will let me go home.'

'Indeed, it does, I'm afraid,' Romulus sighed, 'although I hate to say it my dear, but there is no way that you can return through the Doorway between worlds. To achieve that level of training takes many years of dedication and patience. I'm sorry, my dear, but returning to your family will come at a price.'

'But why can't The Robin *do* something to help me get back?' Laura asked desperately, 'I don't want to be a Robin. I don't even know what they are exactly!'

'Robins are healers, bards and travellers throughout all worlds.' Romulus answered calmly, 'we are charged by the Divines to guard and respect the Barriers between the worlds and to make sure that no one mistreats or misuses the Barriers' power. Robins seek to restore balance and justice, to aid those in need with the tenets of the old faith. Some of us say we protect the weak and preserve the worlds' existence, but I find that a bit far-fetched.'

'It *sounds* interesting.' Laura said slowly, 'but I'm not sure if I could do all that.'

'I can see that you would be a welcome addition to our Order, if you so decided,' Romulus replied, 'you have the certain characteristics we look for: curiosity, intelligence and...' He paused again, deep in thought.

Loneliness, Laura thought, being without a home or family. As well off as an orphan. But when Romulus' answer came, it surprised her.

'Faith.'

'Faith?' She thought for a moment that she had misheard.

'Faith that we will restore the wrong committed by taking you from your own world, by returning you to it.'

'How would I ever be able to explain something like this to my parents though?' Laura sighed, already knowing deep down inside, that she never could come up with a reason for her absence. Romulus merely shrugged.

'Ah, there are the female dormitories.' Romulus smiled, obviously relieved to change the subject. He pointed to the building which reminded Laura of the false Tudor impressions back home. Laura gasped as they approached; the building gave off a silvery gleam as if it reflected the rays of moonlight. Again, she felt a strong pull of something deep within her. She was propelled to move faster, to hurry to reach the mysterious building.

'Do you feel it too?' she asked, not taking her eyes off the silver light which beckoned invitingly.

'No,' Romulus replied, 'what is wrong, child?'

'Nothing,' Laura said, glancing downwards, certain that she was suffering from mere nerves or delusions. The sensation grew more insistent, so she walked faster, her breathing hitching up a beat in anticipation. What was this feeling? Suddenly it stopped and she felt as though a cord had been savagely cut. Her hand touched her chest in slight shock.

Romulus, not noticing Laura's unease, opened a large oak door which gave a low creak as it pushed inwards. The corridor they stepped into was lit dimly by lanterns hanging from the ceiling. The floor was carpeted in a lilac colour and felt softer than the carpets she'd had back home. As she looked around, Laura felt the stirrings of that strange feeling again. It didn't pull her anymore, instead it resonated through her body and mind with one word which made Laura freeze.

Home. The word repeated itself within her soul; *home.*

Laura was too shocked to think about anything else.

'Here is the Common Room,' Romulus whispered, indicating a large room to her right, where several armchairs and couches were placed in front of a smouldering pile of coals. Apparently, the fire had died out a little while before. Some older girls looked up from the table in the centre of the room, to stare, unabashed, at Laura and Romulus.

'And here is the bathroom,' the elderly man continued, after winking at the girls, who had turned away, once again poring over their work. Laura's eye followed Romulus's finger and she saw another large room with a large pool in the centre. A statue of a dolphin was in the middle of the pool, and a steady stream of water escaped from its mouth.

'The privies are in an adjoining room.' Romulus said, as Laura stepped from the carpet onto the bathroom's marble floor.

'It's beautiful,' she murmured, suddenly realising that steam was rising from the pool with the scent of rosemary.

'There are hot springs deep within the mountain,' Romulus smiled, 'so our water is always heated.'

'Then why doesn't it smell of sulphur?' Laura asked, brow furrowed; back home it always stank around hot pools.

'That's because we mask the smell with bath salts and soaps.'

'How did you get the water all the way up here?'

Romulus tapped the side of his nose. 'With a little bit of magic and delicate engineering, Miss Jefferies,' he smiled as he ushered her out of the bathroom.

'There are two floors downstairs,' he said softly, 'both have four rooms, because it isn't often that women are here to study. They find it harder to leave their families.' He smiled sadly, and Laura looked once again at the floor. 'Anyway,' he went on, 'this is where I will leave you. By The Robin's decree, male Robins are not allowed in the female dormitory. Your bedroom is on the bottom floor, first door on the right. Sleep well.'

Laura nodded as tiredness raised its sleepy head inside her. 'Goodnight, then.' She yawned and stumbled down the staircase, which twisted like a snake, gradually going lower and lower before reaching a short corridor. Laura finally halted in front of a relatively short door, which only seemed to be about one and a half metres tall. It was lucky that she didn't have to duck her head as she carefully pushed it inward.

The door opened smoothly, casting a pathway of light into a dark room. It was large, with two four-poster beds and a window built into the mountainside, overlooking the distant rocky crags. She noticed immediately that her clothes were next to the empty bed. She slumped down onto it and undressed before slipping under the covers, utterly exhausted.

'Psst! Are you the girl who came with that Robin?' A voice came from the opposite bed, shattering all hopes of immediate peaceful slumber.

'Yes, I'm Laura.'

'Oh my *God!*' Was the reply, and then there was a rustling sound. Laura was too tired to be bothered by her roommate's antics, and closed her eyes. Suddenly, her hand was caught in a strong grip and vigorously shaken. 'I'm Natachatet, but you can call me Tash.' A voice right next to her ear said eagerly, 'you don't know how lonely it's been in this room ever since Finika left last winter.'

'Well, that's a long time,' a surprised Laura admitted.

'I know, but now that you're here, I'm hoping that you'll stay for a while. It'll be fun to study alongside someone new.'

'I'm not here to study,' Laura said, 'I don't even know why I *am* here. I never wanted to be a Robin. It was just that The Robin wanted to see me. You should've seen Kylan's face when he got the letter,' she chuckled.

'The Robin was the reason you came here?' Her roommate asked, awestruck. Laura nodded, until realising that Tash couldn't see it in the dark.

'Mm hm,' she added.

'Wow,' Tash murmured, 'do you know how rare it is for The Robin to see anybody? He's so secretive up there; we always wonder what he does.'

'He invited me to meet him tomorrow,' Laura whispered.

'Really? That's weird,' Tash replied.

'How old are you?' Laura asked impulsively, hoping that Tash would be the same age as her.

'I'm twelve; it's my birthday next week.'

'My birthday's coming up soon too,' smiled Laura. 'Then we'll be the same age.'

'Amazing, we could almost be sisters!'

Laura giggled, she had always wanted a sister, and it would be good to have a new friend in this place, especially one who hadn't had anything to do with bringing her to this world.

'Maybe,' she replied. 'If I can stay.'

'I bet we'll be best friends by the time of your birthday!' Tash promised as she ran back across the room and jumped into her own bed, which creaked at her enthusiasm. Laura smiled and closed her eyes, hoping that her roommate's optimism would infuse her with something similar.

Chapter Six

'I want you to study under my guidance, Miss Jefferies.'

Laura gazed up at The Robin in surprise.

'But I don't want to be a Robin.'

The Robin laughed, 'that's what I once said. And look where I've ended up.'

'What would I study?'

'First you must accept my offer, Miss Jefferies.'

Laura paused for a long time before asking, 'will I ever get the chance to see my family again?'

The Robin flinched and said, 'If you decide to not be a Robin, Laura, the path to see your family shall always remain closed.'

She nodded, unable to hide her disappointment. If she accepted there was a chance that one day, in the far-off future, she would see her family again. Maybe. It was worth a shot at least. Besides, it may be exciting to learn how to become a Robin. Lukas had made it seem interesting. She tried not to imagine her parents' disappointed faces that she wouldn't be continuing with normal schooling. She would never be a lawyer or a paediatrician like her mother had hoped. Taking a deep breath, Laura replied,

'I will accept, but can I ask something first?'

'Very well,' The Robin replied, 'ask away.'

Laura pondered for a while as to how to word her question, she had been sure that of all people, The Robin would understand.

'When I arrived yesterday,' she began, 'I felt something strange. I'd never felt it before, it was a sort of tugging *here*,' she indicated her chest, 'it pulled me towards the Temple and then the female dormitories. When I reached the dormitories, it stopped. But it was so strong. What was it?' She halted, breathless, and looked at The Robin expectantly. His face was shrouded but she thought that through the darkness, his eyes were full of strongly suppressed emotion.

'What you felt is not normal for many who come here to study, Miss Jefferies. The only others I have known to feel such a connection to the Temple of the Nest was myself and my predecessor. You felt the pull of old, elemental magic, which attracts people who would be not only good, but great, Robins. That is truly excellent, Miss Jefferies.'

'So I felt… magic?' Laura asked, astonished. 'Why now? Why not when I was on Earth, or when I arrived in Venetica?'

'The Temple is situated over a mountain where the old magics still are strong and undisturbed. Throughout the rest of Venetica the connection to the old magic has dwindled so that only a few may feel its pull. Does that temporarily satisfy your curiosity?' Laura nodded dumbly as she tried to take it all in. The Robin continued without waiting for her to reply, 'now for your initiation— hold out your left hand, palm facing upwards, if you please.'

She did as he instructed, and he gingerly held her hand with utmost care. She wasn't sure what he intended to do.

'As proof of the fact that you're now an apprentice in the Temple of the Nest, I'll have to brand your left palm.' The Robin said calmly, 'there is no need to be afraid.'

'Wait, what?' Laura jumped, confused. She was suddenly unsure about whether she'd made the right decision. She had heard about branding before but couldn't quite remember what it was.

'It's a tradition that whenever The Robin chooses an apprentice, they are marked as an initiate who is special, different from the rest.' The Robin explained with surprising gentleness, 'I had the same brand when I myself joined. See?' He pulled off one of the gloves that he wore and turned his hand to show a four-pointed star imprinted on his palm. 'I will sing an incantation which will dull the pain for several hours, so that we can tend to the injury before you feel any pain.'

Out of the fire he brought a brand which resembled the four-pointed star on his letter to Kylan and the mark on his own hand. Laura's breath quickened in panic and she stepped away, shaking her head forcefully.

'No, no,' she muttered, terrified. The heat of the fire was once more against the heels of her feet, and the panic as she struggled to escape the flames filled her again. She pulled away from The Robin's outstretched hand, a sob rising in her throat. He sighed, clasping her hand in a vice-like grip.

'It won't hurt,' The Robin murmured comfortingly, starting to sing in a low tenor as he pressed it onto her palm. Laura cried out in shock as the brand was pressed against the smooth, clear skin. Stunned, she watched in horror and wondered how it was that it only felt like her hand was on a hot window. It didn't hurt at all. A part of her was horrified and another part fascinated.

'Put it in some cold water,' she heard The Robin say as he indicated a nearby bowl. Obeying him, Laura dunked her hand into the water. The Robin muttered something under his breath and the water got even colder. Her fingers started to go numb as she tried to process what had happened. The panic was fading now but the shock still remained.

'What shall you teach me?' Laura asked after a moment, turning her head to stare at The Robin.

He hesitated before answering, 'in the mornings you'll have meditation with the other apprentices, which shall be followed by lessons in how to cross the Barriers. You shall be taught several languages, three main tongues from three different worlds. They are Erethianian, Hïala and Damas.

'You are my apprentice, so whenever you want to leave the Temple, my permission must be sought first. That includes when you wish to attend world trips with the other apprentices...'

'What are "*world trips*"?' Laura interrupted eagerly.

'On your planet they are called field trips,' The Robin replied, raising one eyebrow in disapproval. 'A couple of Robins will accompany the apprentices through some of the closer Barriers. Normally a world trip will last a couple of weeks, depending on how advanced the students are.'

'Do they go to the same worlds?' Laura asked, confused. 'I mean, if they are only going through the Barriers closest to the Temple?' The Robin smiled despite himself.

'I gather that Kylan did not tell you much about Venetica. You see, Laura, Venetica is the central world amongst all of the others. It is like Sol in your universe.'

'Sol?'

'The Sun.' The Robin snapped, then, on seeing Laura's expression, softened his tone and raised a hand to his forehead. 'Forgive me, I am not used to having people ask questions or interrupt. I am not... I have not had much experience with apprentices in recent years.' His voice drifted away for a moment and Laura watched him, intrigued.

'I always found it hard to speak to people after I was alone,' Laura said quietly, wondering if sharing this about herself would make him feel less ashamed of his sudden vulnerability. 'And since coming here everything's been difficult. It's all new and people treat my home like a curiosity, like they don't understand what's so wonderful about it. And every time I talk about it, I remember, and I miss it all the more.'

The Robin watched her for a moment and then said, 'I'm sorry that you were taken from your world, Laura. It should not have happened, but fate can be a many-layered thread and the tapestry it weaves will, I'm sure, help you to find your way back home. In the meantime, I will teach you to harness your connection to natural magic and I hope that in time, you will come to see the Temple of the Nest not only as a refuge, but as a home too.'

It seemed that this last statement caught in his throat, as though he were suddenly overwhelmed with emotion. With a short cough, he continued his original point as though Laura had never interrupted. 'The other worlds orbit around Venetica, like the planets around the Sun. Venetica is the strongest force of natural, elemental magic in the universe. The other planets are drawn to this power, which means that planets with little or no magical energy very rarely come close to Venetica.'

'Planets such as Earth?'

He nodded. 'Exactly. Likewise, the planets with similar amounts of magic frequently border on the Barriers into Venetica. Therefore, the Barriers are constantly changing, so one day a Robin could enter through a Barrier to your world from the Barrier outside of the Temple. But the next day, if another Robin went through the same Barrier outside the Temple, one might enter Erethia, or Kinet.'

'So you can never know which world will be next in the rotation?' Laura said, eyes wide.

'No.' The Robin said, seemingly satisfied with his explanation, 'now, back to…'

'But what if you wanted to come back from the world you had been visiting and the Barrier home was no longer outside the Temple? What happens then?'

The Robin gritted his teeth together and Laura bit her lip to stop herself from smiling.

'Then the Barrier home will be at another point in Venetica. Or not there at all. The Robins will escort the apprentices back, as they have a vast amount of experience. This way, students can learn not only about other worlds but Venetica as well. The Barrier may be on the other side of the Western Marshlands, the Northern Alps or the Eastern Seas. Perhaps it will be the desolate Southern Desert. Who knows? But wherever the Barrier connects with Venetica, the Robins will be more than able to lead everyone back to the Temple.'

'But how…'

'Miss Jefferies,' The Robin's thin shred of patience seemed to have snapped, 'I feel that I have described more than necessary. If you still have questions then we can discuss them later, when you understand more about Venetican geography and culture. But now I must *insist* that we return to the final rule of your residence in the Temple.' Laura leaned back with a sigh and observed him with obvious reluctance. She wanted to know more about world trips, not hear more rules.

The Robin looked at her with stern eyes. 'There's to be no inappropriate activity with any of our male residents. That is a very important rule.'

'Gross! I'm twelve!' she said, appalled. 'Besides Mum said I couldn't have a boyfriend until university.' As if any boys she had met would even be interested in her that way anyway. Amelia's words of *she's not even attractive* echoed in her mind and she clenched her fists tightly, noting the slight ache from her palm in the water bowl.

'I'm glad that you were raised well,' The Robin nodded condescendingly. She rolled her eyes and changed the subject, eager to learn more, now that all of the rules and regulations were over.

'When does my first lesson start?'

'Today. Now, if you wish.'

'Oh, yes please.'

'You're an eager girl, aren't you?' he regarded her closely. 'Very well. As we have already started on the topic of Barriers and different worlds, there is no reason why we cannot continue with that topic. Sit down.' Laura sat down in one of the carved wooden chairs from the night before. The Robin tossed his dezmian in the air and a desk appeared in front of her, complete with a quill, ink pot and parchment. Laura picked up the quill and twiddled it through her fingers, wondering if she really was expected to *write* with it. What happened to pens and pencils? The Robin was watching her, and she realised that she *was* expected to write with it and hurriedly opened the inkpot, dipping the quill into it carefully.

Her teacher nodded almost imperceptibly and began. 'There are multiple worlds, and like an invisible wire fence, there is a Barrier around each one. They protect the world from any outside threat, like invasion from another side. These barriers are almost impenetrable, unless a Robin, or someone just as skilled, can use The Way to make a Door between worlds. They were created by the Gods when the inhabitants of one world went on a rampage of blood and terror, determined to conquer each world and claim it for their own. That's why Robins were created, we were given divine instructions to protect the Barriers and to only create Doorways between worlds to promote peaceful interactions between the inhabitants.'

'How can you open up a Doorway?' Laura questioned, beginning to enjoy herself as she took notes, ignoring the blotches which splattered across the page as she jotted down his different points. Who knew if she would be tested on this stuff?

'With the use of song. You need to have the ability to sing in the Ancient Tongue. This skill normally takes years for an initiate of the Order to learn. Once someone has gained control of the Song, and can create a Doorway between worlds, they must be able to respect the culture and language there. Any Robin must be able to blend in with the inhabitants, who, in the majority, are unaware of their otherworldly companions.'

'How long are Robins allowed to stay in the worlds?' Laura asked as she scribbled across the parchment.

'One month and no more. Otherwise, they shall begin to fade, due to being in a different realm. The small supply of magic they hold within themselves begins to lose its strength.

Robins are safe in the world of their birth or this one— Venetica.' He glanced at the clock, 'my, my, look at the time. It's lunchtime already. From now onwards the students are studying, you can go and relax. Try and make some new friends, I cannot guarantee how much longer Kylan will stay on with Timothy Crow. Dinner is at six. Please come here at ten each morning and be prompt. Make sure you've had breakfast first and have attended your meditation and language classes. That will be all. I'll see you tomorrow.'

She nodded and fled the room, running down the stairs two at a time, bubbling with excitement to tell Tim and Tash about her first day and initiation.

'He branded you?' Tash asked over a serving of a type of fish stew. 'But that's barbaric.'

'Weren't you branded to become an apprentice?' Laura asked.

'No, all we had to do was sign a contract with our name and a drop of our blood. But we weren't *burnt.*'

'Well, what does it mean?'

Tash leaned forward eagerly, jet black hair just missing her food. In the daylight, Laura could finally see her clearly. Her deep brown eyes glittered, her skin was dark, and her teeth flashed white in contrast.

'I think that, as you're *his* apprentice, you'll be the next Leader. The Robin's replacement. Though why he chose you, I don't know. No offense, but, well, you're too old to become an apprentice.'

'I know, I should've been eleven.'

Tash laughed suddenly, 'maybe he was hypnotized by your beautiful eyes!'

'No,' Laura replied, 'I'm not beautiful.' The memory of Amelia in Yorket came back to her mind.

'Poppycock! In a few years all the men will be coming after you.'

'Who'll be coming after who?' Tim asked, as he sat down next to Laura.

'No one,' Tash said conspiratorially.

Tim turned and with a mouth full of food said to Laura, 'I heard about you becoming The Robin's apprentice. Congratulations. Kylan had to sit down when he found out; I was scared that he would faint.' He smiled, 'but he's very proud of you, glad that some of the rumours about your new mentor aren't true.'

'Thanks,' she responded. 'The Robin's not so bad, just a bit anti-social, I think. Is it as good here as you expected?' The thought of Kylan nearly fainting in shock just reminded her of what he'd done. The anger she felt was still there, gnawing into her breast.

'Even better!' Tim cried enthusiastically, at a volume which earned a few frowns from elderly Robins. 'I mean,' he added, more quietly, 'there seems to be more books than I could ever read.'

'Too true,' Tash said. Suddenly her eyes tightened and she snarled, 'can't *he* just leave us alone?'

'Who?' Laura asked, glancing around.

'Glenroy Mintz,' Tim answered, suddenly grim. 'He's been watching us for a while.'

'Why?'

'You're The Robin's new apprentice,' Tash replied bluntly, 'I just wish he wouldn't have that glint in his eyes.'

'Where is he?' Laura whispered, eyes still darting around the room.

'There.' Tim growled, pointing out a scrawny looking boy on the other side of the room, whose dark eyes scrutinized Laura. She felt like a biology specimen and was more than a little uncomfortable. He brushed his greasy hair out of his eyes, and his eyebrows came together in a frown.

'Why does he look so angry?' Laura asked Tash, turning back to her companions. He looked scary, and she instinctively didn't want to be alone with him.

'It's part of his nature.' Tim replied, glaring back at Glenroy, 'it's best to ignore him, Laura.'

'Since when did you have time to get to know him?' she asked Tim, 'we haven't even been here for a full day.'

'I had three classes with him today, he's sleeping in the room across from mine and he still hasn't even condescended to say hello. He's not very welcoming.' Tim replied, 'I don't know how the others have been able to stand him for so long. I can't bear his company after just twenty-four hours!'

Laura blinked, surprised at his outburst.

'Don't worry, Laura. I'm sure that he's just curious, probably everyone is.' Tash comforted, laughing at Tim's expression.

'Yeah, I suppose.'

'You're very lucky with your roommate, Laura,' Tim whispered to her, 'Natachatet's one of the smartest apprentices here.' He cast her new friend a blazing look.

Laura rolled her eyes, 'you're impossible, Tim.'

'Well, I have to keep up my reputation.' Tim grinned, puffing his chest out. She hit his stomach and he deflated immediately.

'Meanie,' he grumbled, but Laura saw the cheeky twinkle in his eye.

As she was lying in bed that night, Laura decided that she should try to come to terms with the fact that she would not be able to return immediately to her family. Every Robin and apprentice she met in Venetica seemed to agree on the point that she could not go home without years of experience, and the idea of ignoring their advice and disintegrating on her way through the Barrier was not how she wanted to reunite with her family. Her parents would want her to make the most of her life– wherever she was– if it meant that she could see them again. Her classmates would move on to high school without her, moving in new social circles, and would probably soon forget Laura Jefferies from primary school. Of that, she was sure. If she accepted it, then it would be easier to study without the worry and sadness which over-whelmed her whenever her thoughts strayed towards images of her past. She should at least give it a try.

'I love you Mum, Dad and Fred,' she whispered, 'but you must understand why I have to let you go for the moment. I'll work hard so that we can be together again soon. Good-night.'

No tears fell as she spoke, and for that Laura was relieved; she had already cried so much. Sitting up to gaze at the full moon over the mountains in the cold night, a sad smile crossed her face.

Tomorrow would be the start of her new life, and, hope-fully, time would heal any other wounds in her heart.

Part Two

Six Years Later

Chapter Seven

It was the day before Laura's eighteenth birthday. She and Tash were sitting at their normal table in the hall, eating a well-earned breakfast and relishing the fact that, at long last, they had finished their essays for Magical Studies.

'How do you think you did?' Tash asked as she took a gulp of apple juice, 'I hope I didn't fail. I wasn't sure whether I should have included the translated interview with Iobhan, you know, the man I met when we went to… what was the name of that world? Yarshni… Yarshi …'

'Yarishnak,' Laura answered, her eyes travelling over the faces of the other apprentices until they rested on one in particular. 'It was there that you interviewed ten people about their views on magic and overuse of the Barriers.'

'And it was *so* hard choosing which one to include!' Tash replied, 'but then I reread what Iobhan said, and I mean, who doesn't want to know…' Laura zoned out from the sound of her friend's voice as she watched the man stretching in his chair, muscles tightening beneath his tunic. He flicked his dark hair out of his face and lazily sat back, laughing at some pun his friend, Harrison, had said. She felt her heart beating faster and her hands started to sweat, and she rubbed them along her skirt impatiently. What was wrong with her? Tim turned and caught her staring at him with a playful smile and she ducked her head, embarrassed.

'See something interesting?' Tash drawled, as she watched her friend squirm in her chair. 'It must have been fascinating; you went all gooey-eyed for about a minute.'

'Don't!' Laura replied, covering her cheeks with her hands before draining her own apple juice. 'Let's just talk about something else for a while, OK?'

'Fine,' her friend grinned and Laura felt her spirits lift slightly, she wasn't in complete trouble for not having listened to the engrossing story of ten separate interviews.

'Are you going to Boowlra tomorrow?' Tash asked, suddenly all seriousness, 'it would be horrible if you couldn't. I know that The Robin doesn't like you to go out *too* much but surely for your birthday treat he would reconsider?'

'I'll ask him next lesson,' Laura smiled, 'I *do* need new ingredients for alchemy classes.'

'And perhaps some new jewellery?' her friend joked, as she lifted Laura's pendant up to the light, forcing Laura to lean forward over the table.

'Perhaps,' Laura smiled and, deep down, she felt a small twinge of regret as she openly considered wearing something different to her parent's final gift to her. As she gently pulled the necklace back from Tash's grasp, she imagined how it would feel to wear something new and shiny. Perhaps that would make her feel more appealing, more attractive than she normally felt. Maybe Tim would notice.

The bell started to ring for classes to recommence and, with a brief hug, she and Tash parted ways; her friend to the library and Laura to the tallest tower. As she began to climb the twisting stairs, she rehearsed what she would say. But, while gasping for breath on the final step, Laura found that all thoughts and explanations had left her mind completely. She'd have to improvise.

On entering, she immediately located the dark presence of her mentor and, as she normally did, felt a sudden desire to see what he looked like, for, even though she saw him daily, Laura had never yet seen his face properly. It seemed that he would be eternally cloaked in that ever-present shadow.

'Laura,' he said, and she thought she could almost detect the smile in his tone, 'right on time. Are you ready to begin?' On seeing Laura's nod, he continued, 'As you probably remember, the ancient world has faded into the bare recesses of memory, as technology and human inhabitation has changed the natural order. Nowadays, the worlds are still there, but a lot of the cultures and traditions have been lost. It happens all the time in history, in every world, you understand.'

While he was speaking, Laura moved to her desk next to the window and drew out her quill, ink and parchment but paused as she lowered her bag to the ground.

'Sir?'

'We shall be starting with the world of Ulsert...'

'Sir,' she repeated, forcing herself to speak louder and stopping him mid-sentence.

'Yes, Laura? Surely you have not already learnt about the lost Hunami civilisation in Ulsert?'

'No, sir,' she replied, 'I just wanted to ask your permission to go to Boowlra with the other apprentices tomorrow. I thought it would be a good place to celebrate my birthday. I need to buy some supplies too, and I hoped that I could do it there.'

'You know that I do not usually approve of you attending these trips into Boowlra,' The Robin replied, and Laura nodded. 'But as you shall be eighteen tomorrow, I see no reason to deny you that pleasure.'

'Oh thank you!' Laura cried, overjoyed. The Robin withdrew a small pouch from which came metallic clinking noises as he gave it to her. She took it and stowed it carefully in her bag, slightly shocked at its unexpected weight.

'Consider it as a birthday gift,' he said, 'but return before nightfall. Boowlra can change from being completely safe in daylight, to the harsh opposite with the coming of night. And there are some areas where the magic is weaker; there's something in the stonework in parts of the city which interferes with the natural magics. Try to keep to the main street and shopping precinct.' Laura nodded excitedly, and, as he started to speak again about the world of Ulsert, she soon forgot his warning.

The day of her birthday dawned clear and bright and Laura and Tash ate their breakfast as quickly as they could, desperate to not waste any time. Together they hastened to the stables and joined the small crowd of apprentices who were getting ready. As they mounted their Willowings, Laura locked eyes with Tim who was laughing with his roommate, Harrison. They grinned at each other.

'Laura, I'll race you to the pinnacle!' Tim called, and leapt into the air before Laura could say anything in response.

'But you've got a head-start!' she laughed, nudging her Willowing, Elaret. 'Fly, Elaret, my darling, let's catch him.' Elaret's wings beat mercilessly at the air, racing towards Tim and Iris, and she stroked the beast's neck lovingly as he strained against the wind. Elaret had been her first gift from

The Robin when she turned thirteen, not long after she arrived at the Temple. Although she had not been able to ride Elaret for several months, due to him being a newborn Willowing, she soon realised that Elaret was not just her transport, but a companion as well. Soon, one of her favourite places was the Willowing stable, where she could sit for hours on end, sometimes grooming or tending to Elaret's needs, sometimes just lying back in the hayloft and talking to Tash.

'Hurry up, Laura!' Tim called, flashing her a smile. He'd reached their destination first; once again she felt her breathing catch.

'Oh, come off it, Tim!' she shot back playfully, 'you only won because of the head start.'

'I'm not so sure,' he replied.

'Aren't you? Well, how about I race you back to the group?' she cried, turning Elaret and sweeping back to the line of apprentices, making their way towards Boowlra.

'Cheat! Cheat, I say!' Tim yelled after her, but Laura heard the smile in his voice.

'No need to be overdramatic!' she called back. Suddenly a memory of her brother telling her the same thing, filled her mind, and her heart ached. She shook her head, shattering the thought, and urged Elaret faster, trying to escape the memory.

Once they were back among their friends, Glenroy Mintz turned to face Tim.

'So Crow,' he scoffed, 'why were you just acting like you were five? You're twenty, for God's sake.'

'And you have a problem with that, Mintz?' Tim asked mildly, 'there's no one around for miles except us.'

'And you're dragging Laura into your idiocy. She should be consorting with others who are not as irresponsible or reckless as you. You shouldn't interfere with her. She's intended to do great things; she can't be dragged down by the likes of *you*. I believe that she would be far better off…'

'I hope you realise that I'm right here, Glenroy,' Laura snapped. 'Amazingly enough, Tim and I have been friends for a long time, so I'm used to his "idiocy", as you put it.' She didn't notice the pulse that beat in Tim's temple or his clenched jaw as he glared at Glenroy. Tash, on the other hand, did.

'I was only trying to keep your best interests at heart, Laura.' Glenroy replied with a smile, eyes lingering on Laura's face.

'Leave us be, Mintz,' Tash hissed. She spat out his surname as if it couldn't leave her lips quickly enough.

'Fine,' Glenroy snarled, turning to give Laura another honeyed look, 'I'll see you around.'

After he had retreated, Laura shivered, repulsed. 'What is his *problem*?'

'You know that he's admired you for twelve months now, Laura.' Tash answered, 'it's been pretty obvious.'

'Oh God, don't remind me,' Laura held up her hands in disgust, 'he's been trying to do everything for me, even though I'm perfectly capable of doing it myself. Remember that time we went into Kinet and he insisted on rubbing Elaret down every night? And how he would always walk me to my room to be courteous? I couldn't walk quickly enough.' Tash laughed.

'Actually,' Tim interrupted, brow creased in thought, 'I think that he's been enamoured with you since we arrived at the Temple.'

'Ugh! Stop!' Laura cried.

'He's detestable,' Tash agreed before pointing ahead. 'Look, there's Boowlra.'

Laura grinned, all of the past conversation quickly forgotten as they hastened towards the city. Boowlra had stone buildings sprawling in every conceivable direction. The cobbled streets stretched out below them and the group of apprentices angled their Willowings downwards, aiming to land outside the large stables. They landed with a clatter of hooves on cobbles and dismounted, each giving the stable hand a bronze coin. He led their Willowings off into stalls and Laura turned around to face Tash.

'What do you want to do first?' Tash asked eagerly as Tim moved away to speak with Harrison.

Laura watched him leave out of the corner of her eye and then said decisively, 'let's get some new clothes and supplies for alchemy classes. After that we can have some fun.'

Excitedly, the two friends hastened into the city, towards an old shop labelled 'Leonora's Aromatics'. Tash opened the door, and they entered a room which had shelves reaching from floor to ceiling. They were all piled with different plants, bottled animal organs and labelled jars containing strange things varying from 'Vampyre Saliva' and 'Crushed Animata Bones' to 'Sun-Dried Machilata Pods'. Their noses were assaulted by the combination of crushed herbs, vinegar and burning oil. The shopkeeper was leaning over a small cauldron, stirring the contents clockwise and counterclockwise, muttering incomprehensible words under her breath as she added liquids from small vials into the potion.

'Welcome, ladies. Look around,' she said without turning around, 'there's a sale on all herbs from the Atenski region until Sunday.'

'How did she know that we were in here?' Laura asked Tash, 'the door didn't have a bell or anything.'

'Maybe she felt the draft as we opened it,' her friend replied as she took out a long list and started browsing the shelves.

'Give your lists to my assistants, girls,' the shopkeeper said, her back still to her visitors.

'But there aren't any...' Tash began, but her words were cut off as a flock of crows flew in through an open window. They snatched the girls' lists out of their hands and flew up the shelves, snapping up the ingredients and placing them on the counter in rapid succession. Dumbstruck, the two girls watched as the pile of ingredients rose and their lists were dropped on top of it.

'How will you be paying for that?' the shopkeeper asked as she walked behind the counter and looked at them expectantly. Laura felt a shiver run down her spine as she gazed into the woman's eyes– she was unsettling to say the least. One of her eyes was dark brown and the other a bright blue. Her hair hung in a long plait which brushed the back of her knees and her rough, calloused hands stroked one of the crows. Her head bent to the side as another bird hopped onto her shoulder and squawked into her ear. She nodded as if she could understand what the bird was saying. Laura's eyes moved to the almost hideous birthmark that stretched across the shopkeeper's face from the bottom of her eye to her ear. Or was it a burn?

'Are you quite finished?' the shopkeeper asked wryly, and the two girls jumped, embarrassed. Laura suddenly found a rather interesting floorboard to stare at, from the corner of her eye she noticed that Tash was doing the same.

'Sorry,' they said together, feeling like chastened young children.

'Do not be sorry,' the shopkeeper, 'everyone reacts in different ways when they see me. I had a child faint once.' Her mouth stretched in a grin, 'that was a fine day.'

Tash and Laura exchanged nervous glances. The shopkeeper continued, 'back to the merchandise, how will you be paying for it?'

'How much is it?' Laura asked cautiously.

'It may be the price of your eyes or your memories of your first love. Perhaps you can pay with your hair.'

'Our hair?' Tash asked, aghast, 'what would you do with our *hair*?'

'You'd be amazed,' the woman replied, smiling. Laura got the impression that she was being perfectly serious but was having fun at the girls' discomfort.

'What about gold?' she asked, 'how much in gold?'

'Ah, always the easiest option,' the woman sighed, 'no one is interested in the more interesting methods of payment. Very well, it will be thirty retzma. For five extra I can include a brief fortune telling for you both. You never know what the cosmos has in store.'

Tash and Laura looked at each other, and then they shrugged their shoulders and added an extra five pieces to the pile of silver coins in her hand. The woman smiled to herself and Laura felt another chill, like a draft of cold air had just entered the room; she shivered and noticed that Tash was doing the same. She glanced back at the woman, who was watching them intently.

'Boys, arrange their purchases,' she said, and the crows flew downwards, lifting all of the ingredients on the counter and placing them into a canvas bag. The shopkeeper stepped out from behind the counter and led Tash over to the fire where the birds placed two stools. Feathers flew in all directions as the crows became frenzied, dumping the bag alongside one of the stools. Tash was covering her eyes and flinching away from the loud rustling of wings. The shopkeeper gently made her sit down and turned to Laura who was still frozen by the counter.

'Would you mind stepping outside for a moment, Laura?' she asked, 'I fear that if you were to stay it would interfere with your friend's prediction.'

Laura stepped back as the flock of birds swooped her, forcing her to flee out of door, which slammed shut behind her. She gasped for breath, her heart racing as she leaned against the door and feverishly brushed away all traces of feathers on her clothing.

I hate birds, she thought to herself, the image of being surrounded by large crows pecking her out of the door was still too fresh in her memory for her to calm down. She thought of Tash who was still in the shop, and wondered how her presence could interfere with whatever the woman predicted. She was staring through the shop window in an effort to see what was going on when another thought struck her.

How had the shopkeeper known her name? As far as she could remember, neither she nor Tash had called each other by their names during their time in the shop. How could she have known? She tried to think about different ways the woman could have found it out, but each time she came up with a new idea it always seemed more ludicrous than the last. Eventually, it was the door opening that caused her to come back to reality and she smiled in relief on seeing Tash's face. Her friend looked confused, and she bit her lip in thought, wondering what the prediction could have been.

'Your turn,' Tash said, leaning in and adding, 'I don't know how reliable it is though, she seems like a bit of a fraud to me.'

Unsure how to respond, Laura merely nodded and re-entered the shop, glancing around at the shelves for a sign of the crows. She didn't want to get swooped upon by them again. To her relief, there was not even a feather in sight.

The shopkeeper was sitting on one of the stools by the fire and Laura approached her, taking her spot on the other stool. The shopkeeper stared into the fire and didn't seem to notice Laura's presence.

'Um, hello?' Laura asked cautiously, wondering whether the woman was in a trance or simply daydreaming.

'Leonora.' The woman said, 'that's my name, Miss Jefferies, you don't have to be afraid to ask.'

'Err, right,' Laura replied, confused. 'How did you know my name?'

The only reply was the lifting of an eyebrow as Leonora turned to face her. Laura was starting to feel more and more uncomfortable, the heat from the fire causing beads of sweat to run down the back of her neck. Leonora tilted her head on one side and watched her closely, so that Laura almost felt like getting up and leaving, when Leonora spoke. 'You need not worry about how I learned your name, after all a name is merely something on the surface, a farce.'

Laura sat up a bit straighter, 'I actually happen to *like* my name,' she snapped, 'it was my grandmother's and is important to me and so is learning how *you* knew it!'

'There's no need to get theatrical,' Leonora replied coolly, 'how I learned of your name is of no importance. What matters is what I can tell you about your future.' She reached into one of her pockets and drew out a large crystal which encased seven dezmians. She placed it on her lap and with a sudden fleetness, reached forwards and plucked a hair from Laura's head.

'Ow,' she said as she rubbed her head, 'what was that for?'

'The crystal will only tell the future of one who has had something taken from them unwillingly,' Leonora replied, 'but if the person knows what will happen, the prediction will not be accurate.'

'Uh huh,' Laura said, not really listening. Instead, she watched as the strand of her hair was placed onto the crystal. For several seconds all was silent as both women held their breath, then the crystal began to hum and glow with white energy. Laura blinked as the light became a blinding flash and then muted to a faint glow. Leonora leaned forwards and stared intently into the heart of the crystal, hands reaching out to hover over the strand of Laura's hair. Her eyes rolled backwards into her head and she fell back against her chair with a primal cry. Laura jumped and a part of her longed to run for the door, to escape. Yet another part of herself held back, incessantly eager to see what happened next.

Her gaze was caught by Leonora's eyes opening once more, except now they were both a brilliant blue and flashed with some unknown power. Laura felt her skin starting to itch and tingle and knew instinctively that the magic contained within the crystal was very strong and very old. Leonora's mouth opened and her voice was deep but clear as she said,

'You who are not from this world,

'Cut off from those you love,

'Have yet so far to go.

'A long journey awaits,

'Through the course of time,

'Before you judge it so.

'Many things will cause dismay,

'And some will mislead,

'Yet none hurt you alone.

'But your hope remains,

'When at a loss,

'It will lead you home.

'Hold fast to dreams,

'And hopes of return,

'And he who holds you dear.

'Together with all three,

'You will find the way.

'Yet lose that which means the most,

'When it is too late.'

There was a crack like thunder and the strand of Laura's hair burst into flames, shrivelling into a thin line of ash within seconds. Laura sat back in her chair, heart pounding, as she tried to comprehend what Leonora had just said. She couldn't start to understand the prophecy's complexity nor what it actually meant. The shopkeeper jolted and blinked several times before focussing on Laura, who now watched her uneasily.

'Did you hear what you hoped?' Leonora asked, and as Laura shook her head, she sighed, 'oh well, I guess the future will always hold secrets for everyone.'

Laura was still staring at her, unable to understand how she did not seem to know what she had said mere seconds before. It was almost like the shopkeeper had not been present at all, as if her mind had been someplace else entirely.

'You don't remember?' she asked hesitantly.

'Of course not,' the woman opposite her replied with a smile and a slight shrug, 'no true fortune teller can ever remember what happens during the time when they look into the crystal. It would be dangerous you see,' she continued as she rose to her feet and picked up some ingredients from one of the shelves and added them to the steaming cauldron over the fire. 'If we knew exactly what was going to happen and *remembered* it, then it could cause a rift in the voids between worlds and time. It would be too unpredictable, magic would get out of control and who knows if anyone would purposefully try to change the future, based on what the fates had predicted. It would be too dangerous.'

'But what about the people who have their fortunes told?' Laura asked, 'surely they will try to change their futures if they don't like the prophecies they're given?'

'Many try,' Leonora conceded, 'but they do not possess the same power as us seers. While you can only *try* to change your futures, if we knew how to harness the magic within the crystal, we *could* have the power to change any future, be it for good or bad. Such power though, will always come at a price, and if transferred into a human body, will gradually eat away at the human soul until there is only a shell of a person left.'

'That's horrific,' Laura was aghast, 'who would ever wish to have that sort of power, which is more curse than blessing?'

'Many, child,' Leonora replied, 'but no one has ever succeeded. It is always easier to leave that power within the quartz, for it can absorb endless amounts of magic, storing it all up. It won't break at all.'

'So that was why the magic was so powerful,' Laura murmured, cautiously touching the crystal with her forefinger. Now it felt like any other rock except for a faint tingle that reached into the marrow of her bones.

'Prophetic magic always is,' Leonora replied absently as she stirred the potion counterclockwise. 'Yet I hope that whatever you heard will be helpful in the long run.'

'So do I,' Laura replied, brows furrowing in thought as she pondered the possible meanings of her prophecy. There was a sudden tapping on the shop window, and she looked up, startled to see Tash waving at her from the other side of the glass and beckoning with her hand.

'Thank you,' she said dutifully as she rose to leave, 'it's definitely been an experience.' As she exited the shop she was followed by the sound of Leonora's laughter.

'What took you so long?' her friend asked impatiently, 'I've been out here for nearly half an hour!'

'Sorry,' Laura replied sheepishly, 'I wasn't really aware of how much time was passing.'

Tash nodded. 'I could second that,' she said as they started walking down the street towards an inn for lunch, 'when I was in there, I had no idea what she was talking about. I know she told us it was meant to be a fortune telling session,' she kicked at a loose stone on the ground, 'but what she said sounded nothing like the future I've been preparing for since I became a Robin.'

'What was it?' Laura asked, 'what did she say?'

Tash glowered at the cobbles and didn't immediately meet Laura's eyes, 'you promise not to laugh?'

'Cross my heart,' Laura replied.

'She said:

"Hearts wild,

"'Lovers flawed.

"'Contamination tamed,

"'Hope is wrought.

"'Help too far,

"'Leaving too soon.

"'He who awaits,

"'Each turning of moon.

"'Beware the night,

"'Be cautious of day.

"'When all strays,

'"You will stay." It's not what I expected at all. I hoped…'

She cut off and returned to staring at the ground.

'What did you hope?' Laura asked, stunned that her friend had been able to remember all of what had been said to her. Although, when she thought about it, the words from her own fortune telling remained stuck in her mind like glue. Perhaps it had been the same for Tash.

'I hoped it would be about me becoming one of the greatest Robins of the century!' Tash burst out hotly, startling Laura out of her thoughts. 'I *thought* she would tell me that my wishes would come true and that I would travel to many worlds, saving lives and keeping the Barriers intact!' She paused for breath and kicked out at a lone pebble, which clattered away with a vengeance.

'You may still do that,' Laura consoled her friend, 'it's just you'll probably meet someone along the way.'

'Yeah, someone who awaits the moon,' Tash replied stonily, 'I can *really* see us hitting it off.'

'You like going outside at night,' Laura said, 'or don't you remember going into the forest after we were sure Romulus was asleep?'

A smile tweaked up the side of Tash's mouth, 'and that time we were nearly caught by our old meditation teacher? I thought we swore never to do it again after that.'

'Which only lasted for a week,' Laura replied, laughing. She was still laughing as they entered the inn, walking into the aroma of ale, roasting meat and wood smoke. The room was almost packed, but they squeezed into some chairs at a small table near the window.

'The usual?' Tash asked, and Laura nodded in reply. Her friend stood up and pushed her way through to the bar where several men leaned back with tankards in their hands, watching as she gave her order and returned to the table, dark hair swaying.

'But apart from it not really mentioning exactly what your future would be like,' Laura said, bringing the topic back to Tash's fortune telling, 'what's so bad about it?'

'I just don't understand it,' Tash said, 'How can I? All I understand is that it is about love, and it being mightily difficult to do so. I mean, I have to stay when everyone else is gone. What is *that* meant to symbolise?'

'I don't know,' Laura said sadly, 'I wish I did.'

'Me too,' Her friend replied, 'I wouldn't have thought that love would be so difficult to find though.'

'At least your prophecy didn't say you would lose it.' Laura sighed, and her friend leaned forward, eyes scrutinizing her face.

'What did yours say?' she asked and Laura repeated it, word for word. At the end there was a slightly awkward pause, which ended when their food was placed in front of them by a barmaid who gave them tankards of ale too.

'Well,' Tash said thoughtfully, 'we don't necessarily *know* that you will lose love, it does say that you will only lose the thing that is most important. Perhaps love may not be on top of the agenda.' She shrugged and Laura felt a slight twinge in her chest.

'Although I think we can clearly understand at least two parts of your prophecy,' Tash grinned.

'Which ones?'

'Isn't it obvious?' her friend replied, 'the part about hope leading you home and the man who holds you dear.'

'Who?' Laura asked.

'Are you serious?' Tash cried, 'you don't know that...' But the first part of Tash's reply suddenly hit Laura and she leaned forwards, cutting off her friend,

'It says that hope will lead me home.' She said intently, 'do you really think after all this time that I *could* go back?' Tash didn't say anything but stared back at her, eyes full of understanding.

The door to the inn opened bringing with it a rush of cool air, causing Laura and Tash to shiver as two men entered and headed immediately over to the bar. As the taller one paid for their drinks, the other noticed Tash and Laura and waved. Laura heard Tash swear under her breath, but she was already waving back at the boy, smiling.

'Harrison!' she called over the noise in the inn, 'come and join us!' Harrison nodded and said something into his friend's ear. With a broad smile, the other man turned and approached them, carrying two tankards of ale with him. Harrison slipped in beside Tash and indicated for his friend to sit next to Laura.

'This is Michael,' he said, 'he's one of my old friends from before I joined the Order.'

'Hi,' Michael grinned as he sat back lazily, casually placing one leg over the other. Tash raised her eyebrows in distaste and began cutting up her steak with savage ferocity.

'Hello,' Laura said, as she too began eating her lunch. Out of the corner of her eye she saw the two boys exchange glances. She also noticed that unlike Harrison, who upon entering the inn had removed his jacket, Michael surreptitiously pulled his sleeves down. She smiled to herself, knowing full well that only one person would be doing that when it was sweltering inside.

She looked across at Harrison. 'Where's Tim today? I thought you were going to investigate that new shop for Magical Studies on the High Street. They brought in new types of dezmians,' she informed Tash, 'that don't require to be turned thrice in mid-air in order to correctly channel magic. Instead, you need only rotate it clockwise and anti-clockwise three times for it to work. That would be so much easier, don't you agree? So one could rotate it in their pocket, and no one would know a thing. Isn't that fascinating, Michael?'

Tash snorted with laughter as Michael transformed back into Tim, who glared at them. Laura bit back a smile as she took a mouthful of steak and chewed it, averting her eyes from Tim's look.

'How did you *know* that?' he asked, 'that shop just opened *today* and we were the only apprentices from the Order there.'

'The Robin knew,' Laura replied, 'he told me about it the other day after he read my essay on whether the channelling of magic should be used through dezmians in worlds other than Venetica. He wasn't in favour of the new idea, though he can sometimes be a bit old-fashioned in his views.'

'What was your opinion?' Tash asked before Tim or Harrison could voice their outrage at The Robin's dismissal of their new dezmians.

'I said we could do without them in other worlds,' Laura said, 'in most of the books I've read– and from what I've experienced– most worlds do not have easy access to magic like we do. If they can go without using magic there, then so can we. It also adds to the whole *immersion* experience. That is *why* we have world trips after all, isn't it?'

There was a silence as she finished speaking and her companions' exchanged glances. Laura pretended not to notice and started slicing up the carrots on her plate.

After a while Tim broke the silence with an awkward laugh, 'well, did we trick you at least for a moment? The new dezmians are so easy to use I thought that it might've been a con or something.'

'You definitely fooled me,' Tash nodded, 'I wouldn't have noticed any difference at all if Laura hadn't realised.'

'Well,' Harrison grinned, 'I *did* add a wonderful backstory to make you believe us.'

'It was very realistic,' Tash agreed begrudgingly, 'but I would hardly call it *wonderful*. I mean, you didn't even mention *how* you knew him or…'

'I did!' Harrison retorted, 'I said I had known him from before I joined the Order.'

'Well, *that's* saying a lot,' Tash replied sarcastically, 'why didn't you just add that you'd been best friends since birth?' Harrison choked on his drink and began to reply angrily yet Laura barely noticed. Her senses were on high alert as Tim leaned over and asked very softly,

'And you, Laura? How did *you* know it was me?'

Her breathing caught in her chest and she stared at her plate, forcing herself to appear calm.

'Your sleeves,' she replied steadily, 'it's so hot in here and yet you still pulled them down.' She turned and looked into his eyes, surprised to see how close he was. Should she lean to the side, her head would be resting on his shoulder. Swallowing, she continued, 'you're the only person I know who does that.'

He was smiling now, 'So if I hadn't pulled down my sleeves, you would have believed me to be someone else?'

'Perhaps,' she grinned, 'unless you did something else which would define you so obviously.'

'Which would be?' He was teasing now, she could tell.

The effect you have on me, she thought in reply. Yet all she said was, 'I don't know,' which, accompanied by a light-hearted shrug, ended their conversation.

Tash and Harrison were still arguing, and Laura was starting to feel that if she had to remain in the stifling inn any longer, she would scream.

'I've got to get some air,' she said as she rose to her feet. Immediately Tash stood up too and with a flick of her dark hair, left Harrison speechless with fury as she strode out. Laura smiled to herself and followed.

'I can't believe Harrison,' Tash cried as soon as they were safely a hundred metres from the inn door, 'he's just so, so…'

'Unbelievable?' Laura asked wryly. Tash screwed up her nose.

'Ha ha, very funny,' she said sarcastically, 'my sides are splitting.'

'Why does he always get on your nerves like this?' Laura asked, 'you always seem to find fault with one another. Maybe you should just ask him out and be done with it. It's obvious that he likes you.'

'I. Don't. Want. To. Date. Harrison.' Tash replied through gritted teeth. 'If *he* is the man my prophecy refers to, I'll… I'll…' she was speechless with fury as she plucked a leaf from a bush and savagely tore it up.

'Calm down,' Laura laughed, 'I was just kidding.' On seeing her friend's unconvinced expression, she added hastily, 'I mean it, Tash, I really do.'

'*Fine*,' Tash growled, 'but I wasn't the only one to get male attention today. Don't think I didn't notice how you and Tim were almost kissing each other.'

'We weren't!' Laura cried, mortified. The mere thought made her break out into a sweat and her heart began racing.

'Of *course*,' Tash smirked, and Laura knew full well that she didn't believe it for a second.

'Well,' Laura said angrily, 'we don't like each other in that way at all. Didn't he date half of the girls at the Temple already? I wouldn't want to be another conquest.'

'He's only dated four girls,' Tash grinned, 'and the way you act when you're around him makes it kind of obvious you'd like to be the fifth one…'

'Stop it,' Laura said, she could feel herself getting angrier by the minute, 'just *stop*, Tash.'

'You like him, admit it!' Tash exclaimed, sensing success, 'just *say* it, Laura!'

Laura felt her hand moving into her pocket and touching her dezmian, which throbbed with power, promising to lay waste to anything and everything. Her eyes shut as she tried to control her breathing.

'What are you doing?' Tash asked. Laura opened her eyes and immediately her hand pulled back, flinching away from the dezmian as if it were poisonous.

'Nothing,' she replied, but Tash drew away, shaking her head and looking confused.

'You were reaching for your dezmian, weren't you?' she asked in a surprisingly small voice, her normal bravado gone. 'You were going to do something. Like you did when we were fourteen and Patrick pushed you into the lake.' Laura wanted to deny it, she opened her mouth but no sound came out.

The silence between them went on and on; finally Tash forced a smile and said, 'I have a lot of homework to do.' They both knew it was a lie, Tash always completed her work within a day of having received it. 'Give me your dezmian, Laura, in case you do something stupid.' Wordlessly the dezmian was passed over and Tash continued, 'I might head back early; I'll see you at dinner though, alright?' Without waiting for a reply, she hurried off without a backwards glance. Laura didn't try to call out to stop her; she knew that they both needed time to think and contemplate. She walked towards a jewellery shop, mindless of where she was going. It didn't matter; all that did was that she had nearly used magic on her best friend, all because she didn't want to admit her feelings for Tim.

She stopped in front of the window and remembered the day before when Tash had teasingly suggested buying some new jewellery. Perhaps if she bought something it would help ease the tension, let Tash know that she appreciated her opinion. Anything to end the awkward silence that they had just shared and which, she knew, would recommence at the Temple. She checked her watch surprised that it was nearly mid-afternoon. But no matter, she would still have time to get back to the Temple in time for dinner.

Once Laura had finally decided what she wanted to buy and bought it, it was twilight. She was proud of her pur-chase– a fine dark red pendant which she immediately hung around her neck, for the first time replacing the now rather decrepit, locket. She admired herself in the mirror, utterly content.

Deciding to try the shortcut to the stables, she headed down a side alley. Her map of the city was faded, and as

Laura peered at it in the dying light, trying to distinguish the streets, she realised that she should've taken a right turn instead of a left, three streets before. Silently cursing herself, Laura turned back, but the buildings seemed to loom higher than ever, closing in and trapping her in the alleyway. Her breathing increased, and she started to panic. The alley darkened, and she remembered The Robin's warning all too late.

Suddenly she jumped, dropping her map in fright as halfway down the alley, a man staggered in from the other end. He was breathing heavily, and even from where she stood, she could smell the oppressive stench of *grigori*, the strongest liquor she knew of in Venetica.

'Hello darlin',' he drawled as he reached her, and she realised that she recognised him.

'Glenroy!' Laura exclaimed, 'what are you doing? We need to get back to the Temple before night comes.'

'Stuff it,' he sniggered, raising a finger to brush a lock of hair from her face, 'how about you and I go to an inn for the night. Eh? Get my meaning?' He pressed himself up against her, grinding into her. Laura jumped back, disgusted.

'Glenroy, stop it!' She raised a hand and briefly slapped him across the cheek. 'Leave me alone,' she tried to hide her revolted shudder. She might be repulsed by this man, but it would be her responsibility to get him safely back to The Temple, Romulus never approved of students staying overnight on their trips to Boowlra.

'So now The Robin's apprentice thinks she's better than me,' he growled, eyes full of desire as they raked the full length of her body.

'Come on,' Laura whispered, terrified, praying silently as she walked away that someone would come and help her, she didn't want to be alone with him any longer.

'Stop right there,' he answered, 'I have the impression that you don't know where you're going.'

'I… I… of course, I was heading for the stables.'

'I knew it! You're going the wrong way. Come on, trust me, I know this part of the city very, *very* well.'

'I'm not so sure…'

'Do you want to get back to the blasted Temple or not?' Glenroy snapped, rapidly losing patience.

Laura realised belatedly that her hands were empty and that she had dropped her map. Mentally, she slapped herself. What an idiot she was! Why hadn't she picked it up?

'Hurry up, darlin',' Glenroy growled, reaching forward and gripping her hand in his rather sweaty one. She promptly pulled away. They were now in a very desolate and secluded part of the city and the dark shroud of night had already fallen.

Suddenly Glenroy stopped and turned towards her, pushing her against the hard wall making her shriek.

'Laura,' his voice was slurring, 'I love you. I always have. Marry me and we can leave the Order.'

'What? No!' she replied sharply, suddenly scared, 'you're drunk, Glenroy. You have no control over what you're saying.'

'But I have control over my body,' he growled, and he pushed her savagely to the ground. Her bag dropped from her grasp as she fell, and she cried out as she collided with the rough cobbles. When she looked upwards, her fears were confirmed; Glenroy's eyes glowered at her lustily, and she felt herself go cold. This could not possibly be happening, but it was.

'I *did* offer you a bed for this, darlin'.' Glenroy drawled, 'but you refused. Obviously you'd prefer to feel a bit more rough.'

'No!' Laura shrieked, as she struggled backwards, trying desperately to get away. Glenroy followed her, smiling. Never in her life had she seen a more frightening smile, and her movements became frenzied as she scrambled back, trying to get to her feet to run. His gaze locked with hers as she hit a wall. It was a dead-end street.

No. Laura's mind cried frantically, *no, no, no! Run! Push past him and run!*

But she was frozen, paralysed by Glenroy's expression. She couldn't move. She couldn't do anything. She was terrified. One desperate idea came to her mind, and she sent out a wordless plea, begging elemental magic to come to her aid. She felt the faint tug in her gut and realised that she must have ventured into one of the areas of town which The Robin had warned her about.

'That's right, Laura, just stay still and I won't hurt you too much.' She didn't respond. Where was everybody? Would no one come? The magic was too weak here, she couldn't protect herself. Why had she given her dezmian to Tash? Of all the times she needed magic, she was cut off from it! She stared into his eyes and realised that he had known all along that she would not be able to use her magic here.

He had almost reached her, and she curled into a ball, locking her arms around her legs, knees planted firmly beneath her chin. She could hear his breathing increase, could smell the foul stench of his breath. No one would help her. No one would hear. It was hopeless.

She closed her eyes and screamed.

The living hell felt like it went on forever. Again and again she cried out for help which did not, *would not*, come. At the start she had thrashed like a wild animal, hitting Glenroy over and over until he tied her hands behind her back with a torn strip of her own dress, where they soon became red and raw. Within the first few minutes she realised that he hadn't intended for her to be unharmed, and so she suffered for all the pain that she had caused him. He barraged her with talk of her misdeeds in the past six years: shunning him, laughing at him, detesting him and, all the time, taunting him and driving him to breaking point.

And the pain. Oh, the *pain*, she didn't know how she could bear it.

Suddenly it ended, when a well-known voice cried out of the darkness, 'Glenroy! *What the hell* are you doing?'

Tears of joy this time formed in her eyes, and she let out a relieved sob. It was Tim.

'I hate you.' She whispered to Glenroy. He roared and punched her in the ribs. Something cracked loudly and more pain rushed through her.

'Get off her!' Tim shouted, racing forwards and wrestling Glenroy to the ground. Laura pulled herself away from them over the cobbles, trying and failing to ignore the pain she felt. Behind her she could hear fist meeting flesh, and then hands touched her elbows, pulling her upwards. Blindly she struggled, pulling away with a violent scream.

'Laura, it's me,' Tim's voice said, somehow still reaching her through the different voices and sounds haunting her mind. 'Trust me, I won't hurt you.' Laura shook her head, stepping backwards. Glenroy had said almost the same thing and look what had happened. She was despoiled, hurt and scared. Why should she trust someone else?

'The Willowings are at the end of the alley,' Tim's voice continued, softly, calmly. 'I came back to find you and Glenroy and to bring you back to the Temple. The Robin sent me. Glenroy won't bother you on the way, he's unconscious. His fate will be decided when we return to the Temple.' He paused, but Laura made no move towards him or the waiting Willowing. Finally, he took a deep breath and asked, 'will you come back with me?'

She couldn't speak, nor meet his gaze, only nodded before bursting into tears. Tim untied her hands carefully and threw the scrap of material as far away as possible. He whistled for the Willowings and threw Glenroy's unmoving body over one, tying him onto the saddle and attaching the Willowing's reins to the back of his own saddle. She walked as if in a dream towards where her bag had fallen, and picked it up, tying it to the saddle.

'Let's go, Laura,' Tim murmured, eyes meeting hers briefly for a moment.

'I'm scared,' she whispered as he lifted her in front of him, making sure that she sat side-saddle, before holding her securely as they leapt into the air. She froze, and Tim realised what was wrong and removed his hands. Laura didn't meet his eyes but clasped the Willowing's neck as they lifted into the air, leaning forward so that she was as far as possible from Tim.

'Glenroy won't touch you again if I can help it,' he spat through clenched teeth. She didn't respond, still caught up in shock. For the rest of the journey they were quiet, each caught up in their own thoughts and Laura was grateful that Tim didn't try to break the silence.

The Robin paced like an angry lion, overturning furniture in his usually orderly room. Laura got the impression that he had been doing it for a while; his usually immaculate bookshelves had had their books thrown to the floor.

'*He did what?*' he roared, hardly caring that the noise was awakening the rest of the Order. Laura sat on a straight-backed chair, her expression blank, almost lifeless. Her chest was still tender after Romulus had performed healing magic on her cracked ribs. Whenever she moved, even slightly, every muscle in her cried out in protest. She stared ahead, only vaguely noticing the discussion going on around her.

'Glenroy assaulted her, sir,' Tim answered, 'by the time I arrived on the scene it was too late.'

'How awful,' Tash cried, clasping her friend closer and ignoring Laura's rigidity. 'I should've stayed with you. I shouldn't have left… I *should have known* something would happen.'

'Why didn't you come home together?' The Robin demanded furiously. 'Why didn't you *stay* together? The *incompetence*, the *foolishness*, the…'

'Tash wanted to complete homework,' Laura interrupted quietly. It was the first time she'd spoken since she got back to the Temple and her throat was tender, her voice raspy. 'I wanted to buy some jewellery and didn't know how long I would be. I thought it would be better if we split up. You can say it was stupid and incompetent of us but at the time…' she halted in her sentence, a choking sob rising in her throat.

'Then why didn't you have your dezmian? You could have protected yourself, Laura. I *warned* you about Boowlra.' He turned and threw a chair against the wall in savage fury. The wood splintered and cracked, and Laura started to cry uncontrollably.

'I'm sorry,' The Robin said, his voice still unsteady as he reached out to take one of her hands. She pulled away. 'We have two choices. Traditionally those who commit crimes against members of the Order are either put to death or incarcerated for life.'

There was a long pause as Laura calmed herself. Finally she spoke, her voice barely louder than a whisper.

'I think that putting him to death would be just as barbaric as what he did tonight. But I never want to see him again. I want him to regret what he's done.'

The Robin and Tim looked at each other, equally disappointed.

'A wise choice,' The Robin said with forced calm. 'I'll notify Romulus to send Glenroy to one of the prisons in the Western Marshlands.'

'Come on, Laura,' Tash murmured, noticing her friend begin to slump, 'let's get you to bed.'

Laura turned back, 'how did you know that I was in trouble?' she asked The Robin, 'why did you send Tim and not come yourself?'

He was silent for a moment, 'I heard your plea through my magic. I could discover your basic co-ordinates, but I was unable to come myself.'

'*Why?*' Her question resonated with all the words she wanted to say but couldn't bring herself to.

'That is something you need not know,' The Robin answered coolly, and Laura's shoulders slumped.

'Goodnight,' she whispered, before turning to Tim, 'and thank you. I don't know what I would've done if you hadn't…'

She broke off with another sob, and turned around. Tim reached out to place his hand on her shoulder but stopped himself and moved it back to his side.

'You've been through too much, Laura. I'm just glad that you're safe, here in the Temple, where we can protect you. Goodnight.'

Laura didn't reply, and staggered after Tash towards their dormitory.

Tim turned to The Robin and waited. 'Why didn't you go?' he demanded, 'she deserves an answer.' The Robin's eyes met his own, and Tim felt that deep down he knew. He himself had felt the urge to not listen to reason– it would have been all too easy to not bring Glenroy back alive. He had, but now he knew that had The Robin gone, Glenroy would have already been cold and on his way to Death's Gates.

Once she was inside the dormitories, Laura went straight to the pool in the bathroom, undressed and grabbed a damp cloth to wipe away the blood which seemed to be stained onto her skin.

'Oh my God,' Tash whispered. 'He did *that* to you?'

Laura glanced down at her chest, which was bruised and bloody.

'Yes.'

'And your lips?'

Raising a hand to feel around her swollen mouth, Laura felt stabs of pain from where Glenroy's teeth had dug into her.

She continued numbly, finishing her job of cleaning up some of the physical damage from that night. Slowly she lifted the pendant from around her neck. It glistened, red as the blood that stained her undergarments. She placed it aside and never wore it again.

Chapter Eight

The moonlight filtered through the leaves in the forest as Laura tiptoed through the trees, careful to not make a sound in case she was discovered. After what had happened, The Robin had not let her out of his sight, be it in lessons, meditation or when they were in the dining hall. The only time she could be away was in the female dormitory, but even there she was being watched, with the other girls whispering about her behind their hands whenever they spotted her. It was unbearable.

Laura felt her stomach lurch, and she fell to the ground, retching. Wiping her mouth, she shakily got to her feet once more and hurried into the trees. The now familiar path led towards the heart of the forest, halfway down the mountain. She whispered a few words under her breath, tossed her dezmian and felt the invigorating rush as magic swelled within her, easing the restlessness of her stomach. She never went anywhere without her dezmian now. Around her, the trees seemed to whisper amongst themselves in the night, leaves slightly brushing up against each other, before they were caught in the breeze and fell to the ground.

When she had arrived at the Temple of the Nest, Kylan said that the forest was safe, that The Robin himself had enchanted it. But after her first week, Romulus had told her that it was out of bounds, although when she asked why, he did not answer in detail. All he said was that it was dangerous.

But at that time Laura had had just about enough of rules. After all, Kylan had said that it was safe, hadn't he? Though he had lied to her before. Even so, one summer night, she and Tash had snuck out and disappeared into the forest, carefully winding a long ball of string behind them so they would not lose their way in the darkness. That had been Laura's idea, as she had remembered a hero of Greek mythology doing exactly the same thing. Too much time had passed since she had heard the story and now Laura couldn't even remember the hero's name. The funny thing was that, after all of their nighttime escapades to the forest, neither Tash nor Laura found any reason why it could be classified as dangerous.

Tim had come with them a couple of times, but as they got older, things became more difficult. He would have to work into the early hours of the morning to finish essays and homework. And then there was the strange, giddy feeling Laura felt in her chest whenever they went into the forest together, which she could not understand at all.

She remembered Tash saying that she loved Tim and didn't want to admit it. Laura sighed, she wasn't sure if what she felt towards Tim was anything remotely resembling love. And she did not want to pursue it to discover what it could be, especially after her experience with Glenroy.

Laura halted in her tracks as an image of Glenroy came into her mind. She shivered and clutched onto a nearby tree for support as her stomach heaved again. Perhaps it would have been better for her to stay in the dormitory tonight, she thought, as the chill wind bit into her. And yet she needed space once in a while, and at the moment she was craving it.

The path ahead of her curved and she reached her destination: the centre of the forest. A small pool glistened in the heart of the clearing, surrounded by lush moss. Tall stately trees bordered her small paradise, forming a dark canopy overhead, apart from a small hole through which she could see the moon. Her sanctuary.

Laura sighed and sank down next to the pool, gazing at her wan reflection in the water. Over the past two weeks she had lost weight and looked pale and sickly. Her clothes hung around her and she appeared almost skeletal at times.

In the darkness, she wondered what her life would have been like if she hadn't been taken to Venetica. She would be whole. She would be loved. She would have lived an average, normal life. Maybe by that point she would have just finished high school and be planning her future, excitedly staying with friends for weekends or have a normal boyfriend who would never have dreamed of doing what Glenroy had done.

But if she had stayed in Australia, she would have never met Tash or The Robin or Tim. She wouldn't ever have believed that magic was real and she wouldn't know its addictive rush and sense of accomplishment it brought.

A leaf fell onto the pool's surface, casting multiple ripples into action. When they had cleared, Laura looked back at her reflection.

She looked closer. Blinked. Looked closer still. Surely, but no… it *couldn't be… how* could it be…?

The face staring back was no longer her own, but older, greyer with soft eyes and deep lines across the forehead.

An owl hooted from one of the tree's branches breaking into her thoughts. Laura's head snapped up and when she looked back down, her reflection was her own again, staring back at her with wide, fearful eyes. It couldn't have been real. There was no possible way that her mother could have been staring right back at her. She sighed and gazed up at the moon, like she had so many years before, until her head fell into her lap and she burst into tears. She did not hear the quiet crack as a twig broke under someone's foot. It wasn't until a hand touched her shoulder that she cried out and sprung away.

'I thought I'd find you here,' Tash said quietly, 'it always was your favourite spot.'

'I thought you were asleep,' Laura replied, with a wry smile as she resettled herself by the pool. Her heartbeat started to return to a normal pace and she glanced away from her friend, towards the trees. Tash sat down next to her, perching on a moss-covered log, and it was she who broke the silence between them.

'I didn't get round to apologising for the other day,' she said, 'with everything that happened, well, I didn't think you would want me to raise it. But these last few weeks you've been acting so differently. I was wondering if it had been any of the things we said to each other when, well, you know,' she fell silent and Laura felt her eyes watching her carefully.

She looked back at the pool and said, 'I'm sorry too, Tash.'

Immediately Tash leapt up and hugged Laura so hard that she lost her balance and they fell over. Tash burst out laughing at the sight of Laura's expression of complete and utter surprise, and soon Laura was joining her.

'I shouldn't have lost my temper with you,' she said as soon as she had calmed down enough to catch her breath.

'I didn't mean to annoy you with my ideas about you and Tim,' Tash replied at the same time.

'That's okay,' they finalised in unison, before laughing again.

'That's all very well,' a voice said from behind them— a cold, scratchy voice— 'but what will you do now?'

There was a pause and Tash and Laura stared at each other in horror before turning to face the newcomer. At first Laura was afraid that the voice would belong to the one person she was most afraid of, the only person she despised. But it wasn't Glenroy who stood in the shadows, watching the two women returning his stare.

'*Who*,' Tash asked bravely, 'are you?'

'I believe, young lady,' the man replied, 'what you want to ask is: *what* am I?'

He stepped forwards and Laura suppressed a scream. In the moonlight she could see the horns protruding from his head, how his eyes flashed red and his pointed teeth pulled back in a snarl. She stepped backwards, wanting to run and hide. Tash however, stepped forwards, as if provoking the creature to come closer.

'Tash,' Laura whimpered, '*don't.*'

'Watch me,' Tash said daringly, and she took another step towards the creature. Laura stayed rooted to the spot, unable to move in either direction. The creature snarled again, and Laura noticed his tail, which cut the grass behind him like a scythe. His hands bunched into fists and he stepped closer to Tash, who didn't even flinch at his nearing proximity. Laura didn't know how she could do it, had she been alone, she would have long fled.

'You're a Dæmon,' Tash said softly, 'a creature of the night who enters its true form when the moon rises.' Something in her voice made Laura stare at her profile, concerned.

'Your friend is clever,' the Dæmon said to Laura, 'perhaps I shall not drink her blood after all.'

'Oh, what a consolation,' Tash drawled. 'Please don't do me any favours.'

He hissed, tail desecrating the flowers behind him. Laura trembled.

'What do you want?' Tash demanded, 'it's not polite to sneak up on girls at night.'

'Even girls who reject being within the safe boundaries of the Temple, and choose to come here instead?' The Dæmon retorted.

Both girls remained silent and watched as the creature began to laugh. Laura doubted it could even be called a laugh though, it was more like the sound of chains grating across something metallic. She flinched.

'As to what I will *do*,' the Dæmon continued, 'I need you to get The Robin for me. I have the information he sent me to find last summer.'

'What information?' Laura asked, finding the courage to speak up. She received a withering stare in response.

'That is between *your leader*,' the Dæmon snarled, 'and *me*. Now *go* little birds.' Laura didn't wait for another word, she turned and ran back the way she'd come, before glancing back on realising that Tash wasn't following.

The creature was saying something in Tash's ear, its clawed hand holding her arm in a vice-like grip. Her face was shadowed by her hair, but she pulled away with a jerk and ran towards Laura. The Dæmon melted back into the shadows as if he had never been there at all.

'What did he say?' Laura asked as Tash reached her. Her friend was trembling and she put her arm around her as they walked away. She had the impression that her friend had been more scared than she let on.

'He said that he'd see me again,' Tash whispered into the darkness, 'he said that I would need to be strong for the fulfilment of my prophecy.' Her moist eyes glinted with tears in the moonlight as she turned to Laura and said, 'how did he know about my prophecy?'

She couldn't speak, only shook her head in reply. Together they continued in silence until they reached the border of the forest, where they paused to catch their breath.

'You return to the dormitory,' Laura told Tash calmly, 'I don't want The Robin punishing you for being out of bed after hours too. It'll be for the best.'

'I'll see you when you get back though,' Tash whispered, glancing warily at the dark windows of the Order, as if expecting to see Romulus or The Robin staring down at them. When she was content that they had remained unseen, she looked back at Laura who nodded in agreement.

'See you soon,' she said, and started towards the tallest tower. When she reached the door, she watched Tash enter the female dormitories before she continued her own journey. The staircase seemed longer than she remembered, and she knocked loudly on The Robin's door which she opened before he responded.

'Sir?' she called, looking around for her teacher. There was an odd stillness in the room, as though something was holding its breath. She entered one of the connecting rooms and was pleased to see that the moonlight was shining through the window. On closing the door behind her, Laura realised, too late, that she had entered a bedroom. A strong sense of awkwardness filled her and she edged backwards, reaching for the doorknob. She'd go back to the front door and bang on it continuously, because it was obvious that the man lying in the bed opposite was sound asleep. The Robin rolled over and, for the first time, Laura saw properly what he looked like.

His face wasn't shrouded in darkness like it usually was, which made her eyes widen with surprise. The Robin looked like he would be in his late forties and his hair was closely shaven to his skull, although in the moonlight it gave off a coppery tinge.

Her hand relaxed on the doorknob and the awkwardness she had felt was replaced with a strong feeling of safety. As he slept, a long distant memory came to mind and, without thinking, she stepped closer and reached out tentatively towards him.

'What?!' The Robin sat upright with a jolt whilst, at the same time, the moon was covered by a cloud. Laura watched as her teacher lit a candle and held it aloft, but the light didn't pierce the darkness that had covered his face once more. Her sense of safety had fled: the awkwardness returned along with a sense of foreboding.

'*Laura?*' The Robin said, shocked, 'what are you doing here?' His voice became laced with unrepressed anger, 'why are you out of your dormitory? You know how dangerous it is at night.'

'I... I...' Laura stammered, averting her eyes as her teacher pulled on some robes. She regained her composure and said, 'I had to see you.'

'You had to *see* me?' The Robin's voice was emotionless, and she cringed.

Laura silently cursed herself: she wanted to see him? She had to rephrase, to make it clear about why she was there. 'I was in the forest,' she began.

'The forest?' His voice was getting slightly louder, and she could hear the anger threatening to be unleashed, 'I thought that you knew that the forest was off limits.'

'I was in the forest,' she continued steadily, ignoring him, 'and I met a Dæmon who said…'

'A *Dæmon*?' Now The Robin's voice was full of concern, and Laura almost smiled. 'But you're alright,' he said, as if to himself, 'it didn't harm you.'

'No,' Laura said, 'but it told me to fetch you and say that it has the information that you sent it to retrieve last summer.'

'The information,' he muttered to himself, 'yes, that will be the final thing I need. And then…' He stopped as he realised that she was still there. 'Despite that,' he said, 'you broke the rules which were put in place for your safety. A month of kitchen duty and no access to Boowlra for six months should be enough of an incentive to not do it again.'

'Yes, sir,' Laura replied humbly, and she watched as her mentor picked up a hefty travelling bag and began to fill it feverishly.

'I will be away for quite some time, Laura,' he said formally, 'during my absence you will be tutored by Romulus and be expected to keep up your current workload.'

'Yes sir,' she repeated dutifully. No sir, three bags full sir, she thought.

'And Laura,' The Robin had stopped at the top of the stairs and, she guessed, was looking in her direction.

'Yes sir?'

'Never enter this tower after sundown again,' he said quietly. She stood in frozen mortification as he disappeared into the darkness.

Chapter Nine

Time passed slowly, inexorably. Weeks passed, and then months. And yet no matter what tasks Laura set herself, she couldn't shake the memory of that night when The Robin had left. It still went through her mind, and she thought of hundreds of different ways she would apologise when he got back. She had told Tash about her embarrassment and her friend had little to say that was encouraging.

'I'm sure he understood,' was the best she could come up with, and soon Laura gave up talking about it anyway. She and Tash also avoided the subject of the Dæmon, and in particular, his effect on Tash. That hadn't stopped Laura, and she was sure, Tash, from thinking about it.

She was thinking about it one afternoon whilst completing an essay about Venetican history, when The Robin came into the room and sat down by the fire. She stopped immediately, quill in hand, and looked at him– he looked exhausted, and ten years older.

'Laura, can you stop for a minute?' he asked, his voice sounded hoarse and raspy.

She withdrew her dezmian from her pocket, flipped and caught it and picked up a cup of water which had materialised from thin air. She handed the cup to The Robin and sat down opposite him as he passed her an old, faded piece of paper. Looking closer, Laura realised that it was a map.

'Geography lesson?' she asked, but was surprised to see The Robin shake his head.

'There is something that I haven't told you, Laura. I was waiting for the time when you'd be ready, and I needed to get confirmation about its veracity before getting your hopes up.'

'What is it?' she demanded.

'There is a way that you can see your family again.' His words caught her off guard and her head reeled. Even in her wildest dreams, Laura hadn't expected this, and the thought of a family-that-could-have-been made her freeze temporarily.

'My family?'

But your hope remains,
When at a loss,
It will lead you home.

The words rang through Laura's ears for several moments. Could it be true?

'Yes,' The Robin replied patiently, 'there is an old tale about an item which allows one to track and summon specific Barriers. Rumours say that this item also gave its owner the ability to communicate across worlds, which led to it being misused during the inter-world wars. If it fell into the wrong hands, it could have horrific results. Apparently, it was lost many years ago, but one of my associates was able to pinpoint a map which shows its location. You will need to retrieve a treasure from a hidden grotto. That object will help me locate and summon the Barrier to Earth.'

'So, it's like a quest?' Laura asked, remembering vaguely all the adventure stories she'd read as a child. 'All I need to do is find the treasure and bring it back? What is it?' An image of a treasure chest overflowing with gold and precious gems filled her mind. She shook it away, what would The Robin do with all of that? Become a king? She didn't think so.

'The item you shall retrieve will be a bowl; a silver bowl with an inlay of pearl.' He was staring away from her, gazing into the fire which flickered in the afternoon light.

'But couldn't you retrieve it with magic?' Laura asked.

'The bowl has been lost for many years, Laura.' He said, 'I would hazard a guess that it is bound by some protection which ensures usual magic will not find it.'

She pondered that for a moment, then asked, 'what will you do with the bowl once you find the Barrier to Earth?'

'That is no concern of yours,' he said coldly, 'all that matters is that you retrieve it and bring it back to me intact. Then,' he paused as if the idea pained him; Laura perched higher on her seat in anticipation. 'Then you can return to Australia.'

Australia. A barren landscape of red sand and dry fields, surrounded by a vast blue ocean. Summers of immense heat, kangaroos, surfing and iced coffee… Laura's imagination went wild.

'You can't be sure which rumours to trust,' The Robin said, interrupting her train of thought, 'it's up to you what you believe and how you use that possible knowledge.'

'But will they be relatively similar?' she asked.

'They will vary depending on where you are,' he replied unhelpfully, 'you will have to choose what to believe.'

'Will you tell me some of the rumours?' The Robin was not being helpful at all and continued to stare into the flames, but she held her tongue, knowing that he would continue talking to her soon. Finally he spoke again, his voice so low and quiet that she had to lean forward to hear what he said.

'I have spent many years trying to gather information about the mysterious bowl and its precise location. The most common rumour is that the bowl was made by the Ancients—our ancestors. They were sentient, magical, and they constructed many mystical, wonderful things. The bowl, according to legend, was one of them. But then there was the Great War between the Ancients and the Dragutash. The Dragutash were a lot smarter in those days, and far more cunning. They wanted to have a share of the Ancients' magic and were fascinated by the items. The Ancients refused to share them and the Dragutash became furious. They started the war and preyed on the female Ancients, picking them off one by one. But the women were sneaky, fleeing back into the shadows and hiding before the monsters could catch them.

'Eventually, the female Ancients were very few in number. The leaders gathered in a council to discuss what to do about the war, which had been going on for as long as any of them could remember. At last, they decided that the women folk and children should leave with a small group of guards to another world, and take the silver bowl so that they could communicate with those they had left behind. The remaining men would stay in Venetica and dedicate themselves to ridding the land of the Dragutash.'

'Is that all?' Laura asked gently, for The Robin had fallen silent. He jumped and looked at her before shaking his head.

'No,' he continued, 'at first the plan seemed perfect, and it all worked out. However, one of the Dragutash mated with one of the Ancient's Willowings. When they reached the next world, the Willowing gave birth. The Ancients were horrified and tried to kill the baby, but its mother, incensed, took it and fled into the forest. Neither was seen again.

'The female Ancients were worried, as one among them was gifted with foresight and told them that the Dragutash would find them, one day, and try to find the bowl with pearl inlay. So, as a group, they decided to give the bowl to the seer to take far away and hide it. When the seer had hidden the bowl, she was to return and write down directions to it, for, although Dragutash were cunning and sly, they could not read.

'The seer agreed and started out on her journey, traversing many worlds. She met a man in a foreign world and with him sired a daughter, who accompanied her on her endless travels. The mantle of Protector of the Bowl passed from mother to daughter for three generations. Finally, the journey was over, and the great-granddaughter of the seer returned to the village whose location had been passed down the generations along with the bowl. She wrote down the location and was welcomed back into the village with open arms.'

He appeared to be finished. Laura sat back and said, 'so all I need to do is find the message which the great-granddaughter wrote, and then I'll have a better idea of where to find the bowl?'

'That's correct,' The Robin nodded. 'I have heard other rumours which say that a terrible beast was tamed to protect the bowl. Some say that it is protected deep within the earth in a magical cavern which swallows those who try to find it. There are also tales of a mystical waterfall which dissolves those who have cruel intentions in their hearts, leaving only those pure of heart to gain access to the bowl. Sadly, though, I do not know which rumours are true, if any. Apart from the story, everything else concerning the bowl and its whereabouts is a mystery. Except that the seer's great-granddaughter, apart from leaving the message, also drew this. It has taken me a very long time to find the whereabouts of this map.'

Sudden realisation hit Laura and she blurted, 'is that what the Dæmon came to tell you? How to find and locate the map?'

He regarded her coolly. 'What I did took me through many worlds. I could not tell anyone about my mission, which you yourself also cannot do. Others would do terrible things to lay their hands on this map.'

'I understand,' Laura said gravely. 'But why can't you search for this bowl? You've done so much to find it already, why just hand all of the responsibility over to me?'

He was silent for a moment, then said, '*he who desires cannot retrieve, he who retrieves cannot desire*. I learnt that from our Dæmon friend on one of our past encounters.'

'How do you know I won't desire it?' Laura asked. Who would stop her from taking the bowl for herself? Surely The Robin could not do anything to stop it.

'You won't.' He replied simply, with complete certainty evident in his words. She frowned, how could he be so sure?

'Why not?'

He spoke with quiet intensity and each word stuck in her mind.

'Because then you will never get the chance to see your family again. You do not know the correct incantations to activate the magic of the bowl to achieve your heart's desire. Instead, you will not be able to enter your home universe. You will be completely cut off, every possible, slight chance of returning lost forever. Also, you will be rejected from the Temple and cast out of the Order. You see, Laura,' he continued, ignoring her shocked gasp, 'you will be too busy thinking about the life you will have after you give me the bowl to even consider desiring it for yourself.'

Laura was too stunned to say anything in response. Who would have thought there would be all those consequences for just wanting a silver bowl?

'Anyway, now that's all dealt with, I have one last piece of information for you. The map covers different places in alternate worlds, Laura. If you accept this task then, on returning with the bowl, I will name one thing that you must live without from then on. Think of it as something you lose after being in possession of the bowl, a sacrifice made by everyone who has owned it. What do you say?'

'Hang on,' Laura interrupted, holding up one hand, 'so I need to give up something, in order to see my parents and brother?'

'Yes.'

'What?'

'We'll cross that stile when we come to it.' Suddenly he reminded her of Kylan, he'd said exactly the same words when she'd asked what would happen once her leg was better all those years ago.

Absentmindedly she placed a hand over the scar which stretched down her thigh. The Robin wasn't really giving her a choice: she could either do what he asked and be forced to lose one thing or refuse him and lose the opportunity to see her family again.

'Very well, I'll go and find this bowl. But what about my singing skills? I didn't think that I was accomplished enough to open Doorways in the Barriers alone yet.' She still hadn't had her initiation to become a Robin, and she didn't know how she would cope on her own.

'I understand your concern, Laura,' The Robin replied appraisingly, 'that is why I have chosen a companion for the journey.'

'Who?' she inquired, feeling slightly nervous as to whom her mentor had chosen. Please let it be Tash, she prayed, please, please, please, I need her brains! I can't figure this all out on my own.

'I'm amazed you don't know already, Laura,' The Robin laughed, 'it's Crow. One of the first friends you made here. He has recently graduated from his studies and is a fully fledged Robin who can assist you.'

'Oh,' Laura murmured, shocked. She forced a smile. At least she could go on this journey with someone who she could talk to and laugh with. And yet how would she be able to control her emotions with Tim there all the time? It would be almost unbearable. Why was The Robin sending her with a man, anyway? Especially after what had happened on her birthday. Suddenly, she felt filled with anger.

'Why Tim?'

The Robin paused, obviously taken aback. 'I beg your pardon?'

'*Why Timothy Crow?*' Laura asked vehemently, 'I thought you wouldn't want me to be going on a quest with a man, especially after…' She trailed off, her anger dying at the look in her mentor's eyes.

'Do you *really* believe that Timothy Crow would do the same thing that Glenroy Mintz did in his drunken stupor?' he asked quietly. 'If you do, Laura, you will have to rethink your judgement of his character.'

She was silent, mutinous and ashamed.

'You are both to set off at the end of the week. Try to return as soon as possible.' The Robin added abruptly, ending their conversation with a wave of his hand, and Laura rose to leave the tower room.

We can try, she thought.

'I'll miss you, Tash,' Laura whispered on the dawn of the day she was to leave, 'but it's the only way I can see my family again. I wish you were coming with me instead.'

'Well,' her friend replied, 'at least you're doing something to try and see them once more. I wish that I was able to come with you too, but I'm afraid that if I go with you I'll see that… creature, again.'

'And to avoid that it would be easier to stay here,' Laura sighed.

'You *will* come back, won't you?' Tash begged. 'I read so many tales about people who go on adventures and get hurt or lost or killed…'

'That's a pleasant topic for a goodbye speech,' Tim said as he sauntered up to them. Tash turned away, her shoulders shaking. Laura shot Tim an annoyed look and hugged her friend again as they walked towards the courtyard where all of the apprentices, Masters and Romulus had gathered. The only one absent was The Robin, but Laura hadn't expected him to bid them farewell. He had given her his blessing to leave when he gave her the quest, in his eyes, that was enough.

Romulus stepped forward, placed a hand to his heart and touched Laura and Tim's chests. As his hand dropped back to his side, Romulus began one of his customary farewell speeches.

'It has been a pleasure having you both at the Temple. Tim, you've proved to be every bit as marvellous as your mentor, Kylan. I personally know for a fact that Kylan will miss you more than words can describe.' There was a cough in the crowd which made Laura look up. She saw Kylan scraping a hand across his eyes roughly as he watched Tim bow to Romulus. He looked greyer than he had when she first met him and she looked away quickly, the old bitter resentment rising once more within her chest.

'Laura,' Romulus continued, 'even though you came here a year later than your peers, you became The Robin's apprentice. The fact that you are both leaving today symbolises much for our small community. May the wind speed your journey and may the Gods watch over you and provide you with a safe return from your travels.'

Laura and Tim were silent for a moment, their hearts bursting with emotion at the old man's words. Her eyes full of tears, Laura rushed forward and hugged him, while Tim gave an awkward bow.

'Thank you,' she whispered, coming to a choking stop, her feelings getting the better of her. Tim gripped her arm and she leaned against him, grateful for the comfort. He was taking steadying breaths, but everyone present could've sworn that they saw tears in his eyes as well.

'We'll return soon,' Tim promised the group, 'Goodbye.'

Laura mounted Elaret and they leapt into the air, leaving behind the Temple of the Nest, her home for the past six years.

They flew for hours, following the sun's course across the sky, to the west. During that time neither of them spoke, but

Laura barely noticed, as she could only focus on the vital details of the quest. The words of her prophecy kept going through her mind, and like mosquitoes they buzzed around and around, taunting her.

You who are not from this world,
Cut off from those you love,
Have yet so far to go.

She snorted, how far did she *need* to go until she could return home?

A long journey awaits,
Through the course of time,
Before you judge it so.

Laura stared ahead, her eyes watering slightly in the wind. Her journey *had* started long ago, she realised, from the moment she had been carried away from the burning remains of her house by two hooded strangers. Yet it was only now that she began the main journey; the retrieval of a mysterious silver bowl which would buy her access to her home world.

'Laura?' Tim's voice was slightly raspy from the hours of silence, 'we should probably descend, set up camp for the night. It'll be evening soon.'

She nodded and they landed in a wide field which stretched in every direction, there weren't any farms or dwellings in sight. Laura's joints ached from the hours in the saddle, and she felt stiff all over. What she wanted was a nice hot bath, a bed in an inn and a plate of hot, mouth-watering food. She watched as Tim threw his dezmian and shut his eyes, murmuring hasty words under his breath. His skin turned pale, and he trembled as two tents appeared behind him. When they had completely materialised, he sank down, drained. Laura felt a pang of sympathy: he sometimes had difficulty with magic, and it would often leave him feeling weak.

'Don't summon the tents tomorrow,' she said as she gathered wood for a fire. 'You know what magic does to you, Tim. It's dangerous.'

'I'll be ok,' he gasped as he put his head between his knees, 'I'm just out of breath, that's all.'

'Don't lie,' Laura snapped, 'it doesn't, as Romulus would say, befit you. You *know* how you cope with magic and that it drains you. What if one day you accidentally went too far and...' She cut off and busied herself with the fire. Once there were enough twigs and small branches, she withdrew her own dezmian and flipped it, mouthing the words to light a fire. There was a slight wrenching feeling in her gut and the wood burst into flames which devoured the kindling in seconds. Laura added some more wood and soon the fire's hunger seemed to be sated, as it chewed on some larger branches of wood.

'Laura,' Tim said slowly, 'I wouldn't... I didn't mean...'

'It's not safe,' she interrupted abruptly, 'magic can be dangerous, Tim. I thought you knew that as well as I did. Promise me you won't try something as big as summoning, assembling and,' she peered inside one, 'furnishing them again. Please.'

He laughed and she glared at him. 'It's not funny,' She snapped.

'I know,' he grinned, and she was struck by how, even though he looked pale and weak, he still could make her stomach do somersaults, something even magic couldn't achieve. 'I promise I won't do anything too stupid, Laura.'

Satisfied with the knowledge that she had won, Laura withdrew a small pot from her saddlebags and filled it with water before placing it to boil by the fire.

'Have you got the map?' Tim asked. 'We should probably see if it provides any help at all.'

'I'll get it,' she replied, and pulled the faded piece of parchment out of her saddlebag. 'The map covers parts of separate worlds,' she said as she looked at it, 'should we bring out some maps of the worlds around Venetica to see if we can see any similarities?'

'Good idea,' Tim murmured, bending his head to look at the map in the flickering light. Taking it from her, he went into his tent and brought out several large tomes, while Laura added several vegetables and slices of dried meat to the pot.

Once the maps were spread out in front of them, the two friends put their heads together and pored over the books.

'Look,' Laura suddenly exclaimed, 'The Gherna River in Calcityia resembles the river in the map exactly.'

'Yes,' Tim whispered intently, 'and Roshterdam appears to be the city at the end of the river. See how the city appears to be flying? Roshterdam is held up by great propellers and it's the only city known to fly.'

'Okay, so to recap what we have so far,' Laura said, holding up a hand to silence him. 'We know *that* line,' Laura pointed at the added map, 'is the Gherna River, or something that looks a lot like it and that once we go all the way along it, we'll have to travel to Roshterdam. And then?'

'I don't know what the next part of the map means,' Tim muttered, indicating a vertical line of runes down the left-hand side of the map.

'Maybe that's why we need to go to both places,' Laura replied, 'who knows, perhaps some of the inhabitants may have an idea as to what they mean.'

'What makes you say that?'

'After the picture of the city, there are more of those runes. If we can discover what they mean, it'll make the journey a whole lot simpler.'

'Do you think we should head along the river or just travel straight to Roshterdam?' Tim asked.

Laura returned his gaze with wide eyes, 'we must travel down the river. I doubt that it's the city alone which holds secrets. Who knows, the great-granddaughter may have written her message in two different places, or maybe more. If the stories are true and she was running from the Dragutash, then she would have tried to put them off the trail and confuse them.'

After they had picked at a very unappetising meal, Laura retired to her tent and Tim sat and gazed into the fire, pondering her final words.

After all, why would a person write a message next to a river? What knowledge could they find beside a river, when they could find so much more in the city?

The morning dawned, cold and bright.

As they set off, Laura couldn't help noticing the dark rings under Tim's eyes.

'Someone didn't sleep well,' she teased. Tim grunted in reply. 'Were you disturbed by dreams?'

'No,' he answered shortly. 'Just tormented by dreams of good food.'

This stung. 'Well,' Laura snapped, 'I didn't see *you* offering to cook last night. I did the best I could.'

Tim glared at the space in front of them, snapping to Iris, 'come on,' he kicked her sides savagely. Iris screeched in protest and flapped her wings. Laura watched him for a minute, slowly realising that there was something else on his mind.

'What?' Tim growled, scowling at her for a second.

'You're scaring me, Tim,' she said, 'what else did you dream about?'

There was a silence for a long time before Tim murmured, 'I don't want to talk about my dreams. They would scare even you, and the Gods know everything *you've* been through.' There was a short silence while Laura watched him closely and he actively avoided her gaze.

'How far until we reach the Barrier?' she asked, deciding it'd be wise to change the subject.

'It should be up ahead,' he replied, 'hopefully we'll reach it within the next hour.'

And, sure enough, Tim was right. After travelling about five miles, they came across a large invisible wall, which shimmered and wavered in the air, looking very fragile indeed. If Laura hadn't known what to look for, she would have thought it was a heat haze.

'Don't forget the Barrier's power, Laura,' Tim murmured as the Willowings landed. She almost didn't hear him, as she stood transfixed, in awe of the thrum of power swirling through the air. He dismounted and stepped forward, reaching a hand out to find the beginning of the Barrier.

Once his hand touched the invisible wires, Tim began to sing in a deep, rich voice, which Laura had never heard him use before. The notes rose and swelled with unseen power. As if in answer to his song, an archway appeared in the shimmering air.

'That was cheerful,' Laura smiled. He laughed, but was soon serious again.

'Let's go. We haven't got much time until the Doorway closes behind us.'

She grabbed the Willowings' reins and hurried through with Tim following close behind. Once on the other side, the Doorway behind them gave a loud crack and meshed together once again, blocking off all sight of Venetica. They had come out on top of the crest of a hill which provided a wide view of the panoramic vista that spread out below them.

'There's the Gherna River,' Laura cried, pointing excitedly at a slice of blue on the horizon. The river was bordered with a dense forest on either side, which stretched for miles in every direction. It appeared as if the Gherna River was the only straight route through the forest.

'The Chimeté Forest,' Tim whispered in awe as they descended the hill and made their way in the direction of the river, 'I heard stories about its great size but never thought that it'd be this…'

'Huge?' Laura finished, unable to hide even her own amazement.

'Exactly,' he said, 'but it's beautiful as well.'

Laura nodded in agreement, 'it looks magical.'

When they entered the trees, Laura couldn't help noticing that the Willowings were becoming restless.

'What's wrong?' she murmured to Elaret, who snorted and pawed the ground in response.

'I think a species related to the Willowings lives in Calcityia,' Tim muttered, staring into the dense trees, which now surrounded them on either side.

After a few minutes, the sound of a cracking stick rang through the air. Spinning around, Laura couldn't see anything in the foliage. But it was too silent, as if the trees were holding their breath, watching them.

She let her breath out slowly and turned to keep moving.

Another twig broke from the opposite side.

'Tim…' Laura began in a whisper, as though talking would be too loud for this noiseless place.

'I know,' he replied, 'there's more than beauty in this forest. Much more.'

'I'm scared,' she mumbled, 'it's like the trees are waiting for something. There aren't any natural sounds here, not even cicadas, and they're basically everywhere.'

Listening, Tim realised that Laura was right. This place was hauntingly quiet.

'Come on,' he said softly, 'hopefully there's more noise downriver.'

She didn't respond, and they kicked off, leaving the strangeness behind them as they began flying towards the never-ending stretch of water.

As time passed, they talked less and less, watching the two riverbanks and searching for any sign of life. But no matter how hard Laura and Tim rubbed their eyes and stared intently at the forest, they saw nothing.

Once they had set up a camp on the edge of the river that night, Laura gazed up at the stars. She sighed, the slight pang of unease that she had felt earlier still lingering. There was something unwelcome about the forest, almost like something was waiting to pounce as soon as they fell asleep. She noticed Tim watching her from across the fire.

'Tim, can I tell you something?' she asked.

'Anything,' he replied. She almost smiled at the speed of his reply and paused for a moment, trying to work out how to put what she wanted to say into words. Eventually, she settled on the easiest approach.

'Do you remember Glenroy?'

Tim ground his teeth, the peaceful moment shattered.

'How could I forget him?'

'For a while, I thought that he did more that night, Tim.' Laura murmured, turning away to face the water glistening in the moonlight. She didn't want to see his face, his expression.

Tim reached forward to grasp her hand but then drew back, and asked with forced calmness, 'what do you mean?'

She smiled wryly, 'I thought that Glenroy left me with child.'

A long silence ensued, and finally Tim said firmly, 'but you didn't show any signs of being pregnant, Laura. Surely, you'd be several months along by now if... well...' He trailed off, and Laura was glad.

'I know,' Laura said quietly. 'The only person I told was Tash. I thought it was odd, being sick every day. Tash suspected that I was pregnant, long before I thought that I was. She told me that I needed to alert a healer, she said my illness wasn't a good sign, but I couldn't. I still don't know why; maybe I was ashamed that Glenroy had still left his mark on me. I was so relieved when I bled that month,' Tim coughed uncomfortably but Laura couldn't stop, 'but it didn't explain my sickness. So, when The Robin was away, I went to Boowlra one night and went to see Leonora.'

'Hang on,' Tim interrupted, 'that crazy lady who runs the alchemy shop on the main street?'

'The very same,' Laura replied, 'I thought that, even though she's terrifying, she would be the only person other than The Robin who would know what was going on. Her connection to magic and the way she spoke about it was unlike anyone I've met. I was sure that she would have answers to my questions.'

'Why did you go to see her at night? If you'd gone during the day we all would've accompanied you. You didn't have to do it alone.' He sounded hurt and Laura turned to look at him.

'I just knew that I had to,' she said, and her expression was blank, 'besides, I was forbidden from going to Boowlra. Romulus would have noticed and alerted The Robin when he returned. I was meant to be punished, I couldn't risk being caught.' Laura paused, contemplating, 'but she surprised me. It was as though she knew I'd come; the door was open and she sat by the fire making a pot of tea.' She smiled at the memory, 'it was so weird. She welcomed me like one would an old friend, like I wasn't just a strange girl who she'd spoken to once, but someone important. Someone special.' She halted, eyes glazing over as the memory took hold.

'What did she tell you?' Tim prompted after a few minutes of silence.

'She said that I was sick because I had tried sending out a magical plea for help before what happened; I had tried really hard, and I was in a place where the magical energies were extremely weak. I think Glenroy knew that.' She paused again, 'but I drained my magical energies apparently. That was one of the reasons why I was so weak afterwards. I didn't notice for the next few days because I was so caught up in what had happened.'

'So, what happened then?' Tim asked, tone unreadable.

'I was shocked,' she replied softly, 'Leonora had to give me several cups of tea before I came to terms with it. She didn't seem surprised or uncomfortable by my reaction. I didn't take much note of it at the time, but now…'

'Your reaction?' Tim pressed, and she could hear the desperation in his voice. Her instincts begged her to turn over and look into his eyes, yet her back remained turned and when she spoke, her voice was directed to the far-off trees on the opposite river bank. She didn't want to see his reaction to her innermost thoughts or the judgement she was sure he would feel.

'I was devastated,' she whispered, her voice breaking, 'deep inside I wanted to have a child. I didn't blame it for who its father had been, or the way it had been conceived. When I thought that I was pregnant I began to hope, insanely, that I would be able to have a family of my own here. That some part of me might feel reunited with the idea of having a family. I'd virtually lost hope that I could return to see Mum, Dad and Fred again, so the idea of having a baby was somewhat comforting.'

'But it would have been *Glenroy's* child,' Tim said, his voice hard and cutting. Laura flinched slightly but he was too shocked at her admission to notice. 'How could The Robin have allowed you to stay at the Temple with a baby? And what if the baby took after its father?'

'Genes can only determine so much,' Laura said doggedly, 'it's the *environment* that affects a child the most.' She was regretting her confession now, but she couldn't take it back.

'And if Glenroy found out and tried to take the child?' Tim demanded, 'what then?'

'The Robin has made sure that I'll never have to see Glenroy again,' Laura said, her voice suddenly devoid of emotion, 'and I guess we'll never know what could have been because there never was a baby in the first place.' She stood up abruptly and walked to the edge of the river, whose waves lapped gently against the riverbank below her feet. Breathing deeply, she tried to calm herself as her meditation teacher had done for the past six years.

In, she thought, *and out. Breathe and relax.*

'I know I sound unsympathetic,' Tim said after a moment. She heard him stand up and walk closer. The hair on the back of her neck stood on end and she had to focus harder than ever on controlling her breathing.

'You do,' she replied curtly, as she shut her eyes to focus more. Laura felt his presence next to her, and her heart began a marathon.

'I just don't know how I would have coped if you had given birth to a child. Especially if its father was Glenroy.'

His words surprised and startled her, she opened her eyes to find him standing a hair's breath away. She didn't say anything in response, but her eyes flitted towards his and away, fearful of the message that she might read in his eyes. Unconsciously, she stepped back, breaking the moment.

'Do you know what he said to me?' she asked, knowing full well that he didn't. Tim shook his head, eyes on hers, watching as she forced a smile and shrugged her shoulders, feigning ease. 'He told me that it was my fault,' she said, 'that I taunted him and teased him and that I deserved what happened. It was my fault.' Tears began to slide down her cheeks as her calming meditation was destroyed.

'No, it wasn't,' Tim replied as he caught her hands in his, 'it was Glenroy's. *All* Glenroy's. Don't take his words to heart, don't ever believe what he said. He wanted to make you feel guilty and scared so that he had power over you. It wasn't your fault.'

She blinked and then hugged him, sobs racking her thin frame as her head rested against his chest. Tim, unused to being embraced by weeping girls, awkwardly hugged her back, patting her shoulders until the sobs subsided.

'Thanks, Tim,' Laura sniffed, wiping her eyes with the back of her hand and pulling away towards her tent. She felt slightly embarrassed and missed seeing his nod in reply as she ducked out of sight. Silently, Tim watched her before returning to his own tent, thoughts full of what she had told him and how he could possibly try to make her forget all that had happened.

As the moon rose higher into the night sky, and the fire became mere embers, quiet footsteps filled the air. Figures disassembled the tents, and Laura and Tim were picked up and taken into the depths of the Chimeté Forest as they slept.

Chapter Ten

The smell of roasting meat awoke Laura from her slumber.

Opening her eyes, she noticed around her were small huts branching out from the trees. She sat up, panic coursing through her veins; this wasn't the campsite from last night! What scared her more were the looming woven wooden walls. At each end of the village were two gateways, giving Laura a glimpse of pointed stakes facing away from the walls, towards the rest of the forest. Where was she, and where was Tim? Her latter question was answered almost as soon as the thought popped into her head.

'Laura!' Tim called from the other side of the village, and began heading towards her.

'Tim,' she cried, relieved. He didn't seem to be hurt or even worried about where they were. He reached her and they hugged each other tightly. Laura clung onto him as if he would be able to teleport them both away from the village, and the group of its inhabitants who had gathered at their loud exclamations.

Her eyes moved across the group, some heads were nodding with knowing smiles on their faces, while others frowned. They all wore feathers and bones in their hair, and their clothes were made up of woven grass and animal fur, knitted together with lengths of what appeared to be reeds. Her eyes widened as she noticed the men with large decorative tattoos move closer, peering curiously at the newcomers.

All of the people closest to her were women, and they were watching Tim and her even more shrewdly than The Robin had on first acquaintance.

'*Dakka*,' an old lady said to the rest of them, pointing at Tim and Laura. '*Opolini dakka*.'

'*Tis, tis*,' was the answering reply.

'What are they saying?' Laura asked cautiously, but to her astonishment, Tim shook his head.

'It's nothing, Laura, you don't need to know.' She was intrigued that he understood the language, which sounded very nasal and harsh. She, on the other hand, understood nothing. She looked at him and saw that his cheeks were burning.

Ah. Perhaps the villagers thought the travellers were a couple, then.

'No,' she said slowly, stepping away from Tim's side. 'No, we're not... Tim and I aren't...'

'*Nici*,' Tim snapped, hoping to drown out Laura's vain efforts to tell the truth.

The old lady stepped forward and clasped Laura to her bosom.

'*Fereis swei dis vici jilous girla?*' she cried, glaring angrily at Tim, whose look of astonishment made Laura laugh. He stared at her for a moment and seemed to slump in resignation,

'*Justi lici heiri,*' he sighed, '*eidin asihi tica mor seriosici.*'

The old lady glanced at her and then nodded and replied, '*Pecini vericus. Hicini averina grishnam pecim.*'

Tim nodded in assent and reached out to take Laura's hand. The old lady moved at the same moment, pulling Laura with her and smacked his hand away. If Laura had looked back then, she would've seen the momentary look of loss and sadness cross Tim's face.

But she didn't.

The old lady took Laura to a hut at the edge of the village.

'Is this where I'm staying?' Laura asked.

'*Tis, tis,*' the woman replied, nodding vigorously.

Laura took it that the word '*tis*' meant 'yes'. Smiling, she stepped through the small doorway into a building that, although not large, was snug and comfortable.

A braided rug lay beside a small three-legged stool and a few candles, which made mysterious shadows flicker on the walls.

'Thank you,' she murmured, clasping the woman's hands tightly.

With a gesture towards herself, the lady said, '*Mini santelle Élendill.*'

'That's your name?' Laura questioned. The woman looked confused and so Laura repeated herself with embellished hand gestures, pointing at the woman and saying 'Élendill'.

'*Tis,*' Élendill nodded, her silvery hair gleamed in the candlelight.

'OK,' Laura smiled, '*mini santelle* Laura.'

'*Laura,*' Élendill muttered, trying the strange word out on her tongue. '*Laura.*'

Abruptly, with a little wave, Élendill was gone, leaving her to settle into the temporary home. Laura gazed around before sitting down, panicked thoughts beginning to swirl around in her mind.

What would happen to them? Why had they been kidnapped in the middle of the night? And *what* had the villagers been saying about her and Tim? Despite what he had said about it not being important, Laura had a feeling niggling at her that it *was*, in fact, quite significant.

'Laura?' Glancing upward, she noticed Tim in her doorway; how long he'd been there she couldn't tell.

'Tim, come in.' She gestured to the fur rug on the ground.

He entered and slumped down, not caring about ruffling up the rug.

Laura watched him for a moment. 'What's wrong?' Anxiety penetrated her voice and Tim looked up in surprise.

'I'm fine, really. It's just that the locals have odd customs which, as members of the Order, we must respect and abide by. I was speaking to the Elders before you awoke, and they told me what we need to remember.'

'What customs?'

'We aren't allowed to meet in private, Laura. The Taperi, that's this tribe, have strong thoughts on young men and women together. Especially virgins.' He smiled at her wryly.

'But I'm not,' Laura whispered.

'We've got to let them continue to think you are. If the Taperi realise that you no longer possess the sanctity of virginity, then you'll be treated with no respect and will be kicked out of the village.'

'Why?'

'Because, after your little demonstration this morning, it's obvious to the Taperi that we aren't married. Therefore, we cannot pretend to be, so that you don't need to lie. They only allow married folk in the same hut.'

'Then why are you here?' Laura asked, but could tell as soon as the words were out of her mouth that Tim had taken them differently.

'I'm not alone,' he replied tightly, pointing to another figure in the doorway. 'And if that's all, I'll be going.'

'No, Tim, wait, I didn't mean…' she cried after him as he stormed out of the hut.

He didn't turn back, and Laura leaned against the wall, silently cursing herself for being so abrupt with her words. Why did he have to take such offence?

She was like this when Élendill found her.

'*Teferi wiri?*' she asked.

'Oh, talk some sense!' Laura muttered, before sighing in exasperation and looking Élendill in the eyes.

'What did you say?'

'*Tefer?*'

'What?'

'*Tefer?*'

'Oh, just leave me alone!' Laura cried angrily.

Élendill watched the girl for a minute, understanding beginning to dawn on her. '*Veri on slicer?*'

'I don't understand! No! *Nici!*' she pointed at herself and shook her head viciously, 'I do *not* understand.'

'*Ahh,*' Élendill murmured, nodding. 'You… no… understand, *tis?*'

'No!'

'*Nici,*' Élendill corrected.

'*Nici,* then!'

'*Tis, grechi, treil grechi.*'

'*What?*' Laura questioned.

'*Tefer,*' the elderly woman answered, '*tefer… what, veri slicer?*'

'Tefer means "what"?'

'*Tis,*' her new mentor nodded.

'Therefore "*tis*" means "yes"?'

'*Tis*,' Élendill smiled. Laura sighed in annoyance. The last thing she felt like was having a crash course in the Taperi language. The intensive lesson lasted until the sun had barely touched the horizon and Laura's head was about ready to explode.

By that time Laura had learned that '*veroni*' meant 'thank you', '*plicin*' meant 'please' and that '*veri on slicer?*' meant something along the lines of 'you don't understand?' along with multiple hand gestures which she could use to try and express herself.

Élendill led the way out toward a large bonfire in the centre of the village where the men were roasting meat on a spit. Some girls had brought urns full of water back from washing clothes in the river. As they walked past the group, Laura noticed a couple of them lagging behind, talking and joking amongst themselves.

A man laughed at a woman and kissed her cheek playfully. In response the woman grabbed an urn of water and threw it at him, but her irritation was lessened by a smile.

Élendill sighed at the young couple who, on noticing her and Laura, bowed respectfully, their sides shaking with laughter.

'*Necino verion dulce,*' the woman said, glaring at the young man. Laura glanced from the man's mortified expression to Élendill's stern one and remembered what Tim had said about the severe tribal customs.

Thinking about Tim made Laura bite her lip, wishing that she hadn't made a question sound like a cruel remark. But another part of her was annoyed at Tim for not even bothering to listen when she'd called out after him.

'*Supperi,*' Élendill proclaimed, dragging Laura to a seat by the fire, where the aroma of roasting meat was even stronger.

The men all jumped up as they approached, bowing their heads respectfully to Élendill as she reached them.

Laura's first impression of the men was that they were dirty and crude. With no utensils to eat with except for fingers, the men stuffed their mouths until meat was almost spilling out. Laura couldn't help but watch, disgusted yet fascinated, until she noticed Tim performing the same eating habits.

His face was streaked with dirt and sweat, and if she'd seen him earlier Laura was sure that she would've believed him to be a native. But he was still wearing a long-sleeved shirt to cover up his scar. Laura always felt a pang of emotion whenever her eyes fell on his left arm. She could almost see the jagged scar on his skin underneath the linen, and wondered if it had hurt as much as her own scars across her thighs.

Meeting her eyes across the flames, Tim looked quickly away and began to make conversation with the girl next to him. They whispered together and, after having to hear a lot of giggling, Laura decided that enough was enough. She followed the example of another girl and stood up to scrub some plates carved of tough bark. Her new companion looked at her in surprise but allowed Laura to accompany her to the riverside where they washed the dishes in silence.

'*Hemich*,' Laura began, praying that she was using the right word for saying 'hello'. '*Mini santelle Laura.*'

'You don't need to try to speak in Taperi to me,' the girl replied stoutly, although Laura could hear the good humour in her voice.

'Well that's a relief,' Laura smiled.

'Yes,' her companion answered. 'I'm Kiera, I came with Millie.'

'Who's that?' Laura asked, confused.

'My companion, she treats me as a servant, although I'm not.' Kiera's voice was bitter.

'That's awful,' Laura replied carefully.

Kiera shook her head remorsefully, 'it's hard to deny Millie anything. She always gets what she wants.'

'Why?'

'She has her ways,' Kiera said wryly. 'I noticed at dinner that she was getting hold of another man. Didn't he arrive with you?'

'So that was who he was talking to,' Laura mused, 'are you part of the tribe?'

'No, we used to live in Yorket, but that life wasn't satisfactory for either of us.' Kiera began, 'have you heard of Yorket?'

'Yes,' Laura nodded, remembering her time there. She began to recall how irked she'd been when Tim had been with the bar girls, and how one in particular had said something very hurtful to her. But her name had been Amelia, could it be the same girl?

'Anyway,' Kiera continued, 'I was sick of the customers, and Millie was pining over some apprentice who went away. So, we decided to manipulate an elderly Robin into bringing us here. In fact, Millie did the manipulating. It was quite exciting at the time, until the Robin got mauled by Giffleets when we arrived. We were saved by the Taperi and taken in by them. Millie was starting to get sick of the strict laws about men, I think that she was going to try and run off with some of the village boys. But now you two are here.' As Kiera spoke, Laura felt a rush of recognition and the old dislike towards Millie began to return.

'Did you catch onto the language quickly?' Laura inquired, keen to steer the conversation away from Millie.

'Yes,' Kiera nodded, 'I like learning new things and although I can't write in Taperi, I can understand most of what they say now and can speak enough to get by.'

'Why did the Taperi take Tim and I away from our campsite?' Laura asked.

'Don't you know?' Kiera replied but received a confused look in return. 'Well, there are Giffleets. They destroyed our original campsite. If the Taperi hadn't come when they did, we would have been eaten like the Robin.'

'Giffleets?' Laura asked, 'what are they?'

'They're a much more violent version of Willowings,' Kiera replied. 'Nowhere in the forest is safe from them, even though they live on the other side of the river. Some of the Taperi scouts noticed you set up camp and figured that it would be safer for you here.'

'What about our Willowings?' Laura cried, leaping to her feet in panic, the image of Elaret filling her mind.

Kiera laughed, 'don't worry, Laura, the Taperi have stables and the Willowings were smart enough to fly away from your campsite.'

'Oh,' Laura sighed, relieved.

'Relax,' Kiera smiled, splashing some water in her companion's direction.

This provoked Laura to flick water back and soon they were in the middle of a water fight, eventually collapsing, sodden, onto the bank, their sides hurting with laughter.

'Come on,' Kiera said once she'd regained some breath. 'I want to show you something I found when I came here.'

Holding Laura's hand, Kiera led her further into the forest until they came to a desolate clearing where another hut

stood. This building had a different design to the Taperis'
huts. Instead of being crafted out of wood, it was stone and
had a curved roof. It was apparent that no one had lived in
it for a long time, as moss crept up the walls, enslaving the
stonework in its vice-like grip. Grass grew along the roof,
forming a second garden from the ground below. The doorway was dark, and Laura blinked as Kiera led her inside and
lit a candle, which had been on the ledge, subduing the darkness.

Laura gasped in astonishment as the light showed what
was inscribed on the walls. A funny sense of déjà vu went
down her spine and she shivered.

'This was here when you arrived?' she asked, moving forward and tracing her fingers along the walls.

'Yes,' Kiera was surprised by Laura's reaction. 'I think
that it was here even before the Taperi arrived, and from
what I can find out, they've been here for three centuries at
least.'

'Three hundred years is a long time,' Laura murmured.
'Who was here before then?'

'I don't know, but it's pretty amazing isn't it?' Kiera
waved a hand at the room. 'Would you like to head back? I
don't think we should be outside much longer, and it will
take at least ten minutes to walk back to the village.'

'Not yet, I'll stay and examine these for a while longer.'

'Okay, I'll wait outside. We can return tomorrow if you
wish.'

'Kiera?' Laura called as Kiera stepped outside, 'will you
teach me some of the Taperi language, please? Élendill was
trying to, but we don't really understand each other very well.
Knowing the language may help me in the village a little bit,
I think. And thank you for being so kind and welcoming. It's

hard settling in, especially when I don't know how long we'll be here.'

'You'll never leave,' Kiera grinned, but was confused when Laura chuckled and said,

'I'm not so sure. But we *will* stay for a while.'

Laura turned her gaze back onto the walls. She recognised the runes before her. They were identical to the ones drawn on the map.

'What do they mean?' she wondered, wishing more than ever that Tim was away from Millie and helping her. There was a cough from outside and she decided to return the next day with the map.

With that, she took the candle and left the hut, disappearing into the shadows falling into step with Kiera.

Chapter Eleven

'Laura, wake up!' The voice was impatient, scared.

'Hm?' Laura mumbled, rolling further into the blankets. 'Come back in five minutes, it's not dawn yet.'

'Don't go back to sleep,' Kiera shook her shoulder desperately, 'you need to get up. We need as many fighters as possible.'

Now Laura was awake, and she sat up, wiping all remnants of sleep from her eyes.

'What do you mean,' she asked, 'as many *fighters* as possible? I don't fight.'

'The Giffleets are attacking.'

'I thought you said they haven't attacked for the past few weeks?' Laura said.

'Come on,' Kiera didn't answer Laura's question, but dragged her out of the hut and towards one of the walls. 'Élendill and some of the other Elders are arranging the archers. When it comes to Giffleets, the more archers we have, the better.'

'But…'

'Don't say anything. The sooner this herd of Giffleets has been killed or scared away, the sooner I can go back to bed.'

Smothering a yawn, Laura reached Élendill and bowed respectfully, but was not prepared for the bow and quiver of arrows thrust at her chest.

'Hurry, child,' Élendill said, 'take your place next to Finnikin. He shall show you what to do.'

Laura hurried onwards, unable to speak another word to Élendill. When she came to a halt, Laura nodded at the two men on either side. One was a bit older than she was, with shaggy blonde hair and a set jaw.

'Finnikin?'

'Laura.' He replied. Laura turned to the other person and was surprised to see Tim.

'Laura,' he said, 'it's been a while.'

'Hmph,' she grumbled, biting back a retort that it wasn't her fault he hadn't spoken to her for the past week while she had struggled to refine her knowledge of the Taperi language and customs.

She glanced away and saw the Giffleets for the first time.

Standing in the shadows of the forest were creatures which resembled Willowings, with savage horns protruding from their wide heads. Their eyes were glowing red slits and surrounded by thick, dark hair. Instead of wings on their backs, they had three pointed spikes. In a rippling movement, the Giffleets moved closer, and Laura noticed scales which glinted in the moonlight. Suddenly, she remembered the Dæmon from so many months before and shuddered.

'Bowmen ready?' Finnikin cried.

'Fire!' Élendill's voice shouted. Laura fitted an arrow onto the bowstring and drew it back before letting the arrow fly. The bow was heavy, and as the string vibrated her arm jarred, making her grit her teeth. The arrow flew forwards a few metres, and then dropped lamely, hitting the ground without a sound.

'Nice.' Tim snorted, and Laura felt her cheeks redden. Back at the Temple she'd never taken part in any archery lessons and had focussed on her magic instead. The only vaguely violent activity she'd partaken in had been learning basic self-defence with a dagger. Healing, languages, magic and geography had been much more interesting to her than using different weaponry.

'Let me help you, Laura,' Finnikin said, as he placed his bow aside.

'Thank you,' she replied, glaring at Tim, who drew his bowstring back with ease and fired. She gritted her teeth angrily.

'Place your hand here,' Finnikin instructed, moving Laura's hand up the bow and placing her fingers on the bowstring. He reached into her quiver and fixed an arrow onto the string, 'now hold that. Good. Place your feet a bit more apart,' his foot nudged hers into the correct position and poked her rigid shoulders. 'Loosen up,' he smiled, 'it's not the end of the world. I'm sure that Élendill and the Elders just wanted you to see what Giffleets were like. They attack less frequently now.'

'So what is this then?' Laura muttered to herself, 'a VIP experience?'

'Anyway,' Finnikin continued, 'relax and draw back the bowstring.' His hand rested over hers, helping to pull the arrow backwards, till both his and her hand rested just below her ear. 'And release.' He breathed, letting go of her hand not a moment too late. The arrow now flew forwards into the darkness and hit one of the Giffleet's legs.

'Well done,' Finnikin grinned, 'you lamed one. That should make it a lot easier to kill.'

'Thanks for the help,' Laura said, 'I really appreciate it.'

'A reasonable shot,' Tim said gruffly from her other side, 'but you need a lot more work yet.'

'At least Finnikin bothered to help me,' Laura replied coldly. It seemed like only yesterday when they arrived, but he seemed to have soured in every way towards her.

Tim drew the bowstring back and let another arrow loose, killing another Giffleet, lips tight with anger.

'Tim, *darling!*'

Laura struggled not to roll her eyes. No one except Millie could make the words 'Tim' and 'darling' sound so off-putting.

'You're so *brave.*' Millie cried, flinging her arms around Tim's neck, 'killing a Giffleet like that, in one shot too! It's *amazing.*'

Tim looked a little unsettled, but briefly hugged her back before trying to un-entwine himself from her vice-like grip. Glancing back over the wall, Laura snorted. The light of the moon shone down, and the final Giffleet fell. The others were either lying on the ground or had escaped back into the forest.

'What are you laughing about?' Tim asked Laura over Millie's head.

'I may be terrible at archery, Tim, but at least I don't have a limpet following me around. You poor *darling.*' She strode away, trying very hard to stop laughing.

The men were carrying in the bodies of the Giffleets, noses scrunched up at the rancid smell. In death the Giffleets seemed a lot less ferocious, almost innocent. One was still clinging on to life and kicked out at the tribesman who was dragging it into the town. Laura glanced at it and was taken aback when moist eyes stared back. Though the colour of blood, its eyes seemed to be full of terrible sorrow, and Laura wished she could somehow help. She stepped forward, and raised a hand, reaching out to touch the Giffleet.

'What do you think you're doing?' the tribesman asked gruffly, shattering Laura's concentration.

'It looks so sad.'

He laughed roughly, 'this isn't a safe, tame creature, like a Willowing. If given the chance, it will tear you limb from limb.'

'But why can't I touch it now?' Laura asked curiously, 'while you're holding it?'

'Giffleets are known for their cunning,' the tribesman replied sharply, and moved the Giffleet further away, leaving Laura's hand still in mid-air.

'And what could it do?' she snapped, all patience leaving in the presence of anger, 'the poor creature isn't able to escape; you've made sure of that by locking the gates and placing spears along the walls. How can you possibly be so cruel?'

'Because they'd show no mercy to us,' the tribesman barked, 'Giffleets are animals. That's the long and short of it. They can't *think* like humans can.'

'Well at the moment I can't see a difference between them and us,' Laura said coldly.

Laura looked back at the Giffleet, which seemed to be begging her silently to let it go back to its home on the other side of the river. It moaned a low, tragic sound, which seemed to reverberate around Laura's head for hours afterward. As she looked into its eyes, her mind buckled as an image solidified of two newborn Giffleets, one tottering on its shaky legs. Their mother watched its children play together, before the babies knelt down next to her, nuzzling into her neck. Laura cried out and fell to the ground, shocked at what she had seen and horrified at what she knew would happen. The tribesman growled, sounding far worse than the wild creature. He reached out to a comrade nearby and received a sharpened stake. When the Giffleet saw the stake, it thrashed on the ground, moaning hysterically, anticipating that its end would soon come.

'No,' Laura cried, rising to her feet, 'it has a family on the other side of the river, please!' She reached for the stake desperately, but firm hands grabbed her from behind and pulled her harshly backwards. She thrashed like the Giffleet, striking out at the arms which wouldn't let her go.

'Stop it, Laura,' Tim's voice snarled, arms still constraining her every move. 'Leave it be. The creature's as good as dead.'

'That's *exactly* what you'd say,' she hissed, eyes flashing, how could Tim just stand there while an animal was to be put to death? 'But it's still alive, if we let it go free it can return to its family, its babies…'

But she had gone too far. The tribesman roared and brandished the stake at Laura. *'Get her out of here.'*

'With pleasure,' Tim replied, and dragged Laura away. When he let her go, Laura didn't turn around. She was unable to watch as the tribesman brought the stake down. The Giffleet gave one last gurgling moan before lying still, crimson eyes staring glassily at the lightening sky. Only then could she turn and kneel beside the body. The tribesman snarled in disapproval, but now the creature was dead he could hardly complain at her behaviour.

Laura's fingers touched the thickening blood softly as tears filled her eyes. She stroked the scaly skin and felt the sharp spikes on its back before closing its eyes.

'I'm sorry,' she whispered, knowing full well that the creature had gone someplace where it would never hear her words. 'I'm sorry you can't go back to your family.' She bowed her head and wept, because she could understand too well how the Giffleet foals would react when their mother never returned.

When Laura returned to her hut, washed her blood-stained hands and crawled into her bed, sleep evaded her for a long time. Her mind was tormented by images of the Giffleet and its family, and so she was glad when the sun arose and she could get up to begin her daily activities.

The day passed in a blur, but Laura didn't notice. Obviously the tribesman who killed the Giffleet that morning had told everyone about her reaction, and some of the members of the tribe gave her either angry or terrified looks, but she ignored them. She avoided the campfire that evening and took her food to her hut and ate there, not wanting to see the expressions of disapproval or confusion on the tribespeople's faces. She also had no wish to see the daily exploits of Tim and Millie, which was reaching the nauseating stage. Kiera came with twilight, carrying two baskets of dirty dishes, and Laura joined her silently.

'Why did you want to save the Giffleet?' Kiera asked finally as they reached the riverbank and set down the baskets. 'Monarché is saying that you were hysterical, that it cast some sort of spell upon you so that you acted as you did. He said you wanted to set it *free*.'

'I did,' Laura replied calmly, 'before it died it showed me an image of its family on the other side of the river. It had two newborn babies who were just learning to walk.'

'But it's an animal,' Kiera emphasised, 'the Taperi have been fighting Giffleets for aeons, it would be unthinkable for them to even *consider* setting one free.'

'I know,' Laura sighed, as she scrubbed a bark plate with unyielding ferocity. 'But I thought maybe they could make an exception. Even for an animal.'

Kiera sighed in resignation, 'its death really got to you, didn't it?'

'Yes,' Laura replied tightly. Thoughts of her own family were filling her mind, and she pushed them away with the same viciousness as she treated the plates. She didn't need to be burdened by thoughts of them now and so cast around for a new subject.

'On another note,' she began, 'a man called Finnikin helped me with my archery. It was the first time I'd ever used a bow.' Kiera was silent for a moment and placed the plate she had been washing on the grass to dry. 'He was very help-ful,' Laura continued, watching Kiera out of the corner of her eye, wondering if her suspicions were correct. There was silence for a while and then Kiera broke it, her voice slightly unsteady.

'When I first arrived with Millie, I learnt the language of the Taperi from Finnikin. He was friendly, helpful, not like all the men back in Yorket.' She said, 'but then Millie noticed that I was spending more time with him than she was. She got jealous, as she always does, and decided that she would like some *language lessons* as well, and then he seemed to forget that I existed. When you and Tim arrived, she left Finnikin for him. I think she got bored, that's just how she is.' Her lip trembled slightly, and her hands were shaking.

'You still like Finnikin though, don't you?' Laura probed.

'Is it that obvious?' Kiera muttered.

'You should try to talk to him.' Laura urged. 'Before you lose your nerve.'

Kiera thought for a moment, 'Will he get the wrong idea? I mean, I don't want him to think that I'm like Millie.'

'Would you rather you spoke to him at dinner? Or when we serve the noonday meal?' Laura asked, trying to keep the impatience out of her voice. 'Or perhaps when he's about to go off and lead a hunting party?'

'Well no...'

'So will you go to meet him tomorrow morning?'

'You are so bossy, Laura!'

'But will you go?'

Kiera threw up her hands in resignation, 'Fine. I'll probably ruin my chances anyway.'

'You won't.' Laura was more confident than she had been in a long time. Suddenly a memory came into her head, and a question which had never been answered. Tim speaking to the Taperi and indicating to herself and him. Élendill speaking so rapidly– and angrily– before pulling Laura away from him. The look of astonishment on his face which made her laugh until her sides hurt.

Changing the subject rather abruptly, but burning with a desire to know the truth, Laura asked, 'Kiera, what was said when Tim and I arrived?'

'I don't think you'll like what you hear.' Kiera replied, 'I don't know if I can translate it word for word.'

'Please Kiera,' Laura said with a hint of apprehension.

'When you hugged each other, it looked like the two of you were in love. Élendill stated the obvious and Tim denied it, to which Élendill asked what his intentions were. The only reply she got was Tim telling her that you didn't take him seriously. Élendill then said that you would stay with us until you learned to see each other truly.'

There was a long silence as Laura digested what had been said.

'I didn't take him *seriously?*' she asked, bewildered, 'but we don't… he doesn't… I never…'

'I believe that Tim cares about you, Laura,' Kiera murmured.

'But he's in love with Millie,' Laura cried, clinging onto the last shred of a reality she understood. A moment ago she'd been helping support Kiera, now the roles had reversed at an alarming speed.

Kiera shrugged, 'Maybe. From what I can gather, Tim was the apprentice Millie was mooning over all those years ago.'

'That explains it,' Laura sniffed, 'he can't like me if he's lavishing all this attention on Millie. And to put the cherry on top, the Taperi Elders obviously don't approve of their behaviour.'

'I know.' Kiera lay down onto the bank and rolled onto her back. 'I'm sorry to say this Laura, but I've got a feeling that your stay here may not last for much longer.'

'Because of how Tim and Millie have been acting?'

'Yes.'

'But I need to work out the runes,' Laura cried, leaping to her feet in panic.

'What runes?'

'The ones on the hut's walls. They tell a message, an *important* message, but I'm not sure what it is yet.'

'Hang on,' Kiera said, holding out her hand to stop Laura's flow of worry. 'The runes on the abandoned hut's walls tell a message?'

'Yes!'

'Then we should take Élendill there, she might have a clue as to what they mean.'

'Thank you,' Laura said gratefully, amazed that she hadn't thought of it herself.

'We can take her there tomorrow, she'll be resting now. On that note, *I* should probably get to bed too.'

Laura glanced at the sky and was surprised to see stars winking back at her, their light cutting across the midnight blue sky.

'Goodnight, Kiera,' she smiled. 'Good luck for tomorrow with Finnikin.' Her friend nodded her thanks and headed off towards her hut, the baskets of clean dishes in her arms. Laura stared out at the glistening Gherna River for a while, before becoming startled by voices, both of which she recognised. She almost groaned in annoyance as she looked in their direction and saw the two figures coming closer.

'Oh darling!' Millie squealed as she gripped Tim's arm, trying not to slip in the soft mud. The sound of her voice shattered Laura's calm. Eyes rolling, she sat up and began to crawl away, trying not to make any noise.

'Careful,' Tim cried, 'I don't want to explain to Élendill about you getting stuck out here.'

'I don't care. I hate the Elders,' Millie replied. 'Let's forget about them and their stupid rules for tonight.' She began kissing him and he responded fondly, enfolding Millie into his arms. Laura glanced back as Millie pulled Tim's shirt over his head and stared open mouthed at his scar. Laura couldn't help staring herself, it had been a long time since she'd seen Tim's bare arms. It was still jagged and horrific, running from the crook of his elbow to the edge of his wrist. It was obviously the first time Millie had seen it.

'When did you get *that?*' Millie asked, her voice cold and expressionless. Laura could almost see Tim flinch.

'A long time ago.' He said, pulling his shirt roughly back over his head. But Millie put a hand on his arm. Laura noted that it was the unblemished arm she touched.

'Don't Tim, darling. I don't mind.' Tim paused and gazed at her.

'You really mean that?' he asked, and Laura could hear the catch in his voice. She wanted to scream out to him not to listen, to see what, to her was so obvious. In the moonlight Laura was able to see the greedy desire in Millie's eyes and it sickened her. She had seen Millie freeze on seeing the scar, and how she'd leaned backwards, subconsciously reeling from the disfiguration on his arm. Laura nearly cried out in frustration, why wasn't it apparent for him to see that here was a girl who only cared about one thing?

'Of course,' the other girl replied, proceeding to once again remove his shirt. Looking a little uncertain, Tim allowed Millie to continue.

He looked so strong, Laura found herself thinking, before becoming disgusted with herself. Why was she even there? It was apparent that Tim and Millie would want privacy; besides, she didn't want to see anymore. If Tim could allow himself to believe Millie's fake sincerity then he was truly blind to her obvious intentions. Laura wanted to be sick, and turned to try to make a silent get away. There was no way he cared about her now.

Crouching, she melded into the undergrowth to sneak away, wishing desperately that Tim and Millie wouldn't be so loud. She had gone about twenty metres away when she tripped over a branch and there was a pause in the kissing behind her.

'What was that?' Millie asked, concerned.

'I'll go and find out,' Tim said curiously.

'No, Tim darling, you can't leave me, it's not important.' Laura noted the desperation in Millie's voice.

'Sorry,' he replied, rising to his feet.

Not bothering anymore about staying quiet, Laura raced back towards the huts, slightly proud at the small scream that escaped from Millie's lips at the sudden commotion in the trees.

'Who's there?' Tim called out after her, before giving chase.

In their races, Tim had always won, head start or not. But this time, Laura had the advantage. Her breathing came in fast gasps as the feet behind her gradually drew closer. The darkness was choking her by the time she reached her destination. Skidding to a halt, she dashed into her hut, closing the door as softly as possible. Turning, Laura blew the candle out just as the footsteps paused outside her door, before moving on. She stood frozen, waiting for her eyes to adjust as she regulated her breathing. With her heart pounding in her ears at the close escape, Laura realised that she should have headed back to the village with Kiera.

She recalled what Kiera had told her that evening by the river. Could it have been true that Tim had romantic feelings for her? And how did she really feel about him? Laura's forehead wrinkled in thought, but the mysteries in her heart remained hidden, unwilling to tell her their secrets. But of one thing she was certain; if Tim stayed with Millie then her heart would break, because he deserved so much better.

With this troubled thought, she finally fell asleep, cheeks wet with unexplained tears.

Laura was up early, partly due to her desperation to know what was happening between Kiera and Finnikin, and partly due to having had a sleepless night filled with images of Millie, Tim and baby Giffleets. As the first traces of sunlight touched the horizon, she slipped out of her hut and hurried towards Kiera's hut.

She saw Kiera a moment later, huddled in her doorway. Kiera's face was terrified, and she turned to head back inside. Laura couldn't bear to see her new friend give in so easily to fear. She pelted after her, hissing out as she ran, 'Kiera.'

Kiera turned, startled, and then relaxed when she saw Laura.

'I should've known that you wouldn't allow me to try to get out of talking to him.' She said, 'but I can't Laura, I just can't.'

'Why?'

'Pride, I suppose.' Kiera sighed.

'Don't worry,' Laura whispered, peeping around the door, to look down the street. Finnikin had just left his hut, carrying his shirt and a sack of grain as he headed for the Willowings' stable.

'Go,' Laura muttered, '*now.*'

'But…' Kiera couldn't even protest, as Laura pushed her friend out into the middle of the street. Laura flitted back into the doorway to watch the proceedings. She felt a sense of accomplishment from her efforts and could only hope that something positive would arise from them.

Finnikin was oblivious to Kiera's presence as he bent over the water trough, splashing his face and chuckling at a Willowing who thrust its nose impatiently towards him. It nickered, desperate to be the first to be fed from the sack of grain in Finnikin's hand.

Kiera was standing motionless, then jolted herself into movement. For a few steps she seemed to walk like an automaton, slowly and jerkily. By the time she was halfway to Finnikin she'd stopped completely, too nervous to continue.

'Come on, Kiera,' Laura urged, her voice barely a murmur, 'you can do it.'

As if hearing her, Kiera moved another few tentative steps.

Finnikin reached out a hand and stroked the Willowing's neck, before pulling his shirt on over his head. The Willowing butted his hand, snuffling eagerly. He laughed and said something to it, but the Willowing was looking straight at Kiera, behind him. Finnikin turned and jumped in surprise.

Kiera looked at him, then the ground, then back into his eyes. She began to speak, but was too quiet for Laura to hear, no matter how much she craned her neck out into the street.

Finnikin's face was expressionless, not the most *promising* start.

Kiera was wringing her hands behind her back, then tried to keep them still, before the knuckles turned white and she went back to wringing them. She finished speaking and stood uncertainly, raising her eyes to see Finnikin's detached expression. Looking back down, she murmured something, before turning to move away, eyes shut. Laura wondered whether she was trying to keep tears at bay, or silently berating herself.

She headed back down the street, towards her hut.

Finnikin watched her go, a strange look falling over his face. Sorrow? Regret? But it was soon replaced by something new.

He strode after her, calling out her name. Kiera turned, surprised and still embarrassed. Finnikin covered the distance between them in a few strides and grabbed her shoulders, forcing Kiera to halt and face him.

He said something very quietly, before lifting Kiera's chin and kissing her.

Laura gave a low whoop of celebration and snuck out of Kiera's hut, into the shadows in-between buildings.

'Well, I think that's all settled now.'

She slipped over, taken aback by the unexpected voice and she turned to see Élendill, who was smiling, amused.

'How long have you been watching?' Laura asked, hoping against hope that she didn't sound too rude.

'I was watching them from the first moment *she*,' Élendill indicated Kiera, 'arrived in this village. Personally, I think that it's about time, they were both quite unhappy.'

'But what about the rule?' Laura questioned, a little bit worried about Kiera and Finnikin's safety, although, they weren't as bad as Tim and Millie. Yet.

'It can be our secret,' Élendill replied, 'I like to know when a wedding is to be expected in the village. We haven't had one in so many years.'

'Thank you,' Laura sighed, gratitude coursing through her veins.

'No need, child.' Élendill replied, turning to leave.

'Wait,' Laura cried, suddenly remembering what Kiera had suggested earlier. 'Are you busy this afternoon?'

'I have a meeting about the Giffleet attack yesterday. After that I'm free. Why?'

In a few moments Laura had told Élendill about the runes on the walls of the strange building, in the middle of the forest.

Élendill looked surprised, 'I never realised there was a building outside the walls. But I shall go with you this afternoon, child.'

'That would be splendid,' Laura smiled, relieved. Now another thing was out of the way. The only thing remaining was Tim and Millie, and how she could get out of the Taperi Village once she'd discovered what the runes meant. Tim and Millie would obviously want to remain, they had to, it was the moral and right thing to do. Especially after last night. Laura shuddered; they'd seemed so intimate on the beach, it disgusted her to even think about it. Just thinking about it brought back memories of her own experience, of pain and shame and horror. She shook her head to rid herself of the memory and hurried back to her hut to prepare for the oncoming day.

A few hours later, Élendill scrutinized the wall for a second before grabbing the paper and writing down the twenty-six different runes.

'This is our old alphabet, child,' she explained.

'Thank you, but is it the same as our own?'

'Yes, Laura. See, this one starts the twenty-six, your...' Élendill looked at Kiera who interpreted.

'Our "a".'

'Yes,' Élendill continued, 'I'll write them down in their correct order. I hope that it helps with whatever studies you're doing.'

'Thank you, Elder,' Laura said respectfully. 'I really appreciate what you've done.'

Élendill smiled and headed back in the direction of the camp. As she reached the trees, Millie and Tim emerged, his arms around her shoulders. Élendill glared at the openness of affection and turning, she noticed Laura duck back into the abandoned hut.

With a shake of her old head, the Elder moved onwards.

'I'm so grateful for Élendill's help.' Laura smiled, 'thanks Kiera.'

She had seen Tim and Millie but was determined to ignore them. Her mind still spun with emotions from the night before. Her eyes ached from lack of sleep, and she leaned a hand against the wall to steady herself.

'Glad to be of service,' Kiera grinned back from where she had been sitting on the floor.

'You know,' a scornful voice came from the doorway, 'I never understood your obsession with learning that stupid language.' Kiera leapt to her feet, startled.

'Millie, what are you doing here?'

'I might ask you the same thing,' Millie snapped, as she glanced around the room and her eyes settled with distaste on Laura, 'I see you've got company. You're so rude, Kiera, not even introducing us.' Kiera shifted her feet uncomfortably and shot a look full of meaning to Laura. Laura stared at Millie, who was checking her nails in the afternoon light.

'We don't need introducing,' she replied, before Tim or Kiera could say anything. 'Because we've already met. Or don't you remember, Millie?'

'Don't lie, you silly girl,' Millie said coldly, stepping away from Tim. 'I would be sure to remember someone like *you*.'

'Then let me jog your memory,' Laura replied, 'We met in Yorket, about six years ago.'

'You?' Millie cried, 'you're the bitch who stole Tim away from me!' Tim and Kiera's eyes met in combined surprise. He stepped away, and Kiera covered her mouth to prevent a gasp at Millie's dramatic outburst.

'I didn't steal anything,' Laura said angrily, 'and even if I did, you've got him *back* now, so what's the point in complaining?' Millie's mouth opened and closed in silent fury, giving the impression of a stunned mullet.

'Laura…' Tim began.

'Shut up,' Laura snapped, 'if she can't see the truth, I'll have to show it to her.'

'Don't you dare talk to him like that!' Millie cried, flinging herself back across the room to clasp Tim's neck, as if she were a human shield.

'Why don't you just kiss him better then?' Laura retorted, storming out of the door, heading away from the hut and the village. She needed to get away, to breathe and calm down. She'd never felt so much anger before, and her hand was hovering by her pocket, itching to flip her dezmian. It would be like that day all those years ago by the lake when she had been pushed too far. She would make Millie pay. The magic called to her, luring her towards doing something she would regret.

'Laura,' Tim called, standing frozen in the doorway, staring at the pictures of the runes on the walls. 'What are these?'

'Why the hell should you care?' Laura shouted, 'all you think about is *her*.' She spun at the edge of the trees and pointed a quivering finger at Millie, who was rooted to the spot.

'How dare you,' Millie shrieked, 'you're just jealous, you just want him for yourself.'

Something in Laura snapped. She strode back and slapped Millie across the face, before pushing her roughly into the doorway and into Tim's arms.

'You know what?' she said furiously, 'maybe you're right. Maybe I feel *terrible* because every time I see you and Tim together, I regret that he chose *you* to be his girlfriend.' She glared at Tim who, like everyone else, was rooted to the spot. 'You deserve better than her, Tim. She only wants sex, and you know it.'

'Liar!' Millie shrieked, although her face had flushed crimson, 'I bet your mother was glad to get rid of you when you became a Robin. She's better off without having a bitch for a daughter.'

Laura quivered for an instant before glaring into Millie's eyes. Her reflection looked terrifying, dangerous even. It would've frightened her if she hadn't been so angry. The magic was begging her to be unleashed, to make this girl pay for her words.

'You'll regret saying that,' she said quietly, before reaching back and smashing her fist into Millie's face. Satisfaction coursed through her veins when she felt the cartilage break. Millie screamed, clutching her nose as blood seeped down her face. Laura felt laughter rock through her body, cruelly delighted at what she'd just done.

'I hope that you're happy with his love,' she said curtly, 'but know that you don't deserve it.'

With that, she turned and ran into the forest, heading away from everything.

'You really love me?' was the last thing Laura heard Millie say, but then the footsteps from the night before began to follow her again.

'Slow down!' Tim cried out, but it only made Laura run faster.

Her hair was whipping in the breeze, getting into her eyes. She angrily pushed the coppery locks away. Fingertips touching something wet, Laura realised that she was crying. Now that the tears were there, they wouldn't go away.

Soon her vision was blurry and she came to a halt, leaning against a tree for support, making Tim skid in the mud to slow down.

'Laura?' he asked. Once realising that she was crying, he tried to hug her. Laura furiously broke free, panting and shaking her head.

'Why didn't you tell me about the runes?' he asked, annoyed, 'we could've worked on the map toge…'

'Don't you *dare* say "together",' Laura hissed, 'in fact, don't say "we" either.'

'Why?' he asked mildly, which made Laura stamp her foot in frustration.

'It's over, all right? You'll want to stay here with Millie,' she spat, 'I'll continue my quest alone.'

'No, you won't,' Tim growled. 'Where you go, I go.'

'That's not true,' Laura cried, 'where *you* go *Millie* goes. And I don't want to go anywhere with *her*. I didn't break her nose by accident, Tim. Anyway, you showed all your feelings for each other last night by the river.'

There was a long pause before Tim spoke, and when he did his voice was icy. 'It was you?'

'Yes.'

'Why didn't you come up to us?' He ran a hand through his hair, a sure sign that he was nervous. 'Or call out, or *something…*'

'I'm amazed you two didn't *see* me,' Laura snapped ferociously, 'I was sitting down quite serenely until you came along, ruining the moment. The fact that you were both so loud didn't help.'

Tim blushed and a part of her felt stirrings of shame. He replied, 'we didn't do anything, Laura.' In an instant she saw red, her ears roared with a whooshing sound as an irate fury settled over her.

'That's what they *all* say. Don't you dare lie to me, Timothy Crow. I *know* what I heard.'

'And *I* know what I did,' he retorted.

'Then *what* were you doing?' she shot back.

There was another uncomfortable silence, which Laura broke by shaking her head. 'I thought better of you, Tim. She's cruel and she's only after one thing. Why *her?*'

'You don't understand.' Tim growled.

'Then enlighten me.'

'I don't love Millie, Laura.' He paused, 'she's just a friend.'

'Oh, I can tell that you guys are *just friends* when you're all over each other in public. I mean I knew you liked girls, Tim, you've dated at least half of them at the Temple. But Millie? How could you have stooped so *low?*'

'Why do you even care, Laura?' Tim asked suddenly, eyes watching her face keenly.

Laura averted her gaze.

'I don't know,' She snapped, 'I *don't* know, and I *don't* care.'

'Yes, you do.' He moved forward and held her shoulders. 'Look into my eyes and say it again.'

'I don't know, Tim.' Laura's voice had dropped to a terrified whisper, 'I don't know and don't...'

Their eyes locked and suddenly Laura was unable to speak. Blinking, she opened her mouth but nothing came out. Almost immediately her mouth closed, if only to not embarrass herself further.

'I don't love her, Laura.' Tim said softly, but his voice was full of passion. 'I love you.'

'But…' Laura began, however Tim cut her off by placing a finger against her lips.

Then he leaned down and kissed her.

After a moment, Laura relaxed and kissed him back; with closed eyes, she allowed her heart to begin to tell its own story.

It seemed like an hour had passed when they broke away and stared at each other. Almost immediately Laura's mind overrode her heart's desires, and she said, 'I have to go.'

Without another word, she stumbled away into the trees, leaving Tim leaning against the tree, forehead against the bark.

Chapter Twelve

Laura avoided Tim for the rest of that day, choosing instead to spend her time fishing with Kiera and Finnikin. She discovered within a few hours that she would never have the patience of a saint, and therefore would not be a very good fisherwoman. She discovered within a few minutes how awkward it could be to be a third wheel. It didn't help that every time she watched them together– the way they moved to accommodate the other's needs, the slight brush of a hand on arm or the faint blush of colour in Kiera's cheek when he was around– that her mind kept reflecting on what Tim had said to her, and whether she believed it.

During the past six years, she believed she had known Tim well, exceedingly well even. He was kind, funny, had a strong dislike of sun-dried tomatoes and loved roast beef. Yet it seemed that whenever Millie was nearby, he was a different person, someone she barely knew at all. Someone she didn't want to know. It reminded her of their time in Yorket, and how he had acted then, his unkindness and unwillingness to be around her.

Now, however, his behaviour was making no sense. How could a boy sleep with a girl one night and then the next day declare his love for another? It was against every principle that she knew, and was unfair– though she hated to admit it– to both Millie and herself. What was going on inside his head?

The day passed in a blur and night soon fell, but Laura's thoughts still pursued her, like hunting hounds chasing a fox. The ideas, the possibilities, swirled through her mind until she could bear no more.

I will leave him, she decided as the moon reached its zenith in the sky. I will leave him and Millie here, where they can do what they like. As they had already slept together, it felt like the right thing to do. She couldn't believe that they hadn't done anything, like Tim had said. She'd heard how close they had gotten last night, and who was to say that Tim hadn't returned to that secluded spot by the river once he had failed to track her down?

The pleas of her heart were silenced by this thought, and as she lay down her eyes misted up with tears, repenting, pining, longing for something that could never be.

The next morning was bright and cheerful. This particular weather did not sit well with Laura's emotions, and she decided to stay in her hut and begin to translate the runes on the map. As soon as she began, she realised that it was a much longer process than she had first thought. Some runes were very similar except for a miniscule detail, perhaps a dot or a line, which forced Laura to squint her eyes and hold the paper up to the light in order to see them properly. Slowly, agonizingly, she wrote out the letters of the first words. It reminded her of playing hangman with her brother when they were little, and for an instant her eyes squeezed shut as her hand shook with suppressed emotion.

'Laura?'

She glanced up, and the hand holding the quill slipped, causing a long line of ink to spread across the page.

'Damn,' she muttered, before grabbing another piece of paper and scribbling down the words furiously.

Tim sat down next to her and watched as she hastily wrote onto the paper.

'You don't need to rush,' he commented, 'we're not leaving yet. We've got plenty of time.'

'You *would* say that,' Laura grumbled, 'but there's no "we". And you're not allowed in here. Remember?'

'I thought…' Tim said after a moment.

'Well,' Laura interrupted, laughing bitterly, 'you thought wrong.'

'But there's still time, Laura,' he added, with a tone of desperation.

'No, Tim,' She murmured. 'Do you think I'm the only one who noticed how you and Millie were behaving? It's funny that when we arrived you told me we had to respect the rules and abide by them, but you didn't. The Elders aren't happy, so I don't think that our stay here will be for much longer.'

'Our?'

She flung her hands up in exasperation, '*my* stay will not be for much longer. *You* shall probably return to Venetica.'

'I could still accompany you.'

'With Millie? *No, thank you.*'

'Who says that I'll bring Millie along?'

She turned to him, the thought had never occurred to her.

'Well, she loves you. And you lo…'

'Don't say I love her,' Tim said swiftly, 'didn't you listen to what I said yesterday? I love you *and only you*, Laura. It's been like that for years. Now, move over and let's have a look at this translation.' Laura stared into his eyes, unable to fathom whether what he said was true or false, all the while praying that it was true.

As if reading her thoughts, Tim leaned closer until he was only a hair breadth away. She knew he was going to kiss her and she shut her eyes, full of nervous anticipation.

'Well, if that's how you feel, Tim,' a new voice said from the doorway and Laura's eyes opened with a jerk. 'It's over.'

They turned and saw Millie flick her hair dramatically and storm away from the hut. Laura raised her eyebrows at Tim and he stared back, eyes wide with mock horror. Within one second, they were both laughing, and Laura clutched her sides, eyes watering.

'Did you see her face?' Laura gasped, as she caught her breath, 'it was *hilarious.*'

Tim smiled and shook his head in amazement, 'I don't even know how she knew I was here. I haven't seen her since breakfast, she seemed a bit put out after yesterday.'

'Did it take her a long time to calm down?' Laura asked, 'after I left?'

'I believe so,' Tim replied, 'I didn't go back to see.'

'That must have been traumatic,' she smirked, 'especially since her *darling* wasn't there to support her through that difficult time.'

Tim chuckled and leaned across her, arm brushing hers as he pulled the map closer. Laura bit back a smile and picked up her quill, dipping the nib in the inkpot and settled down to write the next part of the translation.

Their peaceful revelry was not long. Within thirty minutes, Kiera crashed into Laura's hut and found them perusing the map and the secret message, which now read: 'In the forest, behind the waterfall in Renderfell.'

'Laura?' Kiera cried as she stumbled through the door. Her face was tracked with tears and her chest heaved with suppressed sobs. Kiera's eyes moved from Laura to Tim, who sat up, concerned. 'What are *you* doing here?' she hissed with vehemence. Tim stared back, his expression of concern changing to utter bewilderment.

'What's wrong?' Laura asked, glancing from Tim to Kiera and back again.

'He's not meant to be in here,' Kiera said, before turning to Tim, 'the Elders want to speak to you.'

'Why?' he asked.

'They have a request for you,' Kiera replied coldly, 'now get out. They won't take kindly to tardiness.'

'What did you do?' Laura asked him.

'I don't know.' He responded as he walked out of the door.

'Why was he here?' Kiera demanded. 'You know the rules, Laura. He isn't *allowed* in here.'

'Well, we've been working on this.' Laura indicated to the map. 'We had a job to do before we came here, and we intend to see it through to the end. Why are you so angry with him? What do the Elders want him to do?'

Kiera stared at her, wide eyed. 'They want him to lead the search party to rescue Millie. She went out of the camp and was taken by a flock of Giffleets. The sentries tried to stop them, but they were too fast. I can still hear her screams.' Kiera paused, gulping for breath, 'the sentries tried to prevent her from leaving but she wouldn't listen. She didn't listen.'

'It's okay,' Laura soothed, and hugged Kiera, who had started trembling with delayed shock. 'They'll find her.'

'The Elders want Tim to lead the rescue party,' Kiera repeated, as if to herself. But her eyes were glued on Laura's expression.

'What if he doesn't want to lead it?' Laura asked.

'The Elders have decreed that it will be so,' Kiera replied, a furrow in her brow. 'He doesn't have a choice.'

'Then I'll go with him,' Laura replied as she took a sip from her water canteen, 'when are they leaving?'

Kiera shrugged, 'ask Élendill, she is going to go with him. I think she wants to see him prove himself worthy of Millie.'

Laura choked and spluttered, '*worthy of Millie*? She isn't worthy for anyone!'

'That's cruel, Laura.'

'But it's true,' she snapped, before another thought hit her. For a moment she looked down, eyes frowning into the dusty ground, trying to discern the different particles as her mind whirled in circles. When she spoke, her voice was slow and strained with tension.

'What do you mean, Élendill is going to watch him prove himself?'

Kiera fidgeted uncomfortably, 'Millie was talking to Élendill the other night and said that she wanted the priest to perform a hand-fasting ritual today.'

Laura had frozen in place, 'she wanted to marry him?'

'It would have only been a matter of time, Laura,' Kiera replied softly. Tentatively she reached out to grasp Laura's hand but Laura jerked away, moving to the other side of the hut.

'Did he know about it?'

'What?'

Laura clasped the inkpot until her hands were white. 'Did. He. Know. About. It?' Her words were enunciated through clenched teeth.

'I doubt it,' Kiera said, 'but I think she would have told him sooner or later. She's head over heels for him, you know.'

'Oh yes,' Laura replied sarcastically, as a load of tension left her shoulders and she slumped down on her bed in relief. The image of Millie's face, twisted with hurt and loathing filled her mind, and she felt a small twinge of pity. It was small, but it was there.

'If she hadn't raised it with Élendill then the Elders would probably force them to marry anyway,' Kiera continued, unaware of her friend's feelings. 'You must admit, it *has* been almost indecent seeing them in public together doing… what they do.' She halted, embarrassed at Laura's cold stare.

'I didn't think that I would hear you say that, Kiera,' she said, 'I mean, we both don't come from this world, and in Venetica people behave like Tim and Millie and it isn't criticised to the same degree as it is here. But what you just said— it makes you sound like you're trying to be one of the Elders.'

'You didn't spend your life working in a bar where drunk men fondled and dribbled all over you,' Kiera said coolly, 'you don't know what it's like to hate your life and to be willing to do anything, no matter how high the cost, to change it. You spent your life holed up in the Temple of the Nest where you had friends, food, lodging and education to boot. And don't forget the wonderful life you have ahead of you: travelling and seeing multiple worlds, being paid to protect the Barriers and such. Well, while you had this charmed life, the rest of us had to struggle with reality.'

There was a long silence, eventually broken by Laura pulling her saddlebags out from under the bed and stuffing items into them haphazardly, not caring whether the inkpot was under the dress or the knife on top of her map. It didn't matter. All that did matter was that she left. Innately, she knew that her visit with the Taperi had come to an end.

'What are you doing?' Kiera asked.

'What does it look like I'm doing?' Laura snapped, 'I'm packing. Once we've rescued Millie, I'm leaving. I don't want to be here anymore. Simple as that.'

Kiera gaped and watched for a few minutes before saying imploringly, 'but you must stay, Laura. I'm sorry for being so rude, don't leave.'

'If you think I'm leaving because of one petty argument then you're wrong,' Laura replied curtly, she didn't have time for this. Who knew when the rescue party would be leaving? 'I can't stay longer than a month in a new world anyway. Robins— as you say— lead a charmed life, but we can't remain in one world for too long, otherwise we fade away into nothing. Besides, why is it so important that I stay? I don't see any specific need or reason. It's not like I contribute to the Tribe's wellbeing.'

Kiera looked at her friend sadly. 'Do you love him?'

For a second Laura was thrown off-guard, then she said, 'I don't know. But I *do* know that while he wouldn't want to marry Millie, he will probably do the honourable thing and save her.'

'But what if Tim and Millie had announced an engagement earlier?' Kiera probed.

'I would already be gone,' Laura said, as she squeezed her last shawl into the saddlebags and forced them shut. She didn't bother looking at Kiera's expression, she already knew what it would be.

'I knew it,' Kiera punched the air triumphantly. Laura was startled, partly from the outburst, but perhaps more from the fact that it was so out of character.

'I knew you loved him,' Kiera continued, 'it's obvious. All one has to do is look at your face when he's around you, it hides nothing.'

Unconsciously, Laura's hands rose to her cheeks, feeling as the blush spread across them. Were her feelings really that obvious? How could they be when she barely recognised them herself?

Her initial response was to deny and keep denying, to Kiera, to herself. Yet something held her back, forcing her to see what had slowly been growing over the years, lying dormant until the time was right for her to know. How could this be happening?

'Laura?'

But he loves me, she thought, he said he loved me and not Millie, so that must count for something, right?

'Laura?'

She had to trust him, she saw that now. If he loved her like he claimed, then he would remain constant, no matter what. But all the same, perhaps she ought to join the rescue party, just in case…

'Laura.' Kiera shook her shoulders and Laura jerked out of her thoughts.

'What?'

'The party's leaving,' her friend replied, pulling on her arm, forcing her to keep up as they ran out of the hut, Laura's heavy bags weighing them down.

'I thought you were meant to be travelling light,' Kiera puffed.

'I packed the essentials,' Laura replied between gasps.

'What would that be?'

'Books, mostly,' she said, 'you can never be too sure

about what might happen and what you might need.'

'How did your Willowing cope coming here?' Kiera asked as they reached the stables. All of the stalls, save Elaret's, were empty. In a feverish haste, Laura drew out her dezmian and tossed it haphazardly into the air muttering under her breath. With a clenching tug at her stomach that left her temporarily winded, a saddle appeared on Elaret's back and the saddlebags flew out of Kiera's hands and settled comfortably behind the saddle.

For maybe the first time since they had met, Kiera was speechless.

'That was… wow,' she said.

Laura hugged her friend briefly, before mounting Elaret and leading him gently out of the stables, Kiera trotting behind.

'Goodbye, Kiera,' she said, 'I don't think that I'll come back here afterwards, no matter what the outcome is. I hope that you and Finnikin have a long happy life, I'm sorry that I won't be here for the wedding.'

'I understand why,' Kiera smiled, and tears filled her eyes, 'I'll miss you, Laura.'

Despite the time they had spent together, Laura did not feel the need for an emotional farewell, one that lingered on the goodbyes and delayed the leaving as much as possible. This wasn't like when she left the Temple; leaving the Taperi, she only felt a slight twinge of regret, which was miniscule in comparison to the relief and excitement at continuing her quest. She had achieved a lot during her stay with the tribe, primarily locating the ancient alphabet so that she could translate the runes on the map. She didn't really need to be with them any longer.

'Goodbye Kiera,' she repeated, not wanting to delay for a

moment. With a slight nudge, Elaret was off, cantering through the village to reach the forest where she could track the rescue party. As she rode past, the Taperi called out, begging her to come back, saying that the forest was not safe, that she couldn't leave now, not with the Giffleet menace so strong.

Yet somehow Laura knew that the forest would not harm her– maybe frighten or shock– but not hurt. She'd felt a connection to the Giffleets ever since witnessing the Taperi killing one. A part of her longed to see its family with her own eyes, to discover if the Giffleets were really as bad as the Taperi said.

As she left the tribe's village and entered the forest, she saw scuff marks in the earth and knew that the rescue party was not long gone. It would be easy to follow their progress, for it seemed that at least fifty Willowings had been here, all racing into the heart of the forest. She could only assume that the Giffleets would live there, for during all the time she had been with the Taperi there had been no trace of the strange creatures close to the river or within the outskirts of the forest.

Elaret whinnied uncomfortably and halted.

'Giddy-up, Elaret,' Laura said, nudging his sides again, 'we have to catch up with them.'

As if he could sense her urgency, her mount obeyed, but she could feel a new tension under his taut skin. For a few minutes all was silent, except for the thudding of Elaret's hooves on the soft earth and Laura's breathing. The forest itself was completely silent, exactly as it had been when they first arrived. The silence seemed to be full of anticipation, of waiting for something inevitable to happen.

Soon Laura could discern the sound of the rescue party

ahead, the crashing of breaking timber as Willowings forged their way through the foliage in hot pursuit of the Giffleets.

'They aren't opting for the stealthy approach, are they?' Laura muttered to Elaret, who snorted in agreement. Together they slowed down, and Laura stared transfixed at the sudden path of destruction in front of her.

The trees should have been thickly spread around her, the ferns on the ground growing tall and strong as they tried to reach the distant sunlight. Instead, the ferns were trampled into the earth and the trees were lopsided, almost as if they had been pushed and battered until they had reached breaking point. Elaret moved closer and Laura saw deep cuts in the bark, like something had cut savagely into it again and again; a memory of the spikes on the Giffleets' backs came to mind.

'So *this* is how they keep the spikes sharpened,' she said, and Elaret shied backwards, snorting in fear. In a moment Laura had dismounted and was stroking his nose, softly murmuring calm words over and over. After a while, the Willowing had settled down enough to move onwards. The forest was now deathly silent, even more so than it had been the day that she and Tim had arrived. This worried Laura; surely she should be able to hear the rescue party, who had not tried to hide their pursuit.

'I don't like this, Elaret,' she muttered, glancing around uneasily, her hand hovering over the dagger sheathed at her belt. She had only ever used it to cut up meat or rope, never against another living creature, the idea of using it in battle sickened her.

Within moments her mind was assaulted with images of home from before she had been taken, before the house had burnt to the ground. Family outings to the zoo when she was a child, a younger Laura laughing as she fed the animals from a small brown paper bag, her parents watching in amusement. Fred stood beside them with a look of boredom on his face– he was ten and far too old for these embarrassing trips to the zoo. Subconsciously Laura smiled at the memory. Even from that age she would never have dreamed of hurting an animal, not even one of the more fearsome ones. It was just against everything that her parents had taught her.

Elaret snuffled into her shoulder and she gasped in shock, drawing out of her thoughts and raising her eyes to see a creature standing not two feet away. It was made from different kinds of wood, which spun and twirled as the creature's human form changed.

One second it appeared like a small round man, with bright eyes burned into the wood, the moss shifted into eyebrows and a crack in the bark curved into a smile.

Then within seconds, just as her eyes had adjusted to his form, the creature changed. It was elongating, stretching upwards until it was almost as tall as one of the trees around her. Roots and vines stretched up the monstrous legs, twisting around and around, apparently holding the whole creature together.

Then the form changed yet again, in a flash of green light. Laura covered her eyes and then a hand– covered in twigs and leaves but still undeniably a hand– gently pulled her arm down. She found herself looking into berry-coloured eyes amid a mass of oak leaves, and promptly fainted.

Chapter Thirteen

A splash of cold water brough Laura back to consciousness with a horrible shiver. She cried out in protest and started rubbing her arms, forcing heat back into her body.

What had happened? Where was Elaret? Where were the rescue party? Questions tumbled through her mind like a fast-flowing stream upon a rapid.

There was a sigh behind her. It sounded like the wind as it passed through the trees on a cold winter's night. *Trees…*

With a deep breath to steady her nerves, which, a mere moment ago had deserted her, Laura rose to her feet and turned.

The tree creature regarded her as she took a step backwards and her hand flicked to the dagger hilt. Her eyes widened as her hand passed through air; her dagger was gone. She was defenceless, at the mercy of this… this… *thing.*

'What do you want?' It seemed the most practical question, after all. She could only hope it would understand.

Its arm rose and pointed at her before indicating to the devastation which surrounded them.

'You want me to repair this?'

It nodded, eyes still watching her intently. Laura's mind raced as she looked around, wondering how to escape. The creature was blocking the obvious path she would take, which seemed to lead further into the forest, further into the devastation.

'I can't,' she replied, 'there is no way that I could move these trees so that they stood tall again. The ferns are all covered by soil and I don't know how to undo whatever caused the lacerations on the trees. It's impossible. I'm sorry.'

There was a piercing shriek and the creature advanced, leafy hair flying in a sudden rush of wind. Laura clutched onto the nearest tree branch as Elaret whinnied in distress and hurtled into the forest.

'Elaret! No!' Now she was defenceless and alone.

The creature clutched her wrist, and she stared into its eyes which were squinting at her in fury.

'How do you expect me to change this?' she cried into its face, her heart pounding fearfully. Would it kill her now? Eat and chew on her bones? Or would she be thrown up into the air and carried away by the wind, which was becoming stronger and fiercer by the second?

The creature let out another eerie shriek, and Laura's hair stood on end. It was ethereal, almost unimaginable, that such a sound could be made. It tore at the heartstrings and brought tears to the eyes. With a sweeping motion of the creature's free arm, the wind came to a sudden halt. For a second they stared at each other, and Laura started to realise what the creature expected her to do.

'Why me?' she asked, 'why not one of the Taperi? Or the Giffleets?'

The look in the creature's eye quelled any further questions. It let go of her wrist and moved closer to one of the fallen trees. It started a mournful cadence, swaying back and forth, stroking the bark with loving hands. Within moments it was joined by others of its kind, each adding their own lonely cries, until the music reached a crescendo, leaving Laura breathless.

The creature stepped back towards her and this time she didn't shy away.

'Have you tried talking to the Taperi?'

A nod.

'The Giffleets?'

Another nod.

'And neither listened?'

The creature shook its head and gestured to the destruction around them. The others copied its example. It was disconcerting and Laura blinked, forcing the entirety of her attention on the leader.

'What are you?' she murmured, edging slightly closer, her voice full of sudden curiosity.

It was almost like the creature before her smiled, and it released another long sigh.

'I can't bring the trees back.' It was a statement, pure and simple.

Another, sadder, nod.

'I've never done anything like this before,' she continued, as her hand reached into her pocket and drew out the dezmian, twirling it absently through her fingers. 'I don't know how much power I will use up, it might be too much, too dangerous, I don't know...' She trailed off, speaking more to herself than the watching creatures.

Her attention was caught when one of the creatures placed itself on top of one of the torn trees. The creature stared at her for a moment before it floated into the trunk, disappearing completely from view.

'You're tree spirits,' she said, awed. 'That's why you care so much about the forest. That's why you're more pacified.' All of a sudden, she remembered last summer when Tash had been reading aloud from one of the many books in the library.

'*Tree spirits,*' she had said, '*are benign creatures often found in heavily shrouded woodland. They are rarely violent yet highly protective of the groves in which they live. These groves are mostly referred to as being sacred, and the creatures who dwell in them are considered guardians of the natural balance.*'

There had been more to it, she was sure, but there was no way she could remember any more than that.

'So this,' Laura said, alight with newfound understanding, 'is your grove.'

This sad, desecrated place, she thought, is their home. There's no way I can't try to make things right. There's no way of knowing how long it will last, but I'm sure they know that.

'Very well,' she said, her voice rang out across the clearing and for a moment she was surprised. 'I will try to help set things right on the condition,' she looked at the assembled spirits, 'that you help me reach the Taperi party who rode through not very long ago.'

The spirits nodded and she was thrown as the heads changed shape again.

I wish they wouldn't do that, she thought. Then she wasn't concentrating on them anymore, in her mind she could picture what she wanted to happen, and with a flick the dezmian left her grasp and turned thrice in the air. With a harsh cry of some guttural words, Laura fell to the ground as her legs gave way. She caught the dezmian and clutched her stomach, which felt like it was being slowly and inexorably ripped from her body.

With a tremendous effort she looked up from the ground and tears filled her eyes.

It was *working*.

Within moments, the clearing was undergoing a drastic change. The ferns and trees shrunk in on themselves, withering away in the light. The leaves turned to mulch and the wood rotted, decomposing into the ground.

Laura's breath came in short gasps and she felt her strength leaving her; but it wasn't finished yet.

Grass and saplings sprouted from the earth, reaching upwards, growing unnaturally fast. Ferns rose around the bases of trees, leaves stretching out to the sunlight. With a resounding crack, the bark on the trees fell off, and as it fell all traces of the lacerations left with it. New bark appeared, hardening into shells around the trees, and at that point Laura's eyesight glazed over. There was a final wrench on her stomach and she was left, exhausted and weak in newborn grass.

The tree spirits gave Laura half an hour's respite before trying to poke her back to life. However it was a soft nuzzling that roused Laura from a doze, and she clutched onto Elaret, stroking his neck feebly. A tree spirit reached down and helped her up, lifting her into Elaret's saddle. After a moment, another spirit was reaching forwards with an offering of water held precariously in a leaf. Laura's hands shook too much when she tried to take it, so all she could do was lean forward and try to swallow as it was poured down her throat.

'Thank you,' she whispered. The spirit shook its head and indicated the group before bowing in her direction. When it had stood up, it pointed at Laura's final contribution to the clearing– a small pond of water, which bubbled upwards from an underground spring– and then back to Laura herself. Once more the creatures bowed.

'It might encourage the Giffleets to drink instead of using your trees as sharpening posts.' Laura said feebly, 'it was the least I could do.'

The spirits sighed in unison before disappearing, save one, back into the trees. Laura smiled at the remaining spirit, who also was the first one she'd met, and watched as it took Elaret's reins from her hands and slowly led the Willowing into the trees.

Once out of the clearing, they followed the path of torn branches and trampled undergrowth.

If it was this easy, Laura thought, I needn't have asked him to show me the way.

But a moment later, the spirit tugged Elaret off the obvious path and hurried them through thick undergrowth, whilst omitting a faint buzzing that sounded like a hive of angry bees.

'What…?' Laura began, but the tree spirit covered her mouth with a mossy hand, efficiently cutting off her words as a crashing of branches filled the air. Laura glanced in its direction and froze.

Thirty Giffleets were on the rampage, throwing themselves with all their might at the surrounding trees. For a second Laura didn't understand what they were doing, until she heard a familiar voice cry out, 'Archers, fire!'

Tim, she thought, and peered closer through the foliage. Sure enough, the rescue party were in the trees, rocking from side to side as the Giffleets smashed against the trunks. A shower of arrows rained down, but fell off the Giffleets' scaly hides, useless.

The archers roared out in unison as they let loose another volley, antagonising the creatures even more. Elaret shied away from the noise, pawing the ground in discomfort. Laura lost view of the fight and frowned in annoyance. The trees had been bending too much, surely they would break soon and the rescue party would be mauled alive. Could she help them? What could pacify the Giffleets long enough for the Taperi to get to safety?

The tree spirit was watching her intently, and she got the feeling that it could understand the direction in which her thoughts had turned. After laying a calming hand on Elaret's neck, she faced it and said, 'what can I do?'

The spirit indicated to the trees and then Laura. Its mossy features contracted, as if it were furrowing its brow, before it nodded and indicated the trees again.

'You want me to climb?'

It nodded, and Laura was flicked by the long strands of leaves on its head. She blinked, ignoring the stinging sensation on her cheek.

'But what would I do once I've *climbed* the tree?' she whispered fiercely, 'I'm not even that *good* at tree climbing. That was always Tim's specialty.'

The tree spirit just looked at her.

'My magic is very weak, I find it difficult to walk on my own and I'm feeling faint. Besides, once I'm up there, what could I possibly do to change *that?* She indicated the scene with a jab of her finger. The Giffleets had changed their tack. Instead of beating themselves into the trees they were now rubbing their backs along the bark. The spikes on their backs were sharpening and the trees weakening. She could see the archers trying and failing to strike them with arrows. It seemed as if those creatures were invulnerable. They didn't even flinch as the arrows struck them, before bouncing harmlessly away.

Suddenly she felt herself rising upwards and she shrieked, clawing at the twiggy hands that held her aloft, floating five metres from Elaret's saddle. Elaret whinnied and lifted into the air, circling upwards towards them.

Laura glared at the spirit, who was clinging onto her as if its life depended on it.

'Put me down!' she cried and forced herself to stop struggling. 'Please,' she added.

The spirit glided over the tree branches until they were suspended over the fight, Laura clinging onto its wooden arm. She shrieked again and this time the combatants below heard it and paused for a moment, glancing around to find the source. Even the Giffleets had halted in their slow destruction of the trees to look from side to side, noses in the air as they caught Laura's scent. With a sudden eldritch cry, one of them jerked away from the trees, and didn't stop until it was exactly underneath where Laura hung. She shut her eyes, grip tightening as the spirit gave a soft, sorrowful sigh. Laura stared into its dark gaze and, too late, realised what it would do.

'No...' she began, but then she was falling, straight past the speechless Taperi onto the Giffleet's back, landing centimetres behind the spikes which glinted in the light. Her body jolted in pain and she was winded from the descent.

'Laura! What on earth...?' Tim cried as her head spun from shock.

The Giffleet gave another loud cry and sped off into the trees, followed closely by its family. Together they ran through the trees and foliage, not pausing for anything. Laura clutched onto the spikes to avoid being thrown off and crushed under the stampede.

She couldn't believe that the spirit had let her be carried away by the Giffleets, that it had dropped her from such a height. She had helped them! After using up all of her magic restoring their sacred grove to its original state and adding a water source to boot, *this* was how they repaid her? It was unthinkable.

There was a swooshing noise from above her head, and she looked upwards. In hot pursuit of the Giffleets was Elaret and behind him…

'Laura!' Tim called, urging Iris onwards, wings flapping in desperation to catch up with the Giffleets. Elaret dived towards them and narrowly avoided being stabbed as a Giffleet jumped over a log, spikes whistling below his belly. Laura watched her Willowing, eyes wide. He had never acted like this before, she hadn't even known that they could be actively aggressive. With an uncanny screech, Elaret turned and swooped again, hooves grazing the Giffleets' scaly hides.

'Laura, take my hand,' Tim said, reaching out towards her, his voice full of fear. Laura stretched out her arm in immediate response, but the Giffleet beneath her, as if sensing what was happening, swerved to the left, putting yet more distance between them.

Branches whipped into Laura's face, catching on her clothes and her hair, as if a hundred hands were pulling and tearing with reckless abandonment. Shielding her head with her arm, she screamed, bending over the spikes as she tried to protect herself. The tree spirits must be angry, she thought, her hand throbbed in pain.

Blood was seeping out of a jagged cut on her palm and she winced. There was no way she could use magic to heal it, so she stuffed her hand into the folds of her skirt, winding it around and around until the skirt had pulled up further than she normally allowed, revealing some of the jagged scars which stretched down her legs.

The Giffleet raced onwards before making a sharp turn and throwing Laura through the air and into a pool of water.

For a moment she was too shocked from the cold to do anything; water rushed into her ears, up her nose and into her mouth. Laura kicked her legs and her head broke through the surface. She choked and coughed as she pulled herself onto the grass nearby, and a small whinny alerted her that she was not alone. She turned her head and saw two newborn Giffleets, staggering towards her on unsteady legs. There was a cry and the Giffleet Laura had been riding jumped between Laura and the babies.

She didn't notice that she was surrounded by the creatures until she got to her feet, albeit unsteadily. Giffleets emerged from the trees, their red eyes burning with hatred.

In the clearing she couldn't hear any sounds of pursuit. It was almost as if they had entered a section of the forest where no one could trace them. This idea did not do anything to soothe Laura's nerves, which were already past breaking point.

'What do you want?' she asked wearily, then more to herself than them, 'I don't know why I'm bothering to ask, it's not as if you can understand me.'

'Of course they understand you,' a voice from the shadows said. 'They want to know what happened to the one who was caught by the Tribesman.'

'Who's there?' Laura cried, 'show yourself!' Her heart was pounding and she took a deep breath, trying to be brave but unable to stop her body quivering.

'I'm afraid I cannot oblige you,' the voice said, a silky whisper in the trees. 'I am not, so to say, of this world, like you.'

'So what?' Laura snapped. 'Why can't I see you?'

The owner of the voice laughed and the sound jangled Laura's nerves. There was something about it that was scarily familiar.

'I am not invisible, but I am not quite visible either.'

'Stop talking in riddles,' Laura muttered. 'Who are you and what do you want with me? Where are my friends? And where am *I?*'

'So many questions all at once.' She could almost hear the smile and glared in the voice's direction. 'Today I am a spokesperson for the Giffleets, tomorrow I will be someone different entirely. You are in their sanctuary, which can only be found by those who have been there before. I would gather that your boyfriend is somewhere out there searching for two women very close to his heart. Now,' there was a snapping noise and the Giffleets advanced towards her, 'what happened to the one who was caught in the last raid?'

'It died,' Laura said quietly, she didn't want to revisit those memories. It had traumatised her then and it did still.

In response to her words, the Giffleets moved away, forming a mass of dark scales, clashing spikes and flaming eyes. They fought brutally amongst themselves, hoof connecting with face, spikes connecting with flesh. Blood spilled onto the grass as the creatures smashed into one another, all moaning in unison. It pulled at the heartstrings and Laura wept, unashamed, beside the pool, unable to watch the violence unfolding.

Two blunt heads butted her roughly and she opened her eyes to see the two newborns beside her. She reached out towards them, but they leapt away, circling her warily.

'Why are they fighting each other?' Laura asked, wondering if the voice would respond. She was in luck.

'This is how they mourn. They battle in the Fallen's honour until they cannot fight anymore.'

'What a waste of energy,' Laura muttered, 'I can think of many better things to do instead.' She stood up and stumbled away from the clearing, glancing repeatedly over her shoulder to check that her absence had not been noticed. The newborn Giffleets watched her leave, omitting high piercing cries.

'If you are looking for the other female then you are going to be disappointed,' the voice sighed in her ear. Laura froze and looked around but couldn't see anything.

'Where is she?' Not that she really wanted to find Millie, but it was worth asking.

'I think that Farsh-Reet would be only too happy to oblige.'

'Farsh-Reet? Who?'

Red eyes stared into hers and she clamped a hand over her mouth to stifle a scream. The Giffleet butted her with its head before kneeling onto the ground. She mounted it carefully, all too aware of the pain in her hand and the ache in her legs. In one fluid movement they were moving through the trees back through the clearing where the Giffleets had taken a respite from their fight. The newborns followed Laura and Farsh-Reet, keeping up amazingly well despite their wobbly legs. The other Giffleets ignored them but continued to make their eldritch cries. Their progress was followed by an eerie laughter that chilled Laura to the bone.

They didn't have to go very far to find Millie. They left the clearing behind and ran through the forest, almost flying beneath the dense canopy of branches. The ground beneath the Giffleet's hooves became rocky and pebbly, forcing them to slow their pace. Suddenly, Farsh-Reet was leaping down a steep slope, which cut downwards with an abruptness that made Laura cry out in shock. She clung on, eyes tightly shut, praying that she would survive long enough to find Millie and return to Tim.

And then, almost as abruptly as it had appeared, the descent levelled onto plain ground and they turned, cantering around the base of something closely resembling a plateau. After about five minutes they came to a halt, and she realised that they had reached the entrance to a cave. Inside there was a high wailing and Laura groaned inwardly, recognising the sound of Millie's theatrics. She dismounted from Farsh-Reet's back and took a step towards the cave.

'Millie?' she called tentatively, knowing all too well that she would be the last person Millie would want to see. 'It's alright, come out.'

The crying continued and rose to an impossible volume so that Laura had to clamp her hands over her ears. There was a nudge from Farsh-Reet, and she realised that she would have to enter the cave. Against her better judgement— she didn't trust the Giffleets as far as she could throw them— Laura ventured warily forwards. It didn't make sense that the Giffleets hadn't attacked her, after everything she had heard and seen it didn't match up. Something wasn't right.

The sounds Millie was making were getting louder and Laura felt a pang of fear. What could have possessed the girl to make her sound like this? It was like she was more animal than human. She brushed against something soft and sticky which clung to her clothes and hair. With a soft cry, she hurried onwards, frantic to get away.

'Millie?' Laura's voice came out as a whisper, 'are you alright?'

'*Arghhhhh.*' The sounds Millie had made paused and died, leaving only an echo behind.

Laura flinched, and then drew out her dezmian, she needed some light, and she needed it fast. Obviously Millie was hurt, perhaps badly so. A ball of light appeared in front of her, and she had to stifle her scream.

Sure enough, Millie was in front of her but not at all in the manner which she had expected. She had been prepared for blood, maybe missing limbs at the most extreme. But not this.

Millie's body was suspended in mid-air, held by a sticky web which twisted around and around, pinning her arms and legs close together. Only her face was visible, her expression slack as if she had been drugged but was on the verge of consciousness.

'Oh God, Millie,' Laura cried, reaching up towards her, 'what have they *done* to you?'

Millie didn't reply. There wasn't even a wail or moan, which made a shiver of unease roll down Laura's spine. She moved closer and saw that Millie's gaze didn't widen or change. Her eyes were staring blankly ahead, unseeing. Laura raised a hand to the girl's face and felt faint warmth. She glanced upwards and stepped back, horrified. Carcasses of animals were wrapped in webbing, hanging from the ceiling. She recognised within moments that most of them were Giffleets. The sound of scuttling reached Laura's ears and she turned, hand hovering over the empty sheath where her dagger had been. This time she didn't try to suppress her scream, it rang out, clear and shrill, causing the giant spider to pause in its tracks, pincers snapping. Dark hair sprouted on its back, eight legs picking their way forward through the web, each one several metres long.

Laura had never struggled with arachnophobia, however that didn't mean that she liked spiders, not at all. The creature advanced, its many eyes glinting in the pale light as Laura flipped her dezmian and summoned her dagger. She swung it in front of her, desperately trying to fend off the spider. If only she could cut Millie loose and could somehow stun the creature so that the way to the entrance would be clear.

Her hands were sweating and she felt her grip on the dezmian slip. The stone fell from her grasp and she cried out.

No!

The access to her source of magic rolled away into the darkness and the ball of light faltered in mid-air, as if trying to decide whether or not to keep shining. The spider watched the goings-on with keen interest and then surged forwards, racing in for the kill.

Laura ran. Not back towards the entrance– the spider was preventing any chance of escape– all she could do was run further into the cave and hope that there would be another way out. She brushed past Millie's cocooned body and felt a pang of regret, there hadn't been any time to cut her loose.

Maybe the spider will be too caught up in following me that it won't think about eating Millie, she thought. Besides, Millie was unconscious and would have been exceptionally heavy to carry. With her slight build, Laura would have found it almost impossible to drag her.

Her breathing came in sharp bursts as she fought her way through the tangled net of spider webbing. Her foot got caught and she fell, crashing onto the rocky floor as her ball of light disappeared completely, flooding the passageway with darkness.

The sound of her pursuer filled the air, echoing off the walls, which only made the noise louder. How could she tell how far away it really was?

She pulled out of the web and felt her ankle wrench, making her cry out in pain. Tears streamed out of the corner of her eyes as she forced herself onwards. Instead of running, she was hopping, one hand holding onto the wall as she struggled forwards. With the other hand she swiped the air in front of her, cutting away any strands in her way.

Oh Tim, she thought, how will you ever be able to find us? You don't even know where Millie and I are. I wish you were here.

Laura was so caught up in her thoughts that she didn't immediately notice the cool breeze which was lightly caressing her face, blowing strands of her hair. There was also a faint glimmer of light in the distance. She blinked, confused and then smiled. It was impossible for any sort of draught that came from the entrance to reach her, she had travelled too far into the cave. And light... that could only mean that...

Something swung out of the darkness and threw Laura off her feet. She flew through the air, terror filling her lungs, and she screamed. Rustling filled the air, and something glinted in the dim light. As she hit the rocky wall and slumped to the ground, her chest burned with sudden pain, making her head spin. Spots passed in front of her eyes, and she gasped. Her hand gripped onto a jagged rock at her side and with her last remaining strength, she threw it in the direction of the glinting eyes. It struck something with a resounding thud and that something let out a shrill cry of pain.

But then she was being lifted by hairy, spindly legs and spun around and around. She wanted to scream, to fight, but her limbs were motionless, unresponsive. Sticky webbing was coating her arms, legs, chest. She could barely draw breath, so tightly was she woven into the cocoon.

I'm sorry, Tim, she thought, so sorry for not believing you. So sorry for not staying put with the Tribe. So sorry that I never told you that I loved you, too.

Her eyes closed, and a darkness blacker than the deepest night overtook her.

The spider finally seemed content with its job and hung Laura from the roof, watching her cocoon sway from side to side. The motion brought Laura back to reality just as the creature approached, pincers clicking together menacingly. Her mouth was open slightly, allowing her wheezing breath to be released. Each breath made her chest ache against the constricting web. Fear filled her, from the crown to the toe, along with the cold certainty that this must be the end.

It seemed that after all she had been through, after she had tried so hard, that she never would get back home. That she could never see her parents, brother or friends again. Or Tim. A jagged pain ripped through her once more, but she could not even make a sound.

The spider was only a foot away now, and she wished that she could scrunch up her nose at the smell of dried blood and filth which suffocated her. Its pincers were a hair's breadth away, hovering over her.

A sudden burst of wind sent Laura's cocoon into motion, swinging her into the spider, surprising it. There was a loud, keening noise which was only too familiar, and Laura's eyes filled with joyful tears, as the spider moved in the direction of its new prey.

She didn't know whether to be happy or scared as the sound of flapping wings intensified, and the spider shrank away. The keening cry pierced her ears again and then a light flared behind her, throwing shadows into disarray.

Wrinkled hands reached up and pulled Laura's cocoon down, and she looked into Élendill's bright eyes.

'Laura,' the woman said, 'what have you gotten yourself into?'

She withdrew a knife and sliced at the webbing, careful to avoid cutting Laura's body. As most of the sticky strands were drawn away, feeling came back into her limbs. Along with her joy at being rescued, her body was overrun with pain, which tore through her like a savage beast on a rampage.

She moved her head to the side and saw the other members of the Taperi hunting party standing over the lifeless body of the spider. Arrows protruded from its abdomen and its many eyes were finally dull.

Élendill started to examine her body, feeling along the bones and noticing Laura wince in response. Her fingers prodded a rib and Laura's eyes rolled backwards, falling into unconsciousness.

New hands were holding her when she came to. Someone was crying over her, rocking her back and forth with her head to his chest. Dazed, Laura realised that the pain was slightly less and she touched the hands which clung to her.

'Tim?' she murmured.

'Laura,' his voice croaked. 'I was scared that I lost you.' He turned her head this way and that, scrutinising every feature. His eyes were full of desperation and Laura raised her hand to his face, touching his cheek. He leaned into her palm, which soon became damp with tears.

Her heart was beating out a new rhythm: one that sang and danced, that made her terrified at the new possibilities ahead. She wanted to hold him as he was holding her, as if nothing else mattered in the whole world.

She didn't want the moment to end, but to remain, suspended forever in her memory. However she knew that she would have to ask, to find out whether her suspicions were true.

'Tim,' he looked up at the sound of her voice, 'is Millie… did that creature…' She couldn't bring herself to say it. It was too horrible to imagine.

'Yes,' Tim said softly, 'we were too late to save her. I only hope that she didn't suffer too much.'

Laura didn't say anything. She didn't want Tim to know that she thought that Millie's last moments had been anything but painless. She remembered Millie's wails and moans and shuddered.

'How did you find me?' she asked, 'I lost my dezmian so I couldn't use magic, and then that monster surprised me so I couldn't fight back. I thought everything was hopeless.'

'It was Elaret,' Tim smiled, as the Willowing appeared behind him and nuzzled Laura's shoulder lovingly. 'After the Giffleets took you away he led the way. It was like he was tracing your scent or something, and he led us to the edge of the forest, close to the Gherna River. He started pawing at some rocks which we lifted out of the way, and then we found the entrance to this cave.' He indicated the rocky passage around them.

'And then he led you to me,' Laura completed, as she caressed Elaret's neck. 'I recognised the sound he made. I never knew that Willowings could act like he did.'

'The bond between mount and rider is strong,' Tim smiled, 'The Robin chose well when he got Elaret for you.'

'The Robin,' Laura repeated, her mind swarming with images and words, reminding her of everything she still had to do.

'Tim, Laura, we have to move out,' Élendill's voice rang out across the cave, 'we must return Millie's body to perform the proper burial rites.'

Laura bowed her head, 'I understand, Élendill, but I'm afraid that I cannot return to the Tribe. I must beg your forgiveness, but it is vital that I leave immediately.'

'But you are injured!' Élendill and Tim cried together.

'I have something that I must do,' Laura said, 'I appreciate the time that I have spent with the Taperi, but it is time for me to take my leave.'

'Very well,' Élendill replied slowly. 'I had hoped that you might choose to make your stay with our Tribe more permanent, I must confess. I am sure that your departure will displease many.'

Laura kept her head bowed for a moment longer before she reached up and held onto Elaret's back. Tim lifted her into the saddle before leaving to mount Iris.

Élendill watched them with a tightly pursed mouth, allowing her disapproval to be apparent as she followed Tim, bombarding him in rapid Taperi. Tim's back was rigid, and he replied swiftly as he led Iris next to Elaret. They both spoke so fast that Laura couldn't understand, but this didn't bother her too much. They followed the Taperi out of the cave, flying away from the darkness and the spider's lair.

The Gherna River was in front of them in the dusky light, glinting and rippling, beckoning Laura to continue her quest. The Willowings landed on the grass and Laura noticed a cocoon of spider web which had attached itself to one of the saddles. She wanted to retch into the grass but managed to swallow back her nausea as she sent out a silent prayer for Millie.

Élendill gave her one last, sharp nod before she led the Taperi away, flying back in the direction of the village. Tim moved next to her, his face pale and blank.

'I'm sorry I didn't want to go back for her funeral,' Laura said quietly.

He didn't look at her, but stared at the river and didn't say anything.

She couldn't bring herself to continue, knowing full well that it would hurt him. The realisation that he had felt strongly for Millie pulled at Laura's heart and she turned away, not wanting to look at him for a moment longer.

'Should we continue onward through the night?' she asked tentatively.

'Yes,' he said immediately, 'I can't bear to stay in this world any longer.'

'We need to go to Roshterdam to see if we can find out where Renderfell is located. Personally, I've never heard of it before.'

'Neither have I,' Tim acknowledged grudgingly.

'I think that there should be a Barrier at the mouth of the Gherna River,' Laura continued, 'where it connects with the ocean.'

'So, to the ocean we'll go,' Tim said gravely.

They kicked off from the bank and flew for a few hours, barely speaking, as the blood red sky became streaked with orange and gold. They didn't speak as the moon rose and the cold of night descended. Instead, they pressed their Willow-ings harder, hoping to get closer to the Barrier. But thick clouds soon covered the moon, and as their source of light disappeared, they landed and pulled out blankets, allowing themselves to be lulled to sleep by the sound of the Gherna River lapping against the two banks. Still neither one spoke a word.

Chapter Fourteen

The smell of hot food awoke Laura from her slumber. Stretching, she yawned and opened her eyes to see Tim watching her. Chuckling, he turned back to the small camp-fire and said, 'you're adorable when you sleep.'

'Stop trying to be funny,' she murmured, crawling over to join him. It was a relief that he seemed in a better mood than he had the night before. She was surprised though, surely he would still be hurt that he couldn't pay his final respects to Millie.

He laughed, 'what makes you say that?'

'I'm hardly *ever* adorable, especially when I sleep.'

'I have to disagree,' he replied with a smile as he handed her a plate loaded with toast.

'Mm,' she mumbled, biting into her food. 'This is good.'

Tim puffed out his chest with false pride. 'I'm a pretty good chef aren't I?'

She poked him in the stomach, 'no need to get cocky.'

'Me? Cocky?' Tim said, 'No, no, no, I don't think so. I am *completely* serious.' He dodged Laura's expected punch, chuckling again. She was reminded of how he had acted when he had been with Harrison, which provoked a small smile. What would Harrison and Tash be doing now? She wondered as she washed the plates in the river and Tim packed up the blankets. Her body ached as she placed them back into the saddlebags.

'Laura,' Tim said coming up behind her, 'hold still for a moment.' She held her breath in anticipation, although she didn't know what for. He muttered something and then the pain in her body lessened, as she heard him catch his dezmian.

'Thanks,' she sighed, as tension she didn't even know she'd had, left her body.

'Here,' he said, placing a dezmian into her hand, 'I keep a few spares, just in case.'

Laura looked at him, not knowing what to say. The stone vibrated in her palm, recognising that it had a new master. He smiled at her as she placed the dezmian in her pocket. Her eyes raised to meet his and, with a small rush of confidence, she leaned forward to kiss him. It was short and sweet but as Laura pulled away, she felt completely satisfied.

'Thank you,' she whispered, suddenly awkward at his silence, and moved away to mount Elaret. He followed her lead, brow furrowed in thought.

For a while they didn't say anything as they flew over the far-spanning forest beneath them. Laura's eyes stayed fixed on the horizon, wondering how far away the ocean would be and whether a Doorway would be there at all. What would they do if she was wrong, and it was somewhere completely different entirely? She could almost imagine the tightening of Tim's mouth and his look of disapproval if they arrived at the ocean and there was no faint glimmering in the air, indicating that a Barrier was present.

'Laura, look!' Tim was pointing downwards at the trees, and she followed his insistent gaze.

Beneath them were hundreds of spirits, each waving after them, as they swayed and danced between the branches, revelling in the wind. A smile lit Laura's face and she waved back, amazed that they had followed them. She couldn't understand the creatures, although they had helped her. Well, she thought, if help counted as being dropped onto a Giffleet's back from the top of a tree. It was amazing that she hadn't been seriously hurt, that she had avoided the vicious spikes as she landed. As if her thoughts had summoned them, the herd of Giffleets sped out from under the trees, keeping pace with them as they flew high above.

'Are those Giffleets following us?' Shock and horror were evident in Tim's voice, and Laura turned to face him. He was reaching for the bow on his saddle, trying desperately to fix an arrow in place.

'Don't,' she said, reaching out and pulling his arm down.

'They're beasts, Laura,' he snapped, 'like the Dragutash back home.'

'If they are beasts then why didn't they hurt me?' This statement made him pause.

'They killed Millie,' he said.

'No,' she corrected, 'they took Millie away to the cave where she was caught by the spider.'

'They still had a part to play,' he growled, aiming downwards once more.

'Don't shoot, Tim!' Laura said angrily, 'it isn't right.'

'Why?'

His question caught her off guard, especially as she had no idea why she was defending the creatures below them. She looked down at them, the entire herd were running along the river bank. Amongst them she recognised Farsh-Reet and the two newborns. A slow realisation started to dawn on her for, as she looked closer, the creatures seemed more benign, less destructive. They weren't knocking trees over or tearing up the earth. It was as if the whole forest had fallen back into balance.

She knew Tim was watching her, awaiting an explanation.

'It wouldn't be right,' she began, 'they may be hunted by the Taperi but that is not our battle. They didn't hurt me when I got carried away by them. Instead, they took me to where Millie was, I think that they were trying to show me that something was wrong. When I went into the cave there were so many Giffleets which had been eaten by the spider; I think that they might have been trying to get help.'

'Or make sure that the spider's next meal wouldn't be one of their own,' Tim snarled.

'But look at how happy they are now,' Laura smiled, 'the tree spirits too. I'll admit, I don't really understand everything that has been going on in this forest. I doubt I ever will, but I'm sure that by killing that spider we have somehow restored a sense of tranquillity here. And listen,' the faint sound of birdsong reached their ears, 'now the forest doesn't have a deathly silence all the time.'

Tim didn't say anything, but she noticed him replacing his bow on his saddle and breathed a sigh of relief. But then she grinned in surprise, for the sky now was meeting the blue of the ocean on the horizon. Within a couple of hours, they had reached the Barrier, and Tim sang open a Doorway that the travellers hastened through, remembering how little time they'd had previously. Laura didn't look back, the Chimité Forest had held too many secrets and dangers which she was eager to forget. She hadn't any idea which world they would find themselves in next but hoped that it would not contain giant spiders or Giffleets or very opinionated tribes.

The next few days they ventured between three different

worlds, barely stopping long enough to look around and enjoy the new experiences. In one, they came out over an ocean which stretched as far as the eye could see. Laura had needed to create a sturdy raft one night for them to rest on, the Willowings struggling with fatigue. Luckily the Doorway had appeared with the dawn, shimmering over the water like a misty haze. In another world, giant mushrooms grew up towards the sky, jungle vines twisting down their stalks, which on closer inspection turned out to be long, green snakes. Laura had paused in fear, before Tim pulled her onward, finding a track through the undergrowth which avoided the scaly reptiles, who watched them pass, hissing softly. That night Laura had been too scared to sleep easily, and so Tim held her in his arms, whispering calming words until she finally dropped off. For him though, sleep did not come, and so he wasn't disappointed when she awoke early and suggested they get moving. When they found the Doorway in this world, it was after almost a week of travel, navigating their way through the strange mushroom jungle.

The last world they had entered was even stranger, where big and small seemed to be inverted. Giant crawling bugs and blades of grass rose high into the air, waving back and forth in a swaying dance. When a centipede appeared, Laura pushed Elaret up into the sky, fleeing the creature as it began to thunder towards where they had been resting, its many feet beating against the ground. Tim had gone pale after this particular encounter, but Laura didn't tease him as she might have done previously– the snakes and the experience with the spider still were fresh in her mind, so she held her tongue.

After two days of searching, they finally found the third Doorway glistening above the long stretches of swaying grass, and Laura was delighted to find that it opened a few miles away from a city which floated high in the air, far above them.

'Roshterdam is ahead, my lady.' Tim grinned with a mock bow, which almost sent him tumbling off Iris.

Laura giggled, 'Stop acting like a complete idiot! Come on, my *lord,*' she rolled her eyes, 'let's see if we can reach the city before nightfall.'

'My sentiments exactly,' Tim added with a cheeky grin, as he spurred Iris on.

As they approached Roshterdam, Laura examined it, captivated by how unique it was. It looked like a huge castle, with curved towers and flags which flew crazily about in the wind. Laura's hair was flying out behind her and the roaring of the wind was deafening. Looking back at the city, she noticed large propellers, rotating at amazing speeds. I wouldn't like to get stuck under there, she thought.

'The best mechanics and architects live in Roshterdam,' Tim yelled over the wind, when she asked him why there were large propellers. 'They wanted their city to be recognised as one of the greatest architectural pursuits.'

'So, they wanted their city to be better than cities in other worlds?'

'Yes,' he replied, 'but it's taken them centuries to get it even this far. From what I've read, the people want to make the city go a lot higher.'

'Is it possible?'

'If they want to die due to lack of oxygen, then yes.' Tim said grimly. 'Also the folk in Roshterdam are supposedly a little bit...'

'What?' Laura asked, as they landed the Willowings onto a side street, hoping that no locals would come up to greet them.

'Their heads are also in the clouds, if you know what I mean.' Tim replied, looking around to check that no one had heard them. 'It's probably because there isn't a lot of oxygen up here.'

Nodding, Laura sucked in a breath, trying to ignore the breathlessness that enveloped her. Shaking her head, she made a beeline for the closest inn, whose sign creaked in the wind. Inside she stood by the door, regaining her breath. It was relatively empty, except for the innkeeper, some men playing pool at the opposite end of the room, and a hooded figure sitting at the bar. Cigar smoke wafted around the room, making Laura cough and hold onto Tim's arm for support.

'Ulrich,' one of the men playing pool called, 'get me another beer, would you?' The innkeeper jolted and began to fill a tankard, placing it roughly on the bar before turning back to cleaning the glasses with a rather dirty cloth.

'Let me do the talking,' Tim murmured, but Laura shook her head.

'I'll do it,' she whispered, sitting down at the bar and leaning across the counter. 'Excuse me sir,' she asked, 'but we happen to be quite lost. Would you possibly know where Renderfell is?' At the sound of her voice, the innkeeper looked up bleary eyed. The hooded man froze and leaned over his tankard.

'Aye, I know of Renderfell,' the innkeeper said slowly, almost like he was as drunk as some of his customers. 'It's to the south-west of here. But it's a dangerous place. Folks tell tales of lights, strange music and otherworldly creatures who dwell in that forest. No one who goes in comes back out exactly the same.'

'We're looking for a special bowl which my grandfather wishes to own in his old age,' Laura said before she could stop herself. 'And we heard that it lay within that forest.'

'Really?'

'Yes,' Tim replied with clenched teeth.

'No need to be brusque, my friend,' the innkeeper laughed, 'I was just curious. Would you mind dreadfully if I bought you and this delightful young lady here a tankard of ale?'

'Well…' Laura began, tempted by the offer. It had been ages since she'd drunk ale, she could put up with the cigar smoke for a while longer…

'No, thank you,' Tim said firmly, gripping Laura's arm and dragging her away. 'But if you could tell us the nearest possible way to reach the forest of Renderfell, we would be much obliged.'

'It's your funeral,' the innkeeper sighed, 'that place isn't safe, especially for young ladies.' He eyed Laura and she shivered, remembering how Glenroy had had the same glint in his eyes. 'It lies about four hours south-west of here. Wouldn't you like to stay the night before heading off on such a long journey?'

'We *do* need to replenish some supplies,' Laura murmured to Tim, but he shook his head briskly.

'We are on a very tight schedule,' he said, and a wave of irritation swept through Laura. It didn't help her mood to have Tim pull her by the arm out of the inn, into the late afternoon sun.

'Why did you do that?' she asked him, annoyed. 'He was just being polite, there was no need to be rude.'

'And there was *no need* for you to ask about Renderfell. I thought I was going to do that for us.'

'You don't always need to do everything, Tim,' she snapped, striding angrily to Elaret's side and mounting him. 'I'm perfectly capable of doing things myself– I'm not a child who needs coddling.'

They flew down towards Renderfell in a chilly silence. The sun began to set, gradually sinking deeper into the western horizon. Laura clutched at her shawl, pulling it closer, craving the scant warmth it provided. Finally, they landed in a small wood, which seemed miniscule after the Chimité Forest– it could only have been a few miles square– and as the Willowings hit the ground Laura felt a familiar sensation. Something, or someone, was watching them.

She turned around as she dismounted.

'I'm sorry,' Tim said, drawing her attention away from their surroundings, 'it's just, I guess sometimes I get a bit protective of you, Laura. I didn't like the way those men were looking at you, as if you were a plaything.' He shuddered slightly.

'I see.' She didn't.

'I couldn't let something bad happen to you again, Laura,' he added, as if feeling the need to explain himself at last. 'Just thinking about what happened in that cave… I almost lost you once, I don't want to again.'

Her dezmian flipped and the tents arranged themselves, it flipped again and the pain in her body faded slightly.

'How are your injuries?' Tim asked, as he held her hand gingerly in his own. She barely felt him pulling off her glove, too caught up was she in his eyes. He gasped as he registered how her magic had removed all evidence of her ordeal in Calcityia.

'I used more magic than I should have,' Laura said, 'when I was following you and the Taperi. My last reserves have mostly been spent on healing some of the things that were wrong with my body, I needed to travel as quickly as possible so…'

'You've nearly run out of magic?' Tim was shocked. 'Then why did you set up the tents tonight? You should be resting, trying to get your strength back. I'll get the food ready.' He placed his hands on her shoulders and pushed her downwards until she was sitting on the ground. 'Stay there.'

'I'm not a dog,' she smiled, but obliged him, remaining where she was.

Tim bustled around their small campsite, preparing a meagre supper for the two of them. Laura watched him silently, noticing how he'd rolled his sleeves up as he fried some meat over a campfire. It was the first time she'd seen him do that in a long time. The firelight played across his pale forearm, casting the scar into glaring clarity. She thought about her own scars, which stretched up her thighs. Not to mention those which couldn't be seen.

What a strange pair we are, she thought, before mentally shaking herself. He hadn't responded when she'd kissed him, merely frowned. What was *that* supposed to mean? Had his feelings for her faded since Millie died? No, she couldn't believe that.

I almost lost you once, he had said. *I don't want to again.*

Warmth filled her, and it didn't come from the fire. She smiled pensively, imagining what it would be like to kiss him again, not a short kiss, but a long deep one which would show the depth of her feelings. She'd run her hands through his hair, pull him closer until they lived and breathed as one perfect entity.

I love him, Laura thought, feeling her heart speed up as Tim handed her a plate of food. She took it, but didn't eat.

Instead, she watched him dig into his own plate, mesmerized. Had his hair always fallen over his eyes like that? Or was it new? She saw that he hadn't shaved in several days and his chin was covered in dark stubble. It suited him, made him look older, more serious.

'Eat, Laura,' Tim finally said as he raised his gaze to meet hers, 'you need to regain your strength.'

'Mm,' she replied, forcing a morsel of meat into her mouth. She chewed and swallowed, barely noticing the taste or texture, too caught up in her thoughts.

Tim took his plate and started to wash it. His back was turned and Laura fell into a daydream again.

'Laura,' Tim said, exasperated, 'don't you like the food or something?'

'No, it's great,' she replied, taking another bite.

'Then what's wrong?'

What's wrong is that I want you, she thought.

'Nothing.'

'Don't play games,' he said, sitting next to her, anxiety in his eyes. 'You've been acting strangely all night. Are you worried about the stories that the innkeeper was telling us before?'

'Hm? Laura struggled to remember exactly what the story had been. 'How people see strange lights and beings in Renderfell?'

'Yes,' Tim replied, 'is that what's been worrying you?'

She nodded, eyes cast down at her plate so he wouldn't see through her lie. How could she admit that she was craving his touch? That would be outrageous, he would be shocked, perhaps even disgusted. Who knew? She didn't want to open herself up to being rejected. It was safer to lie.

But then he took her hand, and it took all of her willpower to contain her need.

'They're just stories, Laura,' Tim murmured, as if to a young child. 'Probably just superstition. It's nothing to worry about.'

A light breeze danced through Laura's hair, and as it passed through the trees she thought it sounded like laughter.

'How can you be so sure?' she asked, not moving her head in case he saw the desire in her eyes.

'I just am,' he said gravely, before picking up her plate and taking it away, placing it in her tent. 'For when you get hungry later. Try to get some rest.' He said, and then walked into the trees, leaving her alone for a while.

Laura let out a breath she didn't know she'd been holding and put her head in her hands. She didn't know how much time passed, but by the time she looked up, the fire was just embers.

All around her was quiet, apart from the slight rustling breeze which played with her hair. She rose groggily to her feet and moved towards her tent, but something made her pause.

The feeling that someone was watching swept through her again and she glanced around warily.

It couldn't be Tim, she thought, he must've gone to bed. She frowned, wondering why she hadn't heard him return, but perhaps he had walked quietly? All the same, she couldn't shake off the feeling that something was wrong. Despite herself, she peeked into his tent, if only to make sure that he was there.

He wasn't.

Laura drew back, heart pounding.

'Tim?' she called, rushing back to the campfire and peering in the direction he had taken. 'Tim, where are you?'

A silhouetted figure appeared in her peripheral vision, beckoning for her to follow.

'Tim?' she blinked, trying to make the figure out clearly. The silhouette moved away into the trees and she followed, wondering why he hadn't replied.

Laura had no idea how long she followed the man ahead of her, for time itself seemed to stand still.

'Tim, where are we going?'

But she was starting to doubt that it even was Tim. What had she gotten herself into?

There were lights ahead, small lanterns which hung from the low overhanging branches, each casting a small mystic glow into the darkness. Laura was reminded of fairy lights, except these ones on closer inspection were made from leaf skeletons which had been strung together with fine gossamer thread. She reached up, gently touching one before drawing back, shocked, as she saw the glow worms who clung to the lantern's sides.

'Amazing,' she murmured.

A twig snapped behind her and she turned, relaxing as she noticed the small procession of doe following her. She stared into their large round eyes, and one leapt back deftly, a fawn shadowing its footsteps. Around her squirrels jumped from branch to branch, their fine bottle brush tails waving slightly as they leapt, ducked and clung on for balance. Laura watched, entranced; she had only seen squirrels in books or, back when she'd lived in Australia, in movies. How amazing they were in real life, such athletic grace combined with furry cuteness. She just wanted to hold one and take it home with her, although she doubted that The Robin would be very impressed.

A few rabbits had joined the doe, crowding around Laura's feet, but leaping away when she tried to reach down to stroke them. She sighed, exasperated, and moved on, vaguely aware of the soft padding of paws behind her.

The figure ahead continued to lead the way further into the wood, which was now lit with many more lanterns. There was a tinkling of chimes in the distance and a soft cadence from something that sounded like a flute. Was that soft thrumming from a harp or lute? She couldn't be sure. And then a rhythm was being beaten out, a rhythm which caused one to stop and listen and made one's feet tap against the ground, desperate to break into a lively jig. Laura's head started spinning and she realised that she had been twirling, arms outstretched, as she danced to the strange music.

Before she knew it, a group of tall, beautiful people emerged from amongst the trees and joined her. Together, they started to dance in a circle, changing partners often and speaking little. But they did laugh, and the sound made Laura's smile wider, and her heart beat in time with the music. She didn't know who they were, but she felt safer than she ever had. Her partner changed and a tall blond man grinned at her, twirling her round and round until the lights blurred into one. The music rose into a fast crescendo and her feet responded, dancing faster and faster until she could barely draw breath.

There was something the innkeeper said about music and lights, the rational part of her brain whispered.

But I'm having so much fun here. It's beautiful, these people seem so lovely. They're gorgeous. The other part of her brain replied dreamily.

The other part of her mind was silenced rapidly, as she staggered to a nearby log for a brief respite. Around her the strange people danced on, and for the first time she could examine them.

Each one had high cheekbones and angular features which made them look regal, and their smiles were blinding, piercingly white in the lamplight. The tall blond man approached her, holding a glass of juice in his hand and offering it to her. Gratefully, Laura accepted, smiling up at him.

'Thank you.'

He nodded and faded back into the crowd. Laura frowned slightly, his behaviour had been odd to say the least. Why didn't these people speak to each other?

She placed the glass to her lips, inhaling the sweet smell of apricot and honey. There were also traces of peach which made her mouth water with impatience, she wondered what it would taste like and whether it would be as good as it smelled.

The doe burst forward and knocked the glass from her hand. Shocked, Laura watched the liquid fly onto the grass. A part of her felt annoyed: she'd been quite thirsty and the juice had smelt amazing, but then she noticed the faint line of steam rising off the spilt liquid, as the grass melted into the earth.

That was when the fear set in.

Who *were* these people? Why had they lured her away with dancing and music and the strangely enticing lights? Was there some sick plot at work here?

No one who goes in comes back the same. Too late the words entered her mind and she mentally berated herself. Obviously no one returned exactly the same, not if they were tricked and tempted by these strange folk. These strange, *beautiful* folk…

The drumbeat was starting to get back into her soul and she felt herself longing to re-join the dancing throng. It took a strong amount of willpower to hold back and remain where she was. The doe nuzzled her shoulder, bright eyes alert, keenly watching the dancers, wary of any danger.

'It's not safe here, is it?' Laura murmured, softly caressing its neck. 'I don't know what they want or who they are, but I can't stay with them, can I?'

Laura sighed, overcome with a sudden, unexpected remorse. She halted in her attention of the doe and gazed back at the dancers, wondering how people so beautiful and happy could possibly be cruel.

The doe gave a low bleat and butted her hand. She looked around and grinned, the remorse fading almost as soon as it had come. The doe's eyes gazed up at her imploringly, as if saying '*don't stop*'. Laura chuckled to herself and resumed stroking its neck.

When she turned back to the dancers, Laura froze. It couldn't be possible.

She was no longer the only human amongst these strange folk, who were too identical and perfect to *be* human.

'No,' she whispered, as fear clutched at her stomach.

A stunning redhead clasped his hand and he followed meekly, like a lamb being herded by a shepherd. His green eyes stared around, barely taking in his surroundings, although he could definitely see the woman before him. His face lit with a smile and the redhead laughed, leaned in and kissed him.

Laura felt a jolt of anger. Obviously he wasn't in control of himself; she'd never seen Tim being *led* by anybody. He always seemed to be one step ahead.

Apparently not this time.

Laura rose to her feet and moved back into the trees, where she hid amongst the foliage and watched the scene intently. She couldn't let herself be tempted back into the dance, where time seemed to disappear along with reason and logic.

Tim joined the revellers, spinning and leaping, whirling woman after woman around the circle. The redhead eyed him hungrily and partnered him for most of the dance, running her hands over his head, torso and arms. Jealousy whispered in Laura's ear and she shook it off, knowing innately that he wasn't aware of what was going on. And yet, mere hours before she had been dreaming about what it would be like to do exactly what the redhead was doing.

The woman laughed again and her dress swayed, highlighting her curvaceous body and muscular legs. Her arms were wrapped around Tim's neck, her mane of hair cascading down her back. Laura stared, knowing full well that this woman's beauty was more than unearthly. It would be impossible for a human to look like that.

'Quite something, isn't she?'

The voice startled Laura, but she recognised it. She recognised the cold, greedy tone and felt terror wash through her. It couldn't be.

'Although she's nothing compared to you, darling.'

Not here. Not now. How was he here?

'Aren't you even going to look at me, Laura? After all we went through together?'

His hands on her body. The pain. His eyes, his words, full of hurt and hate.

'Of course, after what happened, I *could* understand if you didn't want to talk. But actions speak louder than words, don't they?'

Yours obviously do, Laura thought.

A hand brushed her shoulder, and she shrank away, rigid with horrible memory.

'You never could understand though, could you? Your effect on me, on almost every male initiate at the Temple. You didn't *know.*' His words were spoken with something almost like awe.

Laura felt sick.

'I didn't want to hurt you.'

Liar.

'But you made me so *angry.* You were so difficult. You needed a taste of your own medicine. You had to learn what it was like to be used and hurt and angry and afraid. You were too high and mighty being The Robin's apprentice. Although, I've heard, you're much more to him than *that.*'

This was too much.

'You are *sick,*' Laura hissed, whirling to face the man who had haunted her nightmares for months. 'You are a vile, cruel bastard. Leave me *alone.* I thought that The Robin made that clear to you when you last met. I chose to spare your miserable life; you are *indebted* to me.'

'I know,' he smiled, and his cloak shifted around him as he peered through the branches at the revellers. 'That's why I followed you.'

'It was *you* in the inn?' she was shocked, aghast. To think, she had been sitting *next* to him and had no idea. The memory of the cloaked traveller filled her mind.

'Yes,' Glenroy replied, 'imagine my surprise when I heard the voices of the girl I love and my enemy in the same room.' His mouth twisted into a sneer. 'And then to learn that you were coming *here*. To Renderfell. It's too dangerous for us mortals. *They*,' he pointed at the dancers, 'will consume your soul. Dedicate your life to serving their needs and use you like a plaything.'

'Amazing,' Laura heard herself say, 'you have more in common than I originally thought.'

There was a scintillating silence and Glenroy's mouth tightened.

'I …' He paused, obviously searching for the right words to say.

'You?' Laura didn't try to be helpful. 'If you're trying to stumble through an apology for what you did, Glenroy, then it is long overdue.'

He flushed beet red as she raised her head, glaring into his eyes. She wanted to make it as difficult for him as possible. He didn't deserve any better.

'I didn't want to hurt you,' he began again, and she stared at him emotionlessly, not believing a word. 'But,' he continued, 'I'm not sorry. I want you to be mine Laura, only mine,' his eyes flashed to Tim, 'not anyone else's.'

'Well, unluckily for you,' Laura snapped furiously, 'I don't *want* to be yours. I want to be with the man you can't be.' She pointed at Tim and saw Glenroy's shoulders sink.

'Figures,' he muttered, 'pretty boys always win.'

'No,' she corrected, her tone crisp and cold, '*honourable* men win.'

He glared away from her and she didn't mind. She couldn't bear him, let alone his obsession. Yet now she felt something had changed, she did not feel the same fear that had gripped her before. It had faded into repulsion and hatred, and knowing that she had her dezmian in her pocket gave her the strength to say, 'why did you follow us?'

'Because I didn't want *them* to get their hands on you,' he muttered. 'I would've gone through the test to get you back if they had.' His eyes burned with a strange fire and she shivered.

'What test?'

'Why do you care?' he retorted, spitting into her unflinching face, 'you wouldn't have what it takes. You wouldn't know what to do. It's too dangerous, hardly the job for a… a *woman.*'

'What do I have to do?' Laura asked, teeth gritted. Her patience was already on a knife's edge, she didn't know how much longer she could stand his barbing comments. It was vital that she learnt how to get Tim's attention long enough to get him away.

Glenroy's lips stuck together stubbornly.

She leaned closer, inwardly choking on the stench that was rolling off his body. Didn't he *ever* bathe? 'You. Owe. Me.' She hissed, 'whether you like it or not. Tell me Glenroy, or I swear I will tell The Robin about you not really being in the prison in the Western Marshes, and he will hunt you down and tear you limb from limb. He can be *quite* terrifying when he's angry, you know.'

Glenroy shook his head.

Laura continued, 'he'd send out his Dæmons first, you know about them, I'm sure.' His widening eyes told her he did. 'Some people call them Nightwalkers.' She was starting to enjoy his changing expression, 'they hunt their prey at night and drink its blood before beginning on the meat. They are faster than any human and can cross through Barriers in mere seconds. But guess what,' she leaned closer, 'they can always, *always* find their prey once they catch its scent. No matter how long a chase, they will always succeed. How long do you think you'd last once they are hunting you down?'

'Fine,' Glenroy spat. 'Enough.'

Laura leaned back, pleased that her story had been believed. 'How do I save Tim?'

Glenroy seemed to have a spasm on hearing Tim's name, his hands clutched the nearby tree, white with tension.

His eyes were full of loathing as said, 'you can't get his attention by any normal means, he's been put under a spell. That lady he's with,' he pointed at the redhead, 'she's their leader, I think. Her name is Melisande. From what I've heard, you need to confront her and demand to have,' he shook again, '*Crow* again.' The name passed his lips so quickly that Laura had barely heard it.

'How do you know all this, Glenroy?' The thought had just occurred to Laura and she kicked herself for not thinking of it sooner. He spoke about it like he had been amongst them, examined them, perhaps even learnt from them.

'I spent some time with them,' he muttered, 'and when they sent me away, I watched each night as they danced. I saw them lead several men and women into their grove, and send them away just as quickly. Over time, I learnt about what they were and how one could stop them. I tried helping some of the others.'

Laura found this a little hard to believe.

'I knew that if someone stood up to the leader then they were tested. No one ever succeeded, each failed at some point. Their faith wasn't strong enough.' A shred of anger filled his voice, 'it was hard to watch them try and fail.'

'What was the test?' Laura didn't care about his feelings or his life-changing story which was probably invented so that she'd feel sorry for him. It wouldn't work.

Glenroy paused for a moment, dark eyes alight with memory. Whether he found it troubling or remarkable, Laura didn't know.

'She changed them,' he said, 'the person they had enthralled. The other had to remain steadfast and hold onto them, no matter what.'

'So that's what I must do,' Laura murmured. She stood up and made to leave the safety of their hiding place, but Glenroy grabbed her arm and held firm as she struggled.

'Don't do this,' he pleaded, 'please, Laura. Don't.'

'Let go of me,' she growled, yanking her arm away. 'You don't control me Glenroy, I make my *own* decisions. Not you, or anyone else.'

He made a harsh sound, like he was fighting not to reply but Laura turned and walked away, feeling lighter than she had in months. She felt stronger in herself, no longer haunted by the fear that had lingered after that night in Boolwra. Although the rush she felt after defeating her nemesis was brief, she didn't pause or hesitate as she strode through the dancers, fighting off their attempts to coerce her to join them. Instead, she made a beeline for Tim and Melisande.

Before she knew it, Laura was in front of them and the music had stopped. Eyes bore into her, but no one moved. It seemed they all awaited a direction from the woman in front of her, whose haughty features were regarding her coolly.

'Give him back.' Laura demanded, forcing herself to stand firm and remain calm. Her bravado was fading fast, but she had to make sure that she didn't lose heart now.

Tim didn't look at her, his attention solely fixed on Melisande– spell or not, this hurt. As if reading Laura's thoughts, the woman smiled. It was anything but welcoming.

'And why would I do that?' Her voice was like that of an angel, except the cruel amusement in her eyes was hardly angelic. 'As you can see, he is content here.' The crowd laughed amongst themselves as Tim touched the redhead's cheek adoringly.

'All the same,' Laura said, 'I want him back. He isn't yours to keep.'

'Says who?' Melisande asked, raising an arched brow, '*you?* Who couldn't even recognise his love when it was before your eyes? Who hurt him and tempted him but never gave him complete satisfaction? I'd *hardly* claim that to be a good reason to keep him.'

Laura's cheeks went hot, and she stepped forward angrily.

'You don't understand,' she said with forced calm, 'he should be able to make his own choices. I don't want to control him like you do. I want him to be free to love whom he chooses.'

'Even if that isn't you?' Melisande was quick to respond, and her words cut a deep hole in Laura's heart. 'What if he had found the right girl and she wasn't you? If he deluded himself into thinking that his mere lust for you was more important than something far greater. What if he had only realised when she *died,* how strongly attached to her he had really been?'

'How did you know about Millie?' Laura asked.

'There is little,' Melisande caressed Tim's face, 'that men can withhold from me.'

Well, at least she's honest, Laura thought fleetingly. 'Despite that,' she continued, 'let me undertake the test to get him back. He deserves to think for himself.'

'No,' Melisande smiled, 'you don't deserve *him*.'

'Let me try,' Laura said, as panic started to crowd her thoughts.

'Remove her,' Melisande announced as she turned away, leading Tim through the crowd. It was as if Laura were a humble ant in the dirt, who didn't merit the honour of being spoken to. She felt trampled, useless, as hands pulled her, forcing her away from Tim.

Tim, who hadn't even noticed her once or looked back. It was like he didn't know her.

Hard fury stole through Laura, and she fought against the people around her, trying desperately to bridge the widening gap. She couldn't give up. She couldn't fail before she had barely begun.

'Let me *try!*' she shouted, 'I deserve that much. No matter what my mistakes may have been, I love him, and I won't let him go now.' Melisande had condescended to pause and Laura sped on, 'if I pass the test and he doesn't want to be with me, then I will accept it and move on. I swear. If I fail, then I lose him anyway. What can you possibly have to lose? You'll only send him away when you get bored, don't deny it.'

'He won't be faithful to you,' Melisande said coldly as she turned, 'no matter how strong your affection may be. He won't want to remain with you.'

Laura took a steadying breath as the hands dropped away from her and she stepped towards Tim. He looked at her blankly, not seeing the silent tears fall as she grasped him in her arms. She pressed herself against his immobile chest and shut her eyes.

'I love you, dear heart,' she whispered.

Melisande laughed, 'you will need it, mortal. He will revile you, shun you and try to evade you as best he can. Will you be able to remain steadfast, and hold him with the strength of love alone? You haven't accepted or held onto his love before now.'

Laura took another deep breath, 'just let me prove you wrong.'

Melisande's face contorted with unsuppressed fury, and she raised her finger, pointing at Tim.

There was a crack, and Tim was reforming, stretching and moulding into a completely new shape. Laura's hands clasped shaggy fur, and she stared momentarily terrified, into the eyes of a lion. He snarled, revealing sharp teeth mere inches from her face, and she instinctively cringed.

'See how he despises,' Melisande cooed. Laura narrowed her eyes at the jibe and she reached around with one hand, pulling herself onto Tim's back. She wound her hands into his mane and held on for dear life as he leapt around, bucking like a bull in an attempt to throw her off.

There was another crack, and the fur beneath her became scales, which slipped out of her grasp. Desperately, she reached out and somehow got her fingers into the snake's mouth. Her other hand scrabbled along the scales, which slipped out of grasp as Tim thrashed, tail flicking her face, stunning her. Teeth clamped down hard on her hand and she bit back a cry of pain.

'Even now he fights to escape you,' Melisande continued as Tim shook his head, trying and failing to dislodge her.

But despite her now bloody hands, Laura held firm, until Melisande changed him again. Tim's body shrank before her eyes until she could barely see him. It wasn't until she saw a tiny black flea jump on her arm that she found him.

'Watch as he leaps away,' Melisande smirked, 'shunning her company and her *love.*'

Tim jumped again, making a bid for freedom, but Laura's hands cupped around him, containing him. She pressed her hands together, hoping that he wouldn't find a way out. She glanced at Melisande who was starting to look annoyed, and smiled inwardly.

But then she was trying to hold a fish, which was slick with water droplets. It flopped around, almost slipping out of her hands. Laura clutched at the tail and then watched with horror as Tim slid through her wet hands. He fell down her skirt and she jumped, kicking desperately, hoping that a fish might be slightly like a ball. Thankfully he rose upwards, and her hands reached out, once more securing him in a bloody grip.

There was silence now as the spectators watched, impressed. Melisande was seething openly, not bothering with taunts, but her hand was already pointing at Tim.

Searing pain. Blinding agony. She almost dropped him instinctively, as memories filled her mind. The white-hot iron bar in her hands burnt the skin and singed the bottom of her hair. The smell of heat and seared flesh overcame her, and she choked, coughing. Tears streamed down her cheeks and she let out a traumatised scream.

She saw Melisande lean forward eagerly, waiting for Laura to release her prize.

'Feel his suffering because of you,' she said. 'Endure what he has endured.'

It was too much. Her hands drooped lower and her strength was almost gone. As Laura fell to her knees, dark spots floating before her eyes, she remembered the night of the fire. The screaming, crying and panic. How she'd got caught in her window and how her bedroom door smouldered in the heat.

But then she had been saved. It had been Tim who carried her for a while, his arms who had sheltered her from the pain and fear.

He would get no less from her.

Her fingers tightened around the bar and she pulled it against her chest, silently enduring the agony. She didn't want to give Melisande the satisfaction of hearing her cry out. The tears continued, but she stared defiantly into the redhead's eyes, wishing that she could ignore this torture.

Laura had no idea how long she and Melisande stared at each other, it felt like a lifetime and yet she knew it may have only been a few minutes. Finally, Melisande waved her hand in front of her, bringing an end to the test. The folk around her started to disappear into the trees, fading before Laura's eyes.

'He will not be faithful, mortal,' Melisande said, 'none of them are. No matter how much love you think you have, he will always desire another.'

'You lie,' Laura whispered faintly. Tim's body lay next to her, his head supported by her hands.

Melisande laughed, a final, cold laugh. 'Do I?' She started to disappear into the trees, 'just wait and see, Laura Jefferies. You too will lose faith in love.'

As the light of dawn came into the clearing, any evidence of the night before disappeared. The lanterns melded into the trees and there was no sign of the strange folk or even the faintest tinkle of music. There was also no sign of Glenroy. Laura could only hope that he had finally left her be.

Tim stirred and his eyes opened blearily, blinked and then focussed on her face.

'Laura? I had the strangest dream… wait, where are we?' He was looking around the small grove, before he noticed her, 'what happened to you? You look awful!'

'Thanks.'

'Anytime,' he grinned, 'but what happened? I don't remember anything. Did I sleepwalk or something?'

Laura's mouth perked into a little smile, 'something like that. I followed you and was trying to get you back, but you weren't really responsive.' Her smile grew wider as he sat up. She wouldn't tell him what had happened. Not yet. It was still too raw.

'I was worried you couldn't wake up,' she whispered. His eyes narrowed in confusion at the fear in her expression. But then her face cleared and she regarded him with shining exhilaration. She was still amazed that she had succeeded. 'But then you did.'

With that, she kissed him soundly, startling him. She pulled away just as suddenly, examining her hands in astonishment. There was no trace of the burns or bites that she had endured in Melisande's test.

'Magic,' she whispered, as she rose to her feet, glancing around in wonder. In hindsight, the test hadn't hurt her at all, as though it had all been imagined. She thanked her lucky stars.

'Laura?' Tim joined her, confused. 'What's going on?'

'We have to find our way back to the campsite,' Laura said, ignoring him, 'I don't know where it is though. It was so dark last night…' Apart from the lanterns that had been filled with glow worms.

'It looks like we already have a guide,' Tim smiled, 'is she a friend of yours?'

Laura turned and grinned, delighted to see the little doe waiting at the edge of the trees.

'She followed me last night,' she explained. She didn't offer more but Tim nodded, seemingly content. He was watching her carefully, his expression guarded.

'Let's go,' Laura stumbled after the doe, as her exhaustion began to overwhelm her. Tim sighed and walked after her, making sure that she didn't fall over the odd root or rock which barred their path. However, after ten minutes he let out an exasperated groan and strode forwards, lifting Laura into his arms.

'I can't believe how *slow* you are when you're sleep deprived,' he complained.

Even in her befuddled state, Laura could appreciate the feeling of being in his arms. Not slung casually over the shoulder. Not getting a piggy-back. But being in his arms, carried like a child. Or a sweetheart.

Her breathing was shallow and her pulse raced. How could he still have this effect on her? How could he not *tell*?

Her head leant against his chest and she closed her eyes.

'Are you sure we can trust this doe?' Tim asked in a bid to keep her awake.

'Mm-hmm,' Laura mumbled before falling into a brief doze.

Chapter Fifteen

Laura awoke when Tim set her down beside the remnants of their campfire. She watched as he packed up the tents and arranged the Willowings' saddlebags. A part of her wanted to help, yet she knew that he would reject any offer and would tell her quite plainly that she needed to rest and heal. If he knew what she had gone through that night, he would've been even more insistent.

The other part of her was content to stay on the ground and stare up at the clouds, trying to make images out of the wispy strands of white. In the end this part won, although there had never really been any question about what she would do.

'Ready to go, Laura?'

Damn, he'd already finished everything? Laura got up slowly, for the world around her spun, throwing her off balance. She felt Tim's arm come around to support her and his tongue clicked disapprovingly.

'There is no way I'm going to let you ride in that condition,' he muttered, lifting her onto Iris' back and leaping up behind.

'I'm alright, really,' she mumbled, unconvincing even to her own ears.

'Liar,' Tim replied, 'you're riding with me until you have had a good night's sleep.'

Laura couldn't come up with a coherent response, but she

didn't mind. This way she could be in his arms for a much longer period of time.

To her surprise, Iris and Elaret didn't leap into the air, instead they set off at a sedate walk through the wood. Elaret walked close behind them, ears flicked back in the cool morning air. Laura hadn't noticed the chill before, she had been so caught up in her thoughts. Now she snuggled deeper against Tim's chest, trying to evade even the slightest hint of wind or cold. His heart was beating out a steady rhythm by her ear, which seemed to match her own.

'Tim?'

'Yeah?'

Laura's words clogged up in her throat but with some effort she forced them out. 'I'm sorry if I've hurt you.' It was easier to say when she couldn't see his reaction, however she felt the tension in his body as he replied,

'What makes you think that, Laura?'

'I… I've just been…' Damn, this was hard. How could she not tell him about what had happened the night before? That after hearing Melisande's words, a tiny bud of fear had sprouted in her, in case what the ethereal being had said was true. 'I've just been thinking about some of the things that have happened lately.' This much was true. 'And I realised that I haven't always considered your feelings, and thought only of myself.' An image of Millie filled her mind and she pushed it away. 'So, I'm sorry.'

Tim didn't reply and Laura started to worry as the silence dragged into an eternity.

'Say something,' she whispered, her voice a quiet plea.

The tension in his body relaxed and she could hear the smile in his voice, 'don't worry, Laura,' he said, 'you haven't hurt me that badly.'

Somehow, she didn't quite believe him, but decided not to press the subject. It wasn't exactly her favourite topic of conversation; her faults and causes for apology.

'Hey, look,' Tim was pointing ahead to where the path split. One trail led away from the forest, heading straight back to civilisation. The other disappeared within moments, twisting into the dark wood. They reached the crossroads and halted.

'Left or right?' Laura asked.

Tim glanced each way. 'Left,' he finally said, 'it meanders more, and you know I always prefer the longer journeys.'

'Okay,' she replied.

The Willowings set off down the left path, winding between trees and crossing tiny streams swiftly. The light was thinner in this section of the forest, almost as though night had fallen once more.

In her peripheral vision, Laura noticed a cloaked figure dart behind a tree as they rode past. Glancing up at Tim, she realised that he hadn't noticed, eyes intent on the trail ahead. But surely she must tell him about her suspicions, alert him that Glenroy might be nearby. Was he following them?

'Tim, there's something else I have to tell you.' He had to know about Glenroy, he wouldn't be happy to hear it, but he *had* to know.

'Shh,' Tim held up a hand, listening intently. 'Can you hear that?'

Laura paused, momentarily thrown off and listened. Gradually she was able to hear a booming sound, which seemed so much like...

'A waterfall.' Tim grinned, eyes bright in the dusky light.

'Let's hurry there,' Laura said, partly in hope that this would be *the* waterfall, and also in the hope that they would leave Glenroy far behind. Within an instant, the Willowings were cantering away down the path towards the sound. The wind whipped through her hair and she laughed in exhilaration, praying desperately that this would be it. That finally their quest would have reached its final destination.

They ran for a long time, the sound never getting louder or closer, no matter how far they went. It felt like they had been going around in circles. After an hour or two of gradually dwindling excitement, they stopped and dismounted. The sound of water crashed in their ears, sounding like it was now only just out of sight, around the next bend in the path. But Laura knew that it could not be that simple.

'I don't understand it!' Tim growled, as he handed her some sliced bread and cheese. Laura dug in, ravenous, and enjoyed the taste of grainy bread and soft cheese in her mouth. It was over too soon for her liking and so she was grateful when a chuckling Tim passed her an apple.

'There has to be some way to find it,' Laura said between mouthfuls. 'I just have to think. I'm sure The Robin said something about the bowl…'

As she trailed off into silence, she placed her hands on her temples and scrunched her eyes shut. She had to remember, to figure out how to breach the gap between them and the waterfall.

As time passed on, she felt Tim's eyes watching her, waiting patiently for realisation to strike.

With her closed eyes, Laura replayed the last meeting she'd had with her mentor. They'd discussed the bowl, he told her the stories revolving around it and then…

Why can't you go?' she'd asked, and he had replied,

'He who desires cannot seek, he who seeks cannot desire.'

He who seeks cannot desire.

'But I don't desire it for myself,' she whispered. 'I want to get it for him, so he can help me.'

There was a sudden change in the air at her words, the sun shone brighter, and the sound of water was closer.

'What ...?' Tim asked, as he helped Laura to her feet.

'He who seeks cannot desire,' she repeated to herself. 'I don't want to keep the bowl, I don't even understand *why* The Robin wants it. But that doesn't matter.' All that mattered was that she could get back home, although she wanted Tim to go with her.

'Tim,' she began, 'when we get back to the Temple...'

'You'll head back to your family,' he finished. She couldn't read the expression in his eyes or voice, it was like a wall had gone up, barring her from reaching him.

'Yes,' she said, 'but I was wondering, I was hoping...' Damn, why did she have to falter now?

He didn't speak, just waited.

'I would like you to come with me,' she finished, forcing herself not to turn away shyly, but to look up at him.

'Really?' The guard had lifted, his voice was full of gentle, sweet hesitation. 'But I thought that...'

She laid a finger to his lips, silencing him, 'I want you to come with me.'

Elaret whinnied, breaking the moment for both of them. Smiling ruefully, Laura mounted him and headed off down the path.

'The sound is getting closer,' Laura grinned, 'race you there!'

Before Tim had time to argue, she had urged Elaret into a canter, and smiled as Tim came alongside her within moments. They crashed through a wall of ferns and came to a stop, eyes wide with amazement. They had reached a clearing occupied by a dark pool with the waterfall at the opposite end. The waterfall itself wasn't very big, but the noise it made sounded like it was at least triple the size.

'There!' Laura cried as she dismounted. In a sudden haste, she pulled off her dress until she was in her chemise and leapt into the pool. In the moment she forgot all about social expectations and didn't care what Tim would think of seeing her like this. Laura hit the water with a resounding splash and swam towards the waterfall, avoiding the rocks and strong current.

'Laura, wait!' Tim cried, as he swam up alongside her, spluttering.

She ducked under the thundering wall of water, popping up on the other side in a small grotto. Light reflected off the water and made beautiful shadows on the grotto's walls. Laura scanned the rocky surface until she saw the light catch on something quite spectacular on a ledge just out of reach.

Emerging from the water, Laura crawled up and took the item she'd been searching for all that time.

A silver bowl with an inlay of pearl.

Tim hadn't followed her through the waterfall but was waiting on the other side when she emerged. Together they swam back to the shore and emerged, soaking wet. Laura held the bowl like it was a child, wrapping her arms around it. She knelt on the grass and started to rub some of the gritty dirt off it.

'It's beautiful,' Tim admitted, 'but compared to you, it's nothing.'

Laura realised that he was staring at her body, which the wet undergarments were clinging to. In sudden embarrassment, she tried to hide everything with her hands.

'Don't,' Tim murmured, as he too knelt down, reached

out and moved the bowl away.

Reluctantly Laura allowed it to leave her reach. Her heart was pounding with terrified excitement, wary and impatient for what might come. Slowly, she raised her head and looked into his eyes. On seeing the vulnerability beneath her grave countenance, Tim sighed and held her closer, tilting her chin upwards. Laura felt the rush building in her veins, the driving need that had echoed her footsteps for so long. But now that it seemed that Tim felt the same way, she felt scared. Surely it wouldn't be like the first time?

As if sensing the direction of her thoughts, Tim closed the distance between them and kissed her. Her body reacted before she could stop it; a hand ran through Tim's dark hair, while the other held him closer, locking them into a passionate embrace. Her mouth gasped and she clung to him, as if all that mattered was him and him alone. Tim pulled away first, giving her a moment to breathe.

'Laura,' he whispered.

'What?' she asked, had she done something wrong?

'You…' He couldn't find the words to express how he felt, and so kissed her again. A myriad of emotions rocked through her, but desire overruled everything else. He gripped her and they tumbled to the ground, holding onto each other for dear life. As his hand pulled her chemise up her thigh, she drew away, the shadows of her past suddenly threatening to overwhelm her.

'Be gentle with me,' she whispered, touching his cheek with a trembling palm. Green eyes shining bright, Tim nodded and kissed her deeply. She closed her eyes and succumbed, allowing herself to give in to her emotions. And so, for the rest of that afternoon they discovered parts of themselves which they'd never revealed to anyone else.

By nightfall, Laura lay in his arms, sated and content, feeling fuller of emotion than she had in a long time. Tim's hand was stroking her hair, and the sensation awoke even more desire in her. If only she were not so tired, then she might have pursued it.

'I love you,' she whispered, and felt Tim's lips touch her brow.

'I love you too,' he murmured, watching as a smile spread across her face and she fell into a deep, dreamless sleep.

The sound of bird calls awoke Laura, and she stretched.

'Oh Tim,' she said, 'yesterday was *wonderful.*' But, on looking around she realised that he wasn't there. The bowl was also gone from where it had been placed the night before.

Where had he taken it? And where was he? Why hadn't Tim woken her up? Laura thought anxiously, as she splashed water from the pool onto her face. Surely those otherworld folk wouldn't have taken him away again? That wouldn't be fair. Although she doubted that they would care about that.

Iris had disappeared from where the Willowings had been tethered the night before. Surely the dancing folk wouldn't take Iris as well? They had no need for Willowings. That could only mean that Tim had gone, left without even writing a note.

Changing in a hurry, Laura prepared a fire and cooked some breakfast. For a moment she stopped, thinking she had heard the sound of hooves in the distance, but they disappeared almost as quickly as they'd come. It was cruel, not knowing what was going on. But she decided to trust in him, to be patient and not jump to any false conclusions.

She waited and worried beside the pool for a day and night.

Still Tim didn't return.

'Where would he go?' Laura asked Elaret, who didn't have any helpful advice to give her. She paced around the pool fretfully, until she finally clapped her hands together. She'd had enough.

Laura set off for Roshterdam at dawn, hoping to find some trace of Tim there. Maybe he had gone to get supplies. But why would he take the bowl? She'd asked him to return with her, so it couldn't be some sort of ploy to stop her from going back to her own world.

Elaret landed with a clatter and she led him into a stable, placing some coins into the stable master's hand. While she was there, she glanced around, but there was no sign of Iris amongst the assortment of creatures in the stalls. When asked, the stable master had no idea about any male travellers visiting Roshterdam in the past few days.

The air was too thin for her to think clearly, and so she hurried in the direction of a market, asking stall owners if they'd seen a tall man with dark hair and green eyes. Their responses were all the same, 'Why miss, we see so many men like that who come through this way, we're not really any help. But how would you feel about lifting your spirits with this? For a small cost of…' She left them at that point, unable to think of buying anything. What if he wasn't in Roshterdam at all?

Her next port of call was to check the local inns, thinking that perhaps he would have rented a room. Who knew? Sadly, each inn was exactly the same as the stall holders in the market. No one had noticed any dark-haired newcomers lately, although for such a lovely young lady, they could make sure that she found a well-priced room for the night.

Laura thanked them and walked on, barely noticing the

sun crossing the sky until it was setting far in the west. Finally, feeling very dejected and miserable, Laura came across the inn where she and Tim had gone for directions a couple of days before. Not much had changed, the innkeeper was still looking drugged and the pool players looked like they had barely moved a centimetre. Ulrich greeted her very warmly, eyes lighting up as he noticed her, despite her rather bedraggled appearance.

When she asked about Tim he paused and said, 'well miss, he *is* here, but is a little bit… busy, at the moment.'

He was there! Overjoyed but confused, Laura begged to know which room, she should see him directly. He would explain what had gone wrong, why he had left so abruptly. She had spent the past two days trying to tamp down her anger and hurt at his abandonment, in the hope that there would be a good reason why.

'He's in room twelve,' Ulrich finally grumbled, 'but I think he already has company. Oh, and miss,' his eyes suddenly glinted, 'that bowl with the pearl inlay is gorgeous.'

Laura laughed shrilly, to cover up her surprise at the innkeeper's words.

'Yes, it is, isn't it?' she smiled, but her heart began thumping as she ascended the creaky stairs.

On reaching room twelve, she took a deep breath, prepared to forgive him. But Tim would need to give her a good explanation. Especially after their night together.

Laura knocked, and he opened the door. The careless smile on his face immediately changed to one of concern on seeing her.

'Laura, what are you doing here?'

'I might ask you the same thing,' Laura replied lightly, peering over his shoulder, but Tim moved slightly so that her view was blocked.

'What is it?' she asked, worry beginning to get the better of her. Was Ulrich right?

He won't be faithful, mortal, Melisande's poisonous words entered her mind.

'Nothing,' Tim said, a little too quickly. 'I left a note for you at the pool.'

'What note?'

'Didn't you find it?' he questioned, running a hand through his hair. 'I know I left it behind, it explained my… absence.'

No matter how much love you think you have.

It looked as if Tim was about to say more when a female voice called out from the room beyond, 'Who's there, darling?'

He will always desire another.

Laura stared at Tim for a minute in shock before shouldering past him where she saw a woman, wearing hardly any clothing, lying across the bed. The bedsheets were crumpled, as though they had just woken up.

She locked eyes with Tim but he couldn't meet Laura's accusatory gaze. Melisande had been right, she realised, that cruel, beautiful woman had been right. The realisation was a strong punch in the gut, cutting her off from any sort of reasoning.

'Well,' she said resignedly, 'you're just so… predictable, Timothy Crow.'

Anger filled her breast. She relished it. Why did everything always seem to make sense when you were angry? Laura thought.

A part of her wanted to scream and throw a tantrum.

Another wanted to punch Tim and hurt him in every way

possible.

The final piece of her just felt tired. It wanted to go back home, lie in bed and cry until no more tears came.

'Who are you?' the girl asked Laura curiously. She didn't look much older than Laura herself, with wispy brown hair that fell around a face caked in paint and make up.

'I am no one,' she replied, staring hollowly at Tim. 'No one of any importance at all. But I see I was interrupting something, so I'll go once I retrieve one of the things I came for.'

'Yes,' Tim suddenly jumped into action and picked up the bowl from a shelf. 'Here's the key to your journey home. Good luck, Laura.'

He bent to chastely kiss her cheek, but instead Laura snatched the bowl, put it in the bag over her shoulder and stormed out of the room, slamming the door behind her.

'I hate you, I *hate* you!' she yelled, and from inside the room Laura heard his sharp intake of breath. 'You said you loved me, and you lied.' Her voice broke and she clutched a hand to her mouth, stifling the sobs racking through her.

'Going already?' Ulrich called as she strode out of the inn.

Laura didn't bother answering, instead she ran towards the stables, hastily mounted Elaret and flew away from Roshterdam, hoping to never set eyes on it or its inhabitants again.

Chapter Sixteen

Laura cried as she pushed Elaret through the night, barely stopping to eat or rest. She needed to get home to the Temple. She wanted to get as far away from Roshterdam as possible. Then she could return to her own world. To her own family.

When she reached the Barrier, Laura gazed up at it in despair. How was she meant to create a Doorway for herself? She hadn't yet learnt how to do it properly, let alone make the Doorway stable enough to enter.

She landed Elaret, and sat down, thinking deeply. Finally, she realised that she had no choice. She had to get away and wouldn't stay to wait for another Robin to come and sing a Doorway into existence. She had to try.

After a sip of water, Laura leaned against the Barrier, which glowed with power. It was warm, sending tiny vibrations into her body.

Her voice was feeble at first, but soon grew.

In the Ancient Tongue she sang a song of a love gained, how it was like heaven and stronger than anything before. However, it had shattered like a glass being dropped from a high window onto the ground below. When she had finished, her cheeks were tearstained and there was a Doorway in front of her.

Laura picked up Elaret's reins and they ran through the Barrier before launching into the air on the other side. She was surprised to see a familiar mountain range rise up before her. She had entered Venetica and would only have to fly north for several hours to reach her destination.

The Temple of the Nest was first a dot on the horizon, then a faint glow in the darkness, and then suddenly it was below her and she landed, leading Elaret to the stable and heaving the silver bowl out of the saddlebags. She leaned against him, feeling his sweat mingling with hers in the night air as she stroked him lovingly, knowing that this might be goodbye. New tears filled her eyes, but she turned away, brushing a hand over her face roughly. Before any of the Robins could gather outside the stables to welcome her back, Laura was striding purposefully across the courtyard and climbing the stairs of the tallest tower two at a time.

The Robin was sitting beside the fire, staring into its glowing heart. As usual, the firelight didn't penetrate the shadow which cloaked around him, successfully concealing his features.

'I'm back,' Laura said as she sat down opposite him.

'I've noticed,' he replied calmly, turning to gaze at her intently. 'I haven't heard Tim yet, although I expect that he decided to wait and greet his old friends first.'

Laura paused considerably, trying to find the right words, before saying, 'I came ahead of Tim.'

'Oh,' The Robin said, surprised but successfully concealing it. 'Well then, let's get started.'

'Please do,' was the curt reply as she handed him the bowl. The Robin took it, almost reverently, as if he had waited his whole life for this moment.

'I understand that you've been on the quest I wanted you to go on. Now I hope you can appreciate what has happened, and how you've changed.'

Well, Laura thought angrily, I've learnt that men are scheming, lying, cold-hearted bas…

'So, I'm probably right in believing that you still want to go home.'

Laura nodded sharply.

'Now if you remember Laura, I told you that in order for me to grant this privilege, you must give up whatever I name, forever. It is part of the magical contract the bowl requires.'

'I understand,' Laura replied, wishing that The Robin would hurry up. She wanted to be gone before Tim followed her.

'Well Laura,' The Robin said gravely, 'in order for you to see your family, you'll have to give up Timothy Crow.'

'*What?*' Laura cried, shocked.

'Tim. You can never see him again.'

Laura wondered at her good luck, but her voice was firm as she said, 'all right.'

'Did you have a fight?' The Robin asked, confused.

Laura laughed bitterly, 'to say the least, yes. I don't want to talk about it.'

'Very well,' he replied, 'but before I open the Doorway for you, Laura, I think it's about time you knew my name. And I have a personal request; I'd like it if you tell your mother that Corvis sends his love and regards.'

'Okay,' Laura murmured, wondering what had come over him. 'But will I continue being a Robin?'

'Let's see how things turn out. Farewell, Laura.' The Robin glanced away, leaning over the bowl.

'Goodbye,' she whispered, suddenly sorrowful that she couldn't say another farewell to Tash. 'And thank you for everything you've done for me the past six years. I'll miss you.'

The Robin ran his fingers over the bowl, tracing the design along the edge, and began to sing in the Ancient Tongue, conjuring a Doorway to appear in his fireplace. She smiled at the irony: fire had been the reason she left her world in the first place, it seemed only fitting that through fire was how she would return.

Laura waved once and stepped through the Barrier between worlds.

Jane Rallen halted in her tale.

It took a little while for Gretel and Tom to realise that she'd finished.

'Well,' Gretel said slowly, trying to digest all of the information. 'Well.'

'I might copy you, Jane,' Tom smiled faintly, 'I need some sherry.'

'Excuse me, Jane,' Gretel finally said after allowing her husband to pass over some more sherry. 'But should we even be calling you that?'

Tears filled Jane's eyes and her mouth opened, but it was Tom who answered for her.

'You're right, Gretel. She's Laura, our little girl. Although,' he glanced at Laura, 'she isn't so little anymore.'

'Dad!' Laura cried, grasping his hand in hers. 'Mum!' Gretel let out a choking sob and reached instinctively for a tissue. She shook with emotion and Tom embraced her.

'Why did you say you were someone else?' she asked, sniffing into the tissue.

'I couldn't be sure what sort of reception I would get,' Laura replied softly, 'it *has* been six years.'

Gretel took her daughter's hand and allowed tears of joy and surprise to spill from her eyes. She couldn't allow any sort of hurt to enter her mind, not today of all days.

'Laura, my darling, darling girl,' she whispered, sitting down next to her and drawing Laura to her chest. 'I would always recognise my little girl.' Suddenly a thought occurred to her, 'But Laura,' she began, 'how did you know all about the boys who set our house on fire?' Her throat clogged up again, it was because of these boys that the whole trouble had started, really.

'Kylan told me when I was fourteen, in The Temple.' Laura replied, lips curling slightly at the memory of Tim comforting her as she beat out her anger on the trees.

The door opened and they looked up, startled at the interruption.

'Mum, I brought the files like you asked me to.' A masculine voice called.

A man with golden hair walked into the room and paused as he took in the scene before him.

'Who is this?' he asked.

'Fred, don't you remember me?' Laura asked, moving forward to embrace him. 'It's me, Laura. I've come home.'

Fred froze, 'what… but… *how?*'

'It's a long story,' Laura answered, smiling as she helped him over to the couch and sat down next to him.

Fred took a deep, steadying breath and ran a hand through his hair, mirroring Tim's exact movements. Unconsciously, Laura flinched, remembering the man she'd loved.

'But that's impossible!' Fred cried, clinging onto his last shred of reality, reminding himself of everything that he knew. 'Laura was kidnapped from her bedroom on the night of the fire. She disappeared years and years ago… she was just a child.' His voice choked on a sob as he rose to his feet and started to pace, 'the police couldn't find anything but a few blood stains in the alley behind our house and then there was nothing. We were certain she'd died, she was gone so long. She just… vanished.'

'But we never found her body, Fred, or gave up hope that she was alive,' Tom interrupted gently. 'We never had a funeral for that reason.'

'My body was never found,' Laura replied calmly, 'because I survived. It's as simple as that, Fred. I was rescued from my window, where I had caught my dress on the glass, and the two people took me… far away. No matter how much I begged, I wasn't allowed to return home. If you still can't believe me, then wouldn't this necklace be proof enough?' She showed him the well-worn locket which she'd received as a Christmas present so long ago. Fred took another breath and put a hand onto the wall, hoping that he'd remain upright. Everyone in the room was silent, watching, waiting for Fred's reaction.

'But that's… you could've got that *anywhere*.'

'I know it's impossible, but I'm alive, Fred,' Laura stammered, wishing that she hadn't been away so long, long enough for even her own brother to doubt the sincerity of her words.

Fred stared at her for a minute, calculating the truth in Laura's words. Could it really be true? After all of those sleepless nights trying to imagine his sister in heaven, before finally giving up?

He continued to gaze at her and then suddenly asked, 'if you really are Laura, then answer this; where did I keep my favourite oil paints?'

Laura smiled, remembering how her brother had always loved painting.

'On the windowsill behind your bed in a special rosewood box, which Aunt Fiona gave to you at your christening.'

Taken aback, Fred asked, 'but *where* were you? Who took you away? Did they hurt you, Laura? If they did, I swear, I'll make them pay.' Laura blinked, taken aback by the harshness of his tone.

'If I tell you,' she said, 'you may not believe me. But I swear that I never wanted to leave you. I will tell you the story, Fred, but now isn't the time. Do you believe that?'

He watched her, unmoving, and she turned away, saddened. He wouldn't just accept her words as truth. Her memories of Fred reminded her that he'd always wanted to learn the most one could know about anything. Finally, he broke the hushed silence.

'Yes,' he murmured, moving forward to hug her, unashamedly letting tears fill his eyes. 'Laura, my little sister.'

'Well,' Tom said after a moment, 'I think that this calls for dinner out at Grimaldini's.'

Grimaldini's was an Italian restaurant on the main street. Laura had a dish that seemed to be full of tomatoes.

'What happened to the pub?' she asked, recalling the popular place in her childhood where they'd eaten out.

'It closed down two years ago,' Gretel replied. 'The old owner died and his son sold it to a housing company. By the end of the week, it had been demolished. A block of flats is there now.'

'That's awful,' Laura said, appalled. 'I can't believe it.'

There was another silence. Tom turned to Fred and said, 'Well, Fred. Your sister's come home, so what are you two going to do to get reacquainted with each other?' Fred and Laura glanced at each other, surprised and awkward.

'How about a coffee?' Laura inquired, hating herself for feeling like a total stranger.

'I'm free on Friday,' Fred sighed, 'I have a free in the morning before school starts.'

'Fred's an art teacher,' Gretel said proudly, holding her son's hand from across the table.

Laura smiled, pleased. Fred had always preferred arts and painting to sciences. It was great that he could pass on some of his enthusiasm to students. Meeting Fred's gaze from across the table, Laura began to realise that, although her family had taken her back with open arms, she may never fit in perfectly, because things had changed too drastically in the time she had been away.

'Would you like a dessert, Laura?' Gretel inquired, as she sipped her wine.

'No, thanks. Dad, they wouldn't have ale, would they?'

Her mother stared at her, aghast.

'*Ale?*' Gretel questioned. 'Do you like beer, Laura? It's disgusting.'

'*I* like beer,' Fred said, noticing his sister turn red.

'But you're a man,' Gretel argued, 'no daughter of mine will drink beer.'

Tom put a hand on her arm, quieting her. Laura gazed at the table and shook her head, disappointment sinking to the pit of her stomach. She'd forgotten over the years how her mother had had certain beliefs and now that she had lived independently for so long, it was hard to accept them as she once had.

'Of course not,' she said brightly, adjusting to what her mother expected and wishing that her desire for the life in Venetica would dissipate.

That night, Laura lay in the spare room bed, feeling small and insignificant. Over time she had forgotten about the noise and speed of cars, the easy use of electricity and gas, and, of course, readily available hot water. However, she'd adapted to living without these things. She found it hard to get used to the large automobiles which sped down the streets, brakes squealing as they reached a red light. It was strange how living without what she used to take for granted had changed her entire outlook.

She sat up in bed and reached over to her dressing table. Her dezmian lay next to the hairbrush, and she picked it up, twirling it through her fingers. Could she access her magic here? Or was Earth completely devoid of the arcane?

The dezmian flew into the air, turning as she muttered to herself. The hairbrush didn't move towards her as she'd wanted it to. There was no wrenching sensation in her gut, for the first time in six years. Laura watched, horrified, as the dezmian fell down onto the bed sheets. The harsh reality that magic wouldn't work here, no matter how simple the spell, hurt. Her dezmian was as useless as a pebble, which she had once mistaken it to be. Magic had been one of her best subjects in Venetica; The Robin and Lukas on his visits had said that she had strong natural talent. A part of her felt lost now that one of her favourite things was gone.

In the dark she remembered the things she'd done only a week or so ago. Her magic had not been the only thing she'd lost, she realised now that the anger had faded. She recalled the feel of Tim's skin in the afternoon light, the pressure of his lips on hers and the blissful happiness she'd felt, if only for a moment.

Her mind moved on to recollect Tim's movements in the inn, and how the girl had lain on his bed as if she owned it. How the bedsheets had been crumpled as though they had just been doing what she and Tim had done the day before. The anger rose up with a vicious snarl, but then the memory of how the girl's clothes had been on arose, as if she hadn't meant to stay the night. A seed of doubt lodged in Laura's heart, and her brows came together.

Tim's voice resonated in Laura's mind: *Didn't you find the note I left you beside the pool? It explained my absence.*

It explained my absence.

How could his absence be explained?

Two options appeared in her mind.

One was that after the night they lay together, he'd grown sick of her and wanted to leave. Yet that didn't seem like the sort of thing Tim would do. She'd known him for six years. She had been closer to him than anyone else, except Tash.

Or two, there was some other reason as to his, and the bowl's, disappearance.

As she thought on the subject more and more, Laura realised how she'd prejudged him by the company of the girl in his room. How she had allowed what Melisande had said to influence her thinking and interpretation of what happened.

She wished she could talk to him again, to hear him explain everything. To tell her that she'd been wrong, to say that he loved her and her alone.

But The Robin's deal had denied her that wish.

At the time Laura had thought that she'd hated Tim because of everything he'd done. Even now the anger was dormant, lying in wait for the right moment to arise and control her. She couldn't deny that when it came to Tim's association with other girls, she had a very jealous nature. And now, for the rest of her days, would she be tormented by this decision? Would memories of what could have been ever fade into nothingness?

'What have I done?' she whispered to the darkness. Those words haunted her until sleep unfolded its beautiful wings.

What have I done, oh, God, what have I done?

Chapter Seventeen

Wednesday came with dark grey storm clouds covering the sky, denying Gretel the opportunity to hang out her washing.

'I always wash the clothes on Wednesdays,' she told Laura as they shoved the laundry into the tumble drier.

'I remember that,' Laura murmured, 'you'd hang bunches of dried lavender up with the clothes so they smelt fresh when you took them down. It was my favourite.'

'I still do that occasionally,' Gretel admitted, 'but after you went away, the smell of lavender lost its charm. Oh, we did miss you.' Tears filled her mother's eyes, and Laura hugged her, rubbing her back soothingly.

'Are you looking forward to Friday?'

'Having a coffee with Fred?' she asked, 'yes, of course.'

'It'll be good seeing him smile a bit more,' Gretel said thoughtfully, 'we've not had so much to laugh about over the past six years.'

'Really?' Laura asked, suddenly privately guilty of the enjoyable times she had experienced while her family suffered.

'Nothing was the same after that night,' Gretel said.

Laura sighed. If only she had been able to send some sort of communication through a doorway to Earth, so that her family had known that she was alright. But what could she have said? 'Hi Mum and Dad, I'm alright. I'm living in an alternate world at the moment and cannot come back until I'm older and able to pass safely between worlds. I love you.

By the way, did you know that there are hundreds and thousands of different worlds, not just our own?'

No, that wouldn't have gone down well at all. She blinked the thought away and followed her mother towards the kitchen, trying to avoid feeling obsolete as her mother insisted on preparing a pot of tea. Later, as she drank, Laura stared out at the small backyard, hating that all she wanted was to get on Elaret's back and fly far away.

When Friday came, Fred took his sister out to have a coffee. They walked to a small café called 'The Queen's Tearooms'. Fred pushed open the door which sent a small bell tinkling. Laura gazed, wide-eyed at the glass display case where multiple cakes, biscuits and dainty pastries were displayed on a white cloth. Looking closer, Laura noticed some blowflies circling the cakes. She turned away, deciding instantly to not order any food. Aside from the flies, she found the café completely different to the tearooms in Venetica. How different this world was, even though it was her home. Laura shook her head slightly, trying to remove the idea of analysing every detail. This was her home, not Venetica. Besides, the likelihood of returning to Venetica was not on the cards at the moment.

'A cappuccino for me, please,' Fred smiled at the waitress, who then turned expectant eyes to Laura, pen poised on the notepad. She blinked, suddenly brought back to the present.

'Err, the same, thanks,' she said, wishing that the girl would stop looking at her as if she were a biology specimen. Fred chose a seat beside the window, and they sat down opposite each other.

'So,' he began, watching her keenly.

Laura smiled, at a loss for words. How could it be this awkward? What could she say to ease the silence?

'How did you find us?' Fred asked, 'I know what you went through to get back, but Mum said that you finished the story when you went through the fire. So, what happened next?'

'I came out in the bush somewhere. I don't know exactly, but I think it was north of the state. A family was driving past in their four-wheel drive and offered me a lift. I think they thought I was mentally deranged, I didn't even have a water bottle.' She smiled at the memory, thinking about squeezing into the backseat alongside two small children playing on their i-Pads. 'I didn't even have any money to pay them for their help.'

'You were incredibly lucky,' Fred muttered.

'I know.' Dipping a spoon into the froth on top of the cappuccino, Laura worked her way down to the coffee.

Taking a sip, she shuddered, it was so bitter!

'You can put in some sugar if you want,' Fred murmured. Laura nodded, and ripped open one of the sachets of sugar, making sure to stir it into her coffee with the spoon.

Taking another sip, she found the drink slightly more bearable.

Fred laughed at her expression, 'I remember what it was like when I had my first coffee, I bet I looked just like you.'

She laughed. 'Anyway, where was I? Yes, they gave me a lift into Adelaide, which, thank God, was their destination too. I remembered the name of the suburb where we used to live and they took me there. I told them I was looking for my family and the mother gave me the White Pages. I'd forgotten all about them.'

'I'm amazed that they had a spare copy in their car!'

'So, I looked up our name. There were about fifty other Jefferies in Adelaide, so it made the process of elimination quite difficult. But as I went through the addresses, I realised that you had probably moved. I went to every T. and G. Jefferies in the book.'

'But you had different clothes when you came to Mum and Dad's. Where on earth did you get the money for them?'

'I went to a bank,' Laura said calmly, 'and took out a loan. I was sure that Mum and Dad would help me out in paying them back.' Her eyes glittered cheekily, 'I knew they'd be so happy I was home that they'd do anything.'

Fred smiled and shook his head, before a thought popped into his mind.

'You know,' he announced, 'I haven't tried out portraiture yet, outside of the classroom. Would you mind sitting for me? I need something to remember you by if you take off again.'

'Couldn't you just use a photo?' she asked, grinning.

'That isn't the point,' he replied. 'Will you do it?'

'Of course I will. Today's full of first experiences for me,' Laura said happily, 'the first time I've had coffee, I've been asked to pose for an artist and…'

'Laura?' Fred asked, but she had trailed off and her gaze was riveted outside on a man in a long dark coat. His eyes flashed a deep green as they met Fred's and the look in them made Laura's brother feel like he was slowly being electrocuted.

The man ran a hand through his dark, spiky hair and stepped forward, before seeming to change his mind.

All it took was for a mother and a pram to walk in front of the window, and once they'd passed, the man had gone.

Fred noticed the difference in his sister's appearance on beholding the empty air where the stranger had stood.

'Tim.' She murmured, noticing her brother's confused look. 'We were very close for a while, but we had a misunderstanding.'

Ah, Fred thought, it was one of *those* relationships. He remembered his parents discussing it in lowered voices.

'Well,' he said jovially, 'I've got to hurry back to work. I'll see you soon, Laura. And don't forget to prepare yourself for the artist's model business.' He winked mischievously and they laughed.

'I will,' Laura grinned, and outside of the café, brother and sister parted.

Tim had been there.

That was all that went through Laura's mind, for the next few weeks. Although the look on his face had ruined any hope of them trying to reconcile. In her heart, Laura prayed that Tim would call on her, even if The Robin didn't allow it.

However, as the weeks drew into months, Laura's faint shred of hope began to wither, before dying completely. If Tim had stayed all of this time, then he'd have disintegrated because it wasn't the world into which he'd been born.

Fred took photos of her in different shades of light and poses. At other times he sketched her using pencils and sometimes he would use paints. With these studies, he locked himself in the painting studio each night, after coming back from school. It was quite boring at times, but a good time for her to practice meditation. During those long hours, Laura and Fred started to regain their old camaraderie, which used to come like second nature.

However over time Laura felt annoyed that she was yet to see what he was drawing in there, Fred was so secretive with his work. She was even more astonished when he began locking the studio door and keeping the keys on his person.

Gretel was overjoyed to hear about Fred's project. Tom nodded with a grunt and retreated to his crossword in the lounge room, trying to figure out if nine across was lethargic or lassitude.

'I missed the smell of wet paint,' Gretel admitted to Laura as they baked macadamia shortbread in the kitchen. Her daughter glanced at her, wondering how to phrase her questions aloud without potentially causing offence. How could she ask her mother what she wanted to know, to get clarity on several points that had replayed in her mind since she left Venetica? In the end, she decided that bluntness was the best method and so she changed the subject suddenly, throwing her mother off-balance.

'Mum, you know how I told you about the message from The Robin?'

'Yes,' Gretel replied, suddenly pale.

'What did he mean by someone called Corvis giving you his love and regards? What don't I know?'

Her mother could tell almost immediately that this topic had been on Laura's mind for a while.

'Let's sit down, darling.' She said gravely, nodding towards a wooden chair in the corner of the kitchen. 'It's time that I told you the truth, Laura.'

Her mother fidgeted with her oven mitt, 'it all started when I was eighteen— young, just out of school and desperate to see the world. My family was very strict, they wanted me to go to university and get a bachelor's degree in medicine. I wanted very different things, I wanted to hike in the

Himalayas, travel down the Nile and find someone who would love me and not tell me what to do all the time.

'So, I went traveling, after striking a compromise. After one year, I had to return to go to university. If I didn't then my parents wouldn't allow me to have any more money for my traveling. At the time I didn't care, I had two wishes already granted, I had seen the wonderful snow and ice of Nepal, and the pyramids of Egypt. But my heart still wanted more. So, halfway through the year I settled down in Venice. I wanted to go on a gondola and see St Mark's Square. It was in Venice that I met Corvis.

'We met in St Mark's Square, when he pushed past me while I threw bits of bread to the pigeons. I staggered and he turned, already apologizing. I think that the term "love at first sight" was real in our case. When we looked at each other, I think we both knew.

'Corvis and I spent the next few months getting to know each other. They probably were the most wonderful months that year. Finally, I had all the wishes of my heart, and I was content.

'After a while he took me to visit his parents' graves, as they'd both died a few years earlier. His family had been poor, but he told me that he wanted to become a biologist. He was going to go to a university as soon as he could afford the funds.

'Then a crazy idea formed in my mind, what if Corvis and I went to the same university to study? He would study biology and I medicine. My parents may not be happy about it, but if they knew the depth of my feelings for this man, then maybe they would grow to love him like I had.

'It took me a while to convince Corvis to return to Adelaide to meet my parents. He was nervous, especially about the fact that he had basically no money whatsoever to support himself. And you know that my parents were very well-off.

'The meeting couldn't have gone worse; I wasn't expecting it. I thought they'd accept him. Instead Corvis and my father fought over anything and everything. I couldn't bear to watch them, so we left and moved into a small flat in the city.

'We were together for several years until I was thirty. They were happy times, and I gave birth to both you and Fred. But it didn't last. He had a tendency to take off from time to time, and I thought I understood, believing that he must be homesick for Italy. But then I started thinking that he might be seeing someone else. It made what once had been an easy relationship turn sour, and soon we were at each other's throats. And then one night he left and he never came back. It was like he disappeared, like he'd walked off the face of the earth.'

I know what *that* feels like, Laura thought. It was obvious now, Corvis had somehow found a Barrier and sung his way through. When he'd become The Robin, though, was still a mystery.

'Did you tell him to leave?' she asked.

'Yes, and many other things besides,' Gretel sighed. 'I regretted them later of course, but by then it was too late.'

Laura pondered over her mother's words for a minute, still shocked at the sudden revelation, until another thought appeared in her mind.

'What about Dad? I mean, Tom?' Laura asked. 'And what about Fred? Does he know the truth?'

'Yes,' Gretel said, 'but he didn't tell you because he was young and confused, and I thought that it would be better for you to believe Tom to be your father.'

'When did he go?' Laura demanded, she had to know everything.

'You were a toddler when he went away,' Gretel said, 'It was hard for a while. But then my father introduced me to Tom, and he accepted me, along with my past and family. Tom told me that if I married him, he would provide a shelter for me and my children. He couldn't have children of his own, you see. He wanted to provide for you and your brother, to love you like you were his own. So, I married him, and over the years, learnt to love him. I don't regret making that decision for a second.' Her voice was warm, and she smiled in the direction of the lounge.

'Didn't you ever hear from Corvis again?' Laura questioned.

'Never.' Her mother answered. 'It's amazing that you were his apprentice for years and you never knew. I'm sure that he somehow twisted the rules so that he could see you every day.' Her tone became harsh and accusatory, 'but to think that he had you there for six years and didn't even let us know you were alright. I can't forgive him for that.'

Laura nodded in understanding, all of the odd actions and words The Robin had said suddenly making sense. The strange feeling of safety she had felt in his presence; he was her father. How it must've hurt him that she was so desperate to return home to a man who wasn't her father, than stay in the Temple with him. But she hadn't known the truth, so how could he blame her?

Her mind whirled with emotion, disorder and regret and her eyes filled with tears.

'I'm so confused, Mum,' she whispered, 'I don't know what to do.'

Gretel held her child until the choking sobs finally subsided and Laura was able to blow her nose on a tissue.

'Everything will be alright, darling,' she murmured, slowly rocking Laura back and forth.

The beeper on the oven made them both jump with surprise.

'That macadamia shortbread smells good,' Laura muttered.

Gretel held the oven mitts and pulled out the tray of freshly baked shortbread.

'It looks ready, too.'

Carefully they began to cut out the pieces, placing them onto a rack to cool.

'I might go and lie down for a while,' Laura said, and her mother nodded.

As she lay down on the bed she now called her own, Laura sighed and gave in to an exhausted sleep. She was plunged almost immediately into a dream which, she now realised, she had had many times when she was young.

She was a toddler once again, and felt strong arms around her, a deep voice saying, *mio tesoro.*

Now Laura knew whose arms were holding her and whose voice whispered those words. All her life she'd thought it was Tom, but Tom couldn't speak Italian.

It was Corvis.

Chapter Eighteen

Months passed.

Christmas came and went, with the New Year quickly following. Soon it was Lent and then Easter, the weather changing as autumn arrived, chill wind and rain often beating the roof of the Jefferies' house. The leaves turned orange and brown, lining the sides of the streets in piles of soggy mulch.

All this time Laura waited, although she wasn't sure what for, and soon even her family was able to tell when she was thinking about her past.

In her dreams she was haunted by visions of the Temple on fire, Tash screaming and Tim being burnt alive. In the dream, Laura was standing in the tower window, unable to move, and she couldn't save her friends.

Suddenly she was grabbed by the waist and held over the small balcony. Turning her head, Laura saw The Robin, eyes maniacal and wide.

'You want to be a Robin?' he laughed, 'then show me how to fly, little bird!'

The next thing Laura knew, she was plummeting to the ground; sometimes she felt the pain as her lifeblood stained the cobbles, but most of the time she awoke just before she hit the ground.

It seemed as if the nightmare visited her at some point each night. Gretel and Tom were able to hear the sobbing and moaning coming from their daughter's room, and both were worried. She hadn't had night terrors since she was a toddler, after Corvis left. Should they buy some sleeping tablets? Send for a doctor?

But in the end no doctor would be able to cure Laura, because who could control sleep?

'I have a surprise,' Fred announced at the dinner table the night before Laura's nineteenth birthday.

Everyone looked at him expectantly.

'Laura, do you remember how I've been painting your portrait?'

'How could I forget?' Laura smiled. 'You had me modelling nearly every day for at least a month.'

'Well, I have finished. There is, however, more than one, and they're quite a collection. One of my colleagues works part time in the Gallery of National Art. After telling him about it, he's expressed an interest to come and see them.'

'But *we* haven't seen them yet,' Tom objected, 'surely, Fred, as your family we should view them first?'

'I want them to be a surprise.' Fred replied mysteriously.

'When would he come?' Gretel asked, 'because tomorrow *is* your sister's birthday.'

'Well, any time. But he'd rather come tomorrow.'

Laura looked up and her family was surprised to see tears in her eyes.

'Oh Fred, that's *wonderful!*' she cried, moving forward to embrace him. 'It may help your reputation as an artist. This is brilliant, I can't wait to see them. Especially after all the time I've spent sitting still.' She rolled her eyes dramatically and got a smile of thanks in response.

'What time will he come?' Gretel asked, hoping it would be in the morning.

'Ten,' Fred grinned. 'He might bring some other representatives from the Gallery as well.'

'Laura, you need to go shopping, tomorrow morning,' Tom said, an idea forming in his sharp mind. 'I'll give you my credit card, and can you buy yourself a nice dress and some shoes.'

'Sure,' Laura smiled enthusiastically, because she'd always loved clothes shopping, it was just a shame that Tash couldn't come with her. They would have had so much fun together, analysing each shop, trying on the worst possible outfits and then bursting into fits of laughter while the shop assistants would look on disapprovingly. Yes, it was a shame that Tash wouldn't celebrate her nineteenth birthday with her. She had celebrated the previous ones. Laura felt a sinking in her chest, before forcing a smile, trying not to think that almost six months had passed since she left Venetica.

It felt like six years.

Mr Dickinson was the Chair of the National Gallery, as well as an art and design teacher, and took quite a fancy to Gretel's macadamia shortbread.

'Never tasted anything like it, my dear,' he commented with his mouth full.

'Thank you,' Gretel replied, wishing that he'd drop all of the crumbs onto his plate and not the spotless carpet.

'Would you like to see the artwork?' Fred asked, noticing how uncomfortable his mother looked. He himself was impatient for his colleague's opinion.

'First I'd like to meet your model, Fred,' Mr Dickinson said purposefully.

'She's gone shopping,' Tom put in nervously.

'Oh, what a shame,' their guest sighed.

Suddenly the kitchen door opened and Laura walked in, her arms loaded with bags. She somehow managed to balance shoe boxes and plastic bags on one arm while she closed the door.

'Hello,' she smiled, before running up the stairs to put her shopping down.

Gretel watched her daughter with amazement, how many things had she bought? Why hadn't she given the girl a budget? She didn't want to discover that she had a shopaholic for a daughter.

'I take it that you are Laura?' Mr Dickinson asked when she came back down.

'Yes, and you are…?' Laura replied, shaking his hand.

'Harrison Dickinson,' the man informed her. 'And these are my colleagues on the Board: Yasmin Tarles and Benjamin Redford.' He indicated a woman in a tight suit and a man in jeans and a T-shirt.

'Pleased to meet you,' she grinned.

'I see that you've got quite a beauty, Fred.' Harrison announced, looking Laura up and down with an expert's eye. Laura blushed and glanced downward, uncomfortable.

'My sister is a rarity,' Fred laughed, pulling her into a quick hug.

'Well, now that we're all here,' Tom said, 'how about we see what Fred's been spending all his time with lately?'

The group trooped up the stairs and, with a little flourish Fred produced the key before turning it in the lock.

With a creak, it opened and Fred turned on the lighting.

'Wow,' Laura muttered, 'how long did you spend getting everything ready, Fred?' She took in the pale blue couch and twelve paintings on the white-washed walls.

'A few nights of solid work,' he chuckled. 'I had to clean everything up like crazy, who would've thought, eh?'

Slowly Laura made her way around the room. She had never been very artistic, but even she could tell that the artwork before her was finely done. In some of them the brushstrokes were too small to see, and it made the overall effect even more realistic. And then she examined the pictures themselves, marvelling at the scenes which, she was sure, her brother had made up in his head.

The first picture showed Laura glancing over her shoulder on the edge of a cliff by the sea, laughing as if a companion had just spoken a highly amusing joke. Seagulls circled in the background against the cloudy sky, which made Laura's coppery hair stand out bright against the grey.

Wherein the next one, Laura was sitting on a rock beside a waterfall, wearing gauzy white material which shimmered around her like the foam from churning water. Her eyes were large and innocent in this one, long hair dancing in the light breeze. She held a red rose against her chest, and her mouth curved in a smile, but the image of the waterfall caused a painful jab in her stomach, so she hurried along, focussing on the next picture. She was amazed that her brother could make artwork seem to breathe with a life of its own.

The third painting showed Laura kneeling beside a water lily pond, her face reflected in the water. Two ducks were diving for waterweed beside her reflection, distorting the image with ripples.

'Fred, these are incredible,' Laura said, with a soft laugh. 'How can you *do* this?'

The next painting showed her in a different light. Laura's hands were clenched as she stared out of a window at a bustling city life. A letter was on a table beside her, and tears fell from her eyes. Laura imagined the scene in a melodramatic television show and stifled a laugh.

'Lovely emotion in this one,' Harrison admitted.

A bit dramatic though, Laura thought.

'Thank you,' Fred said, cheeks flushed with gratification.

'What's this one?' Yasmin asked curiously.

Laura glanced at the one Yasmin was pointing to, and felt her breathing come out in a ragged gasp. He hadn't. He couldn't.

In the picture, Laura's eyes were bright with excitement and love, reaching over a coffee table in a café to a man on the other side of the glass. His dark hair stood up in untidy spikes and deep green eyes blazed in return, their hands were almost touching, separated only by the pane of glass.

'You didn't take a photo of that,' she whispered, sitting down on the couch.

'I did,' Frederick replied calmly, 'in my mind's eye.'

Laura turned away and examined her hands, practising her deep breathing techniques. *In and out. In and out.*

'Exceptional,' Harrison murmured, before talking quietly with his colleagues.

Fred waited anxiously, now was the moment of truth.

'We'd like to buy these ones from you, Fred,' Harrison offered, indicating five of the twelve. Laura was pleased that the painting of her and Tim was not included. 'They will do very nicely in our collection. I hope that we can do more business together in the future.' He winked at Fred, 'see you tomorrow at the staff meeting.'

He began writing out a cheque for Fred, and handed it to him, before turning to Laura.

'Miss Jefferies, I think that it might be wise for you to join a modelling agency. After some artists see these, I'm sure they'll want you to model for them too.'

'Thank you,' Laura blushed faintly, 'I'd like that very much.'

Their guests departed quickly, each stopping to congratulate Fred.

'How much did they give you?' Gretel asked.

Fred looked at the cheque and gasped, 'four thousand dollars!'

'They're worth more than that,' Tom said instantly.

'Be quiet!' Gretel chastened her husband, 'They're sold and that's that.' She gave him a brief push out of the door and their feet echoed down the hallway.

'How did you know?' Laura questioned Fred when they were alone.

'What?'

'How did you know what Tim looked like when he loved me?'

'I could see it reflected in his gaze when he saw you.'

Laura nodded, and turned away, a few stray tears falling onto her cheeks, which she angrily brushed away.

'Let's go and enjoy the rest of your birthday,' her brother whispered comfortingly.

Together they left the studio.

Chapter Nineteen

'You look beautiful,' Fred smiled as Laura descended the stairs, her strapless black satin dress floating out around her as she walked towards him.

'The shoes are a bit tight,' she admitted, pointing to the pointed black shoes which were very high.

'You're still gorgeous,' Gretel said.

'Thanks, Mum,' Laura grinned, hoping that the lipstick wouldn't smudge on her teeth. Wrapping a silky silver scarf around her neck, she walked out to the driveway and got into the car.

'Are we going to Grimaldini's?' Laura asked as they began to drive, still unaware of her family's plan.

'Yes,' Gretel smiled, 'we booked a table to celebrate. They have a special private function room which we thought might be a nice surprise.'

They reached the restaurant in silence and entered the function room, which was lit with mood lighting. Laura wondered if the restaurant owner had realised that it was a family who had booked it, and not a young married couple.

Her parents and Fred didn't comment, merely sat down at the table in the centre of the room. Laura followed suit, discovering within seconds that bright red walls and gold leaf patterns did not create the most pleasing atmosphere. The white tablecloth was harsh in the light, and she blinked, not sure how long she could stand her surroundings.

'We thought that we would order a feast,' Tom said, he turned to Laura, 'so that way we can share a selection of their best dishes.'

'Sounds great.' Laura wished her enthusiasm wasn't so forced. It was hard to focus on the meal– ever since she saw Fred's paintings, Tim had consumed her thoughts.

Had it really been six months since she last saw him? Already she was starting to forget his smell, the sound of his voice. Was this how it had been for her mother when Corvis left? Piece by piece the memories would fade, leaving nothing in their place.

She didn't want that to happen.

She didn't want to forget the past six years of her life; the things she'd learnt, the friends she'd made. Surreptitiously, Laura reached into her handbag and felt the comforting smoothness of her dezmian. It may not work here, but it could still help her relax, magic or not.

'We've been thinking, Laura,' Gretel began, reaching out and pulling her daughter's hands into her own. The dezmian rolled to the bottom of the handbag, the brief warmth Laura's fingers had provided disappearing almost immediately.

'Since you got back,' Gretel continued, 'you have taken time to adjust back into our normal routine.' She looked at Tom, and then Laura, to make sure she wasn't overstepping the line. Laura waited, curious about what her mother would say next.

'We were wondering if you would like to try and get your high school degree,' she smiled, 'since we don't know what you learnt when you were away. But from what you told us– meditation, geography and languages– none of them are useful here. You learnt geography and languages from other worlds.' Laura could tell her mother had an immense aversion to the idea. 'We think you should learn something more… well, normal. Maths or biology or Chinese. Anything, so long as it is *Earth* related.'

Fiery anger and hurt burnt through Laura's veins, and she had to grit her teeth to avoid snapping in response. They couldn't just expect her to change and become someone different overnight, surely!

'Mum, Dad, what I learnt in Venetica was different from what I would learn here. Of course it was, it *had* to be. The things I've learnt over there weren't a waste of time. I loved learning things that were so diverse and different from fractions and formulas. I *did* do some courses on those subjects,' she added, 'but they never interested me.'

'And what did? Magic?' Her mother gave a slightly hysterical laugh, 'that would be no use to you *here*, Laura! Be realistic. I think we've been open minded enough. You need to learn about things that will help you to get a job and an education. It's time to go out and meet new people and move on with your life here.'

The silence was electrifying. Fred and Tom glanced at each other, raised their eyebrows in unison, and ate with increased vigour, slurping their spaghetti noisily.

Laura had withdrawn her hands from her mother's and clutched the tablecloth, trying to remain calm. The last few months had made her reflect on what she wanted, both now and in the future. She had to tell her family. She hadn't wanted it to be now, but she didn't want them to entertain too many frail hopes.

'Mum, I was away for a long time,' she started. 'During that time, I grew up. I fended for myself and learnt from my mistakes. In that world I had a future, a *life*. A life I could live happily because I had been taught how to for six years. I had to learn how to get on without everything I knew here. Of course I want to learn more about Earth, but I don't think I'll ever fit back in here. Hope of that disappeared long ago, when I was saved by two strangers.'

'Kidnappers,' Gretel muttered.

Laura's eyes flashed. 'They saved me, Mum. No matter what else they did, they helped me to *survive*. I wouldn't condemn them for what they've done; I'd thank them.'

'You can't mean that,' Gretel whispered, 'you lost so much. We didn't see you grow up, go to high school. You have been denied a normal adolescence. That isn't fair on you, darling.'

'I was not *denied* anything,' Laura snapped, 'I was happy there.' She knew instantly that she'd overstepped the line, her mother winced, and tears filled her eyes. 'Mum...' Laura began.

Her mother waved a hand, 'don't, Laura. It's apparent that you would rather...'

'Don't say something you'll regret,' Tom interrupted, 'not after all this time.'

Gretel paused, and with an obvious amount of control, forced a smile and said, 'I'm sorry, darling. It's just hard to hear you talk like that. Like you aren't going to stay.'

'I'll be able to visit you though,' Laura said quickly, 'Don't misunderstand.'

'It's hard not to,' Gretel muttered. This time Laura had the sense to ignore her mother.

'For so long all I've wanted was to come back here, to see you again and let you know I was alright. But I never imagined what would happen after that. Now that my wish has come true, it's been difficult to know what to do. And, if I'm honest,' she halted and glanced at her mother, 'I miss Venetica. I miss the life I had there. I want to go back.'

'But you only just came home!' Gretel cried, shoulders slumping in defeat. Her fears were coming true. Damn Corvis for taking her daughter and keeping her to himself, he had had no right.

'I got back six months ago, Mum,' Laura said gently, 'and I'm not going to cut you out of my life. I *want* to be able to see you and be with you, but I can't stay here.'

'What if we got you a mobile?' Tom asked, 'and you texted us when you got there so we knew you were alright?'

Laura sighed, 'it's not like going overseas, Dad. I don't think mobile connection would *work* there. There isn't any electricity.'

'Oh,' Tom said awkwardly, deciding to devote himself to the bowl of spaghetti instead of making more suggestions.

'Would you try to come back for Christmas, at least?' Gretel asked.

'I'd try,' Laura grinned, it might take them a while to come around to the idea, but she knew that she'd won this battle. Soon, very soon, she would be back in Venetica and having strong words with her… *father*. It felt weird to think of him like that; to her, Corvis would always be a beloved teacher and mentor. Not really a father.

And if she was in Venetica she could see Tash again, while trying to avoid Tim. That would be the hardest part. But there was no way she was going to sit around in her parents' house any longer. She couldn't stand extended idleness. It was a waste of time.

The meal before her had disappeared before she became aware of what was going on. Then her mother's arms were gently helping her up, and they left the horrible function room behind. Laura barely registered the drive back home, relishing the silence. The only issue would be finding a Barrier and getting back to the Temple. Her heart gave a pang when she thought of Elaret, who was probably still waiting patiently in the stable for her to come and ride him.

Tom pulled up in the driveway and they left the car, heading up to the house. When they got into the kitchen, Gretel put the kettle on to make a pot of tea and Laura slumped down on the worn couch in the lounge room, pulling the high heels off in relief. Her feet ached and she lay back into the cushions, too full of spaghetti and ravioli to move.

The sound of the doorbell brought her back to her senses. The clock over the gas fireplace said that it was a quarter past ten. Who would be calling at this time?

She heard Tom walk to the door and open it, his voice a faint murmur. Her eyelids closed drowsily, it had been a long day. She would be glad to go to bed.

'Laura?' Tom had peeped his head around the doorframe, 'it's for you.'

She stood up and headed in the direction of the front door. The rest of her family had taken her place in the lounge, patiently waiting for the tea to brew. Fred rose and followed her, in the pretence of checking on the tea.

Two figures stood in the doorway, and as Laura approached they stepped forward into the light. One had skin the colour of umber, with glittering dark eyes. The other was tall, hands clenched at his sides, eyes devouring the mere sight of Laura.

Laura froze in shock; what in God's name were they doing there? The Robin had forbidden her from seeing him again, and she rested her hand against the door, wondering whether she should close it in their faces and ignore them.

'Laura!' Tash said excitedly, and Laura's hand moved back with a little sigh. She couldn't bring herself to look at Tim just yet, her heart was already having a minor attack with them just being there.

'Who's that?' Fred asked, staring at Tash. All pretence of arranging the teacups was gone, he was gawking at her instead like some schoolboy.

'She's my best friend,' Laura replied, stepping forwards resignedly to clasp her friend's hands. 'What are you doing here?' she whispered, glancing at her friend anxiously, 'you aren't meant to be here. And how did you know where I lived?'

'The Robin told us,' Tash replied, brows coming together in confusion, 'what makes you think that we aren't supposed to be here?'

'It was forbidden! I'm not meant to… I'm sorry, you must go…'

She made to move away and close the door before Tim said, 'Laura, wait.'

She paused, eyes downcast, wishing vainly that they'd never come. He took a hesitant step towards her and was about to say something when he noticed someone over her shoulder.

'Laura!' Fred cried, coming and clasping her shoulder, 'aren't you going to introduce me?'

Tim's eyes, which had been soft and kind when they entered, now turned steely as he glared at Laura's brother. Laura wouldn't have been surprised if he growled. She felt a wave of amusement despite herself: Tim was jealous of Fred!

'Tash, Tim, this is my brother, Fred.'

Tim instantly relaxed and shook hands easily, forgetting that he had just looked as if he wanted to tear Fred's body apart, limb-by-limb. Tash held hands with Fred, enchanted.

'Natachatet,' she murmured, 'a pleasure.'

'Would you like to come in, Natachatet?' Fred asked gallantly.

'But…' Laura began. They weren't meant to be here. They *shouldn't* be here. What had The Robin been playing at, sending them after her?

'Sure,' Tash smiled brilliantly, taking Fred's arm and leaving Tim and Laura alone together. There was silence, neither wanting to be the first to speak. Laura glanced over her shoulder and saw her parents in the kitchen, watching.

'Walk with me?' she asked, stepping past him onto the path, not caring that she had bare feet. He followed her, hands in pockets with an air of nonchalance, but she noticed that the tendons were still stretched tight, betraying his discomfort.

'Why are you here, Tim?' she asked, as they passed the neighbour's picket fence, which glowed in the moonlight. 'Wait no, don't answer that,' she waved a hand, 'you're not *meant* to be here. Not only do you have to explain yourself,' his tension was contagious, she realised before continuing, 'but I also made a deal. I'm not *able* to see you. The Robin…'

'I realised what you'd done,' he interrupted, 'after the incident at the inn.' They both flinched, 'I knew what you believed me to be doing. But I swear on my life, Laura, I wasn't. I was befriending Annabelle, that is true, but not for pleasure. I wanted her to get information about that hooded man.'

'Why?' Oh God, had he realised that it was Glenroy? Why had he been so interested in him?

'I discovered that he had followed us on horseback. Apparently, the man was a collector of rare items, and when you told the innkeeper what we were looking for, this man was fascinated. The way I basically dragged you away, I'm sure only provoked his curiosity.'

'Then why did you leave?' Laura felt herself let out a breath she hadn't known she'd been holding; had Tim really not recognised Glenroy? She didn't believe what he'd heard for a minute.

'When I awoke, the bowl was gone. You were asleep and I didn't want to wake you. So, after writing a note, I found Willowing tracks in the forest and Iris followed his scent to the inn. The whole way there I tried to think of reasons why someone would take the bowl, and I couldn't think of anything. But I knew how much it meant to you, so I wanted to get it back before you woke up.'

'But I never got a note,' Laura interrupted, as the truth became gradually clearer in her mind.

'I don't know what went wrong,' Tim said sadly.

Laura nodded, realising with a heavy heart exactly what Glenroy had done. He'd led them both a merry dance, she was certain. When she'd gone through the strange test set by the otherworld folk, he'd followed them and waited to take the item she'd spent so long trying to find. He lured Tim away, probably circling through the forest until he returned to the pool where Laura still lay asleep, to take the note. She felt an overwhelming sadness, for it was clear that he hadn't tried to redeem himself. On realising that Laura would always prefer Tim to himself, he'd done everything in his power to force a wedge between them.

And he so nearly won, she thought, but he couldn't have foreseen what would happen now.

'Then Annabelle was…?' She left the question hanging, had the girl been paid by Glenroy to be there, or had her presence been completely innocent?

'Annabelle was my inside source, she's a barmaid at the inn and it was she who found the bowl in that man's room, just before you arrived. She told me about the stranger and how he always kept to himself, and that he had brought a package back with him the night before. She'd only just returned when you knocked at the door. At first, I thought it would be him, and that he'd seen Annabelle take the bowl.

'But it was you instead. I didn't know what to do, I knew how bad it would look. Laura, when I saw the expression on your face and heard what you said, it broke my heart. Maybe if you'd thrown a tantrum I would've felt better, but you were so calm— it hurts to even remember. I came to try and tell you a few months ago, but you seemed to be enjoying yourself with Fred. At the time, I'd no idea he was your brother. I thought you'd moved on already.

'In those months that followed, I decided to do something that I swore to do all of those years ago.' He grinned sheepishly, 'I hunted down a Dragutash. Do you remember how I told you that one of those monstrous creatures was the reason behind this?' He showed her the long scar on his forearm and she traced its jagged edge with a slim finger.

'Of course I remember,' she replied.

'Well, I hunted and killed one. It was a quarry I'll never forget,' he pulled back his shirt and showed her his right shoulder, where several new scars were healing. It looked like something had whipped him, leaving deep lacerations in his flesh. Laura's heart did a somersault and she reached forward, examining him closer. It must've been agonizing, and here he was talking calmly about it, as though it were nothing.

'I got my revenge.' Tim continued, 'I was staying in Yorket when Tash found and convinced me to return here. At first, I didn't want to. I was certain that you'd moved on and it was too painful to remember everything I did wrong. To think about what I would do to make it right.'

'It hurts me too,' Laura whispered, looking deeply into his eyes. As he had been speaking, she had been putting the pieces of what really happened that day by the waterfall together in her mind and she knew the truth. She doubted that she would tell Tim about what Glenroy had done to keep them apart for a long time. There was no point in getting caught up in anger at the time they had lost, she just wanted to move forwards and leave all memories of Glenroy in the past.

Tim laughed, unaware of the direction of her thoughts, 'I love you, have always loved you and never will stop loving you.'

'That doesn't completely answer my question,' she giggled, resting her head on his shoulder.

'Okay, I'm sorry to have been the reason to cause so much suffering on both of our accounts, and I swear that I speak the truth.'

'That's better,' she smiled, and kissed him. He responded fondly, fingers entwining in her hair, pulling her closer. She stroked the back of his neck with one hand, and his new scars with the other. It would take a while to get used to them, but they had all the time in the world.

'Wait, Tim,' Laura gasped, suddenly worried, 'The Robin said I couldn't see you again. He made me swear. How can...?'

'I know,' he replied, 'but I went on the quest with you, and he never said it was just *you* who got a favour. I still had to give up something important, though.'

'What did you give up?' Laura asked, fearful.

'I asked to have you back, to be able to be with you. The Robin wasn't happy, but relented eventually. In return, I'm not allowed to return to the Temple of the Nest.'

'But the Temple meant so much to you,' Laura said, shocked.

'Yes, but I can live without it now. I've said the necessary goodbyes, and anyway I don't know how much longer we would've stayed there. I worked out that The Robin will always deny us one of the main things we love. Besides, I'm a fully-fledged Robin now, it was only a matter of time before I left anyway. I can cope with not returning there, so long as I can be with you.'

She nestled closer, any remnants of guilt fading within moments. His arms were around her and, for the first time in six months, she felt complete.

'I did have another trick up my sleeve, in case the first one failed.' Tim said, lips against her temple, 'I know this will come as a shock to you, Laura, but The Robin is your father.'

'I know.'

Tim was astonished, 'how did you find out?'

'My Mum told me.' Laura shrugged.

'I was going to use it against him, blackmail him to get you back.' Tim said sheepishly, Laura smiled at the thought.

'He knows you know then?'

'Yes, it added to my argument, and The Robin was the least composed I've ever seen him.' She couldn't imagine that, despite herself.

'So, we are able to be together now?'

Tim nodded, as they headed back in the direction of her house. When they reached a bus stop, not ten metres from her gate, he got her to sit down.

'What are you doing?' Laura asked, smiling, but then her eyes became serious as she watched him kneel on the pavement. The guarded look that she'd seen on his face so frequently was gone entirely, allowing her to see the hope and irrational fear in his eyes.

'Laura Helen Jefferies, you once told me to choose the right words for everything. I've already told you that I love you. I don't want to lose you again, not even for a moment. I also know that we live in different worlds, quite literally, but that is barely a complication. Not anymore. Will you share my life with me? Will you marry me?' His voice was sweet and hesitant, filling her with warmth.

Laura stared at him, amazed, and felt multiple emotions in her heart, which seemed to be overflowing with happiness.

'Yes,' she whispered, 'yes! How else could you expect me to respond?' She held him close and felt that he was trembling. Carefully she pressed her lips to his cheeks, nose, brow and temple. And then she kissed his mouth, relishing the feeling as he responded, fingers tracing patterns on her body, each touch provoking a wave of heat.

'I got you this, on the off chance you would forgive me.' Tim said as he pulled back, producing a black velvet box. 'Hopefully it fits.'

Laura opened it and saw a silver ring, the bands wove together, plaiting around and around beautifully. It took less than a second for Laura to love it. With a slight awkwardness, Tim took it out and placed it on her left ring finger, where it fitted perfectly. She examined it for a few minutes, inwardly marvelling at the craftsman's skill. It was hard to tell where the metal met in the middle, so finely joined were the silver plaits. For a moment Laura wondered where he had got it but decided against asking. It was better, she thought, to keep some secrets.

'I love you,' Laura murmured as she kissed him again.

'I know,' he replied, returning her embrace.

Epilogue

It was a late night at the Jefferies house that day. When Laura and Tim entered the lounge room to announce their engagement, and, on Tim's side, to be introduced to her family, everyone was sipping cups of tea. Fred was watching Tash, transfixed, and Laura smiled to herself– perhaps she would get a sister as well as a husband. From the sideway glances Tash gave her brother, she could tell that her friend was not entirely unaware of the effect she was having.

Gretel and Tom took the news of the engagement rather well, Laura thought, and she was thankful. A part of her knew that, as soon as Tim had gone to the spare bedroom, her mother would interrogate her and ask whether she was making the right decision. She was only nineteen after all.

But for that moment, everything was perfect. Her hand clasped Tim's and she leaned against him, relishing his comforting warmth.

There was only one final explanation that eluded her, and she knew she wouldn't rest until she found it out.

Why had The Robin wanted to separate Tim and herself? It was all still so unclear. She stared at the small gas fire in the grate at the opposite end of the room. Could he be looking through the bowl now and watching her?

I don't understand! she thought in exasperation, why did he keep us apart and then let us get back together? It didn't make sense.

If only Corvis was able to speak to her through the flames and put an end to all of her troubles. Laura shut her eyes and thought. She thought about the journey she'd been on. It seemed that everything she pondered always came back to The Robin. There had to be a reason behind his actions, but *what?* She stared hopelessly at the flames curling upward.

Watching the flames didn't affect her the way it used to, although she couldn't help wondering why her parents had turned on the gas fire in the house; it wasn't like it was a cold night. She made a mental note to ask her mother about it later. Her eyes strayed down to the new ring on her left hand. Laura's mouth curved instinctively into a smile at the thought of her fiancé, and then the truth and simplicity of The Robin's plan struck her.

As the truth settled in her mind, she remembered other words, which, almost a year ago had haunted her mind.

You who are not from this world,

Cut off from those you love,

Have yet so far to go.

A long journey awaits,

Through the course of time,

Before you judge it so.

Many things will cause dismay,

And some will mislead,

Yet none hurt you alone.

But your hope remains,

When at a loss,

It will lead you home.

Hold fast to dreams,

And hopes of return,

And he who holds you dear.

Together with all three,

You will find the way.

Yet lose that which means the most,

When it is too late.

The prophecy Leonora had spoken in an alchemy shop had come full circle, it seemed. But the ending she was experiencing now had not been included.

Laura's mouth quirked in a smile, it had been true. She had gone on a long journey; it began the moment she left Australia on the back of a Willowing.

In Calcityia she had been dismayed and misled, by tree spirits and Giffleets and a terrifying spider. Not to mention the strange otherworldly folk in Renderfell. In that wood she'd had to hold fast to her hope and dreams, and, most importantly, Tim. How else could she have awoken him from the spell Melisande had placed on him?

Melisande, the leader of the otherworldly folk. Who thought all men were unfaithful and cruel, who was too quick to judge and condemn. Laura wondered what had made the woman like that, but she knew that she would never discover the answer.

It had also been true that she'd found the bowl with pearl inlay soon after, and thought that she had lost Tim. The prophecy was finally finished. Everything had played out as the words had predicted, and yet– aside from six months of distance and unspoken words– Laura and Tim had remained together. Laura smiled again, and felt Tim rub the back of her hand. She wondered if it would shock her parents too much if she took him to her room instead of the spare one.

It was well into the early hours of the morning when everyone went to bed. Tash insisted on using the spare room, casting a mischievous grin in Laura's direction. Laura led Tim up to her room, before leaving him alone for a few minutes. Everyone needed at least a little bit of personal time, and she would be making sure that he dedicated the rest of the night to her. He wouldn't know what was coming until it hit him, and she could push him onto the bed which was much too big for just one person.

She went downstairs and walked over to turn off the gas fire. She paused, kneeling before the flames, wondering if The Robin could see her. Laura looked closer and remembered all that he had done. In a way, he'd been the real mind behind Laura and Tim getting together– he'd sent them on their quest, before deliberately keeping them apart to test how each felt for the other.

A part of her mind could imagine him, recalling the only time she'd ever seen him without the shadowy cloud around his face. His coppery hair, so like her own, and his grave countenance, which even sleep had not been able to change.

There were questions needing answers that only he could give. Loose ends still needing to be tied, but, if she returned to Venetica there would be time. It was only Tim who wasn't allowed to return to the Temple, after all. She needed to spend some quality time with her father.

She smiled at the flames and blew him a kiss, 'thank you, Dad,' she whispered. 'I'll see you soon.'

And in his tower, back in Venetica, Corvis looked into the silver bowl with the pearl inlay and smiled.

The End

Acknowledgements

'Robin' is perhaps one of the stories closest to my heart as it has been a work in progress for so many years. It would not have been possible without the assistance from so many people who have contributed to its development.

I would like to thank Mum, who believed in a fourteen-year-old's idea for a novel and was its first reader. I'm pleased to say that now– fifteen years later– 'Robin' is finally going to be printed and it would not have been possible if you hadn't been there to provide that support to a teenage writer.

To Ian, Natalie, Brittany and the team at The Book Reality Experience– thank you for being open to taking on another fantasy project! I value all of your suggestions and advice and am so grateful for being one of your authors.

To Jordan and our two feline boys, Romeo and Gnocchi, for providing me with regular cups of tea, cooking dinner and cuddles to get me away from the laptop. Thank you for everything you do to make juggling work and writing easier.

To my high school friends who read 'Robin' in its infancy and in particular Ms Caroline Bamford, my Year 9 English teacher, who also contributed worthwhile feedback during those early days. Thank you for believing in me and the encouragement you gave me as I went through the first edits of 'Robin'.

Finally, thank you to the readers who are keen to escape reality with me into Venetica. I hope that you enjoyed reading it as much as I did writing it.

About the Author

A booklover from an early age, Rose began writing stories from the age of seven and this passion continued into a life-long dream of becoming a writer.

When she is not reading a new book, jotting down ideas in a notebook or pottering around in her veggie garden under her cats' supervision, she can be found either on the stage in her other passion – amateur theatre – or teaching English and French to high school students.